According to Mark

Books by Penelope Lively

THE ROAD TO LICHFIELD
NOTHING MISSING BUT THE SAMOVAR
TREASURES OF TIME
JUDGMENT DAY
NEXT TO NATURE, ART
PERFECT HAPPINESS
CORRUPTION
MOON TIGER
ACCORDING TO MARK
PACK OF CARDS

for children

ASTERCOTE
THE WHISPERING KNIGHTS
THE WILD HUNT OF HAGWORTHY
THE DRIFTWAY
THE GHOST OF THOMAS KEMPE
THE HOUSE IN NORHAM GARDENS
GOING BACK
BOY WITHOUT A NAME
A STITCH IN TIME
FANNY'S SISTER
THE VOYAGE OF QV66
FANNY AND THE MONSTERS
FANNY AND THE BATTLE OF POTTER'S PIECE
THE REVENGE OF SAMUEL STOKES
UNINVITED GHOSTS AND OTHER STORIES
DRAGON TROUBLE

According to Mark

A NOVEL

Penelope Lively

Harper & Row, Publishers, New York
Cambridge, Philadelphia, San Francisco
London, Mexico City, São Paulo, Singapore, Sydney

No character in this book is intended to represent any actual person; all the incidents of the story are entirely fictional in nature.

This book was originally published in 1984 by Beaufort Books Publishers. It is here reprinted by arrangement with Beaufort Books Publishers.

 For information address Harper & Row, Publishers, Inc., 10 East 53rd Street, New York, N.Y. 10022. Published simultaneously in Canada by Fitzhenry & Whiteside Limited, Toronto.

First PERENNIAL LIBRARY edition published 1989.

LIBRARY OF CONGRESS CATALOG CARD NUMBER 88-45595

ISBN 0-06-097199-1

89 90 91 92 93 FG 10 9 8 7 6 5 4 3 2 1

To Sheila

1

MARK LAMMING, driving from London to Dorset to visit a young woman he had not met, thought about her grandfather. Gilbert Strong he had not met either but he knew as much about him as it is possible to know about a man twenty-three years dead: his opinions, his tastes, the texture of his beard, his whereabouts on particular days of particular years, his use of the semi-colon, his pet-name for his mistress. Folded into the driving-seat of the Fiat (bought principally for the use of his wife Diana and inappropriate for his long legs) Mark passed from city to the linked suburbias of Surrey and eventually into emptier and profounder landscapes in which despite himself and rather to his irritation he began to think of Hardy. Hardy simply arose from the hills and villages and inhabited the car, also with eerie familiarity: hat, stick, beard, wives, works. Mark, aware and vaguely resentful of some kind of conditioning, pulled into a garage as a distraction, filled up the car and consulted the map once more. There were only four miles to go. He felt, now, unsettled and somewhat apprehensive. He did not consider himself as confident as other people thought him to be.

'I'm afraid,' the man at Weatherby and Proctor had said, a year ago, 'she doesn't seem to have heard of you. But then she isn't exactly the sort of person who would have. Despite the background. She runs a Garden Centre, you know.'

'At Dean Close?' said Mark, startled.

'At Dean Close. It is, actually, a rather satisfactory solution to various problems. Anyway, Mr Lamming, the great thing is that she has no objection. She is prepared to co-operate fully. You have her blessing, so to speak. Guided, if I may say so, by us, as Trustees. We keep very much a watching brief. We advise Miss Summers and er, and her mother, whenever appropriate.'

'I know,' said Mark. 'Thank you.' He stared past the man's head into the murky London afternoon; he knew now with fair precision what he would be doing for the next three or four years. The certainty, though sought, was somehow dampening. He was forty-one, and on occasions thought wistfully of the blithe unpredictability of youth. He had not been much surprised by life for some while now. He was moderately well known and regarded in circles that he himself respected; he loved his wife; he was not financially secure but prepared to accept this as the price of his occupation. He was doing what he wanted to do.

He was a biographer.

For the last four miles Mark thought again about Gilbert Strong, who must have known intimately this line of trees, this bend, this row of cottages. He tried to subtract from the landscape the accretions of the last thirty odd years and refurnish it with the squat and bulbous cars of the last decade of Strong's life, to reclothe the few people that he passed, to reword the advertisements on a hoarding. This could be done, up to a point, but in the process the whole scene somehow leaked its colour and turned a dull sepia, like photographs in the *Illustrated London News*. Those whose professional task is the reconstruction of other times have this problem. The effort of imagination has its own special effects. This century, for Mark, was brown; the eighteenth was a delicate powder blue.

The sight of Dean Close, although expected, took him by surprise. He almost drove past it; past the large green and white sign that said DEAN CLOSE GARDEN CENTRE. OPEN DAILY INCLUDING BANK HOLIDAYS, past the CAR PARK arrow, pointing into the stable yard, past the façade of the house – familiar from photographs – with its half-timbering and gables and rustic pillars, like some superior *cottage orné*, past the glimpsed mountain of yellow plastic bags in the drive. It was these, perhaps, that had clinched his impression that this could not be his destination; a marker beside them said PEAT – £2.50.

He started to go into the car park and then changed his mind and drove up to the front of the house. He sat for a few moments looking at it. It was less ugly than he had expected, shaggy with wistaria and altogether less stark than in pictures. It seemed also to have shrunk a little; the surrounding trees, he realised, had grown considerably.

Her letter was in his briefcase. It was in large scrawly handwriting, on the Garden Centre's business notepaper and said simply that she would be glad to meet him on the day he suggested and as Strong's literary executor she would give any help she could but that actually Mr Weatherby knew more about papers and things than she did. She signed herself Carrie Summers. She had made three attempts at spelling executor and ended up getting it wrong.

He stood on the front doorstep ringing the bell for five minutes. Eventually he gave up and went round the side of the house into the Garden Centre. The stables, he saw, had become the office and sales area and beyond stretched a couple of acres of neatly organised wares, aisle upon aisle of plants in boxes and pots or with their roots shrouded in black plastic, among which cruised a few people pushing supermarket trollies. The contents of the trollies, Mark observed as he wandered uneasily towards a large greenhouse, were as motley as the contents of trollies in Sainsbury's, conjuring up visions of gardens as ill-conceived as other people's weekly diets – one conifer, two dozen pansies and a berberis. Or a dozen lobelia, one winter-flowering jasmine and three hostas. Gilbert Strong, whose personality had been so powerfully with him all day, suddenly evaporated.

For the past eighteen months he had read little that was not either written by Strong or pertained to him in some way. He could quote chunks of his *Disraeli* and his *Napoleon* and of the essays on fiction and on biography. He knew what Shaw said about him and what he said about Shaw and the size of his advance on the first of the travel books and his views on Thomas Love Peacock (admiring), on socialism (guarded), on female suffrage (tolerant) and on Cubism (irritable). He knew the sequence of his infidelities to his first wife and the depth of his friendships. He was so keenly tuned to Strong's name that when the word turned up in any context he reacted: signs referring to Strongbow cider induced a double-take. He had read the manuscripts deposited in the Bodleian and the letters loaned by the various friends and associates whose co-operation had been secured by Mr Weatherby's tactful letter. He had visited several of these people, all of them in their eighties or nineties and as jumpy as kittens about his enquiries. All they wanted to know was what he was going to say and what A, B or C had said about them. Very ancient ladies peered up at him and said plaintively that one just wanted to be sure that one wasn't going to be misrepresented in any way. Men with many letters after their names and long histories of office and achievement implored him to disregard the testimonies of other similar men. He had had no idea that the past frightened people so. The word 'truth' kept cropping up. 'You must,' he was told, 'tell the truth, which was thus.' A labyrinth confronted him; it had been much easier writing about Wilkie Collins, remembered by no one.

'Why him?' Diana had said, way back, when the idea was first aired. 'I mean,' she went on with more caution, 'it sounds rather a good idea, but isn't he a bit, well, on the side-lines? Nobody *reads* him now. Except of course that play.'

'Nobody reads Lytton Strachey or Harold Nicholson,' said Mark, 'and look what's happened to them. In point of fact Strong's very interesting. The novels are pretty awful, and the travel stuff is very much of its time, but the essays are strong meat, the criticism is lively and *Disraeli* at least is a first rate biography. And he was in the thick of things.' He did not add: and the great thing is that he hasn't been done yet. Diana, in any case, would take that point. Indeed, she said after a moment, 'How can you be certain someone else isn't going to write a book about him?'

'Because,' said Mark, 'I shall see to it that they aren't. In so far as that's possible.'

And of course it more or less was possible. Or at least it was possible once he had persuaded the Trustees that he was far and away the best person to take it on and through the Trustees the granddaughter who was now literary executor after the death of Strong's old friend Harold Baxter. No one, knowing Mark Lamming to be working on Strong, would be likely to decide to compete. His Wilkie Collins book had been praised widely and at length; the edition of the Somerset Maugham letters was considered scholarly stuff; he had won a couple of prizes; his publisher was enthusiastic, or as enthusiastic as the publishers of works of literary interest allow themselves to be.

'Did he know Vanessa and Roger and Duncan and Virginia and all that crew?' asked Diana.

'He was sort of on the edges of that.'

'Gawd,' said Diana. 'Poor you.'

Mark had read and enquired and talked and listened and now, on this amiable green and blue May morning he was about for the first time to set eyes on Gilbert Strong made manifest, as it were. What was left of Gilbert Strong; flesh of his flesh.

He entered the large greenhouse, in which a young man could be seen doing something to trays of seedlings. He said, 'I'm looking for Miss Summers. She is expecting me, actually.'

The young man, without turning, called 'Carrie – someone wants you', and from the far end of the long aisle there arose from amid a forest of pots and seed-trays a girl, dungareed and gum-booted, who put down an implement, stared across the vegetation at Mark and approached. She had gingery curly hair, a small face splodged with freckles, very dirty hands and looked about eighteen, which confused Mark who knew from documentary evidence that Caroline Summers was thirty-two.

She said, 'Yes?'

'I'm Mark Lamming.'

'Oh,' she said. 'Gosh. Yes. I was thinking about the man from the fertiliser people, but it couldn't be, really, could it . . . I mean . . .' Embarrassment, now, took over.

'No,' said the young man. 'He doesn't look like anyone from a fertiliser firm.'

'This is Bill,' she said. 'My partner.'

'Hello,' said Mark. He held out a hand, which wavered.

'I shouldn't,' said Bill. 'I'm filthy. Hello.'

Mark, disadvantaged, surveyed the greenhouse. 'I'm most impressed. I hadn't realised you were doing things on such a scale. Fascinating. I'd love to hear how it all came about. I must admit, I'm not much of a gardener myself.'

'Never mind,' said Bill kindly.

There was a silence.

'Carrie,' said Bill. 'You should take the gentleman into the house and give him a cup of coffee.'

She jumped. 'Sorry. Yes. Do come in and have some coffee.'

Mark followed her. They stopped off in the sales office for Carrie to give some instruction to the girl who kept the till and answer a complex enquiry from a customer about species roses. Mark, covertly, eyed her. She bore no resemblance whatsoever that he could see to Gilbert Strong. She looked now not eighteen but about twenty-five. She gave the impression of having been lightly dusted all over with sand; even her eyelashes were a pale ginger. The dungarees, he noted, were not the light-hearted kind in pastel shades with many frivolous pockets sometimes worn by Diana at weekends but the real thing: uncompromising and certainly not flattering. It was not possible to tell if, within them, she was fat or thin. Thin, he thought, probably. Her bare arms glinted with fine golden hairs and were as freckled as her face.

They went into the house through a side door. 'Sorry,' said Carrie. 'It's an awful mess. Bill and I just use this end of the house. We live in the kitchen really.' She went to the sink and filled a kettle. 'Is Nescafé O.K.?'

'Oh, absolutely.' The room was, indeed, untidy – a large kitchen which was evidently several other things as well: office, sitting-room, even possibly bedroom. A huge pin-board was covered with bits of paper referring to orders and to firms supplying fibre pots or slug bait or seed; a couple of worn armchairs squatted beside an old Rayburn stove; in the corner was a divan. Mark felt further disconcerted; the mention of Bill grated in some way – for absolutely no good reason, the chap had seemed perfectly agreeable, had committed no offence whatsoever. He pulled himself together and began to speak the prepared words. He said how excited and pleased he was to be doing the biography, the er, as it were official biography. How grateful he was for her co-operation. How lengthy a task it was. How anxious he was to get it – well, right. Carrie spooned Nescafé into two mugs (chipped), added water and too much milk, and sat down at the table which was covered with what Mark, even in mid-speech, noticed to be real oilcloth, vintage probably around 1949, yellow check webbed with tiny cracks.

'And,' he said, 'if I may say so, this is one of the most exciting moments of all. Meeting,' – his eyes swerved demurely from her face – 'you. At last. I've left it almost deliberately till now. There is so much I want to ask. I've talked to so many people who knew him but you . . . Well, it's of a different order. And your mother, whom I very much hope to meet also at some point.'

'She lives in France.'

'Of course. Anyway . . . You were nine, weren't you, when he died?'

'Yes,' said Carrie.

'You remember him?'

'A bit.' There was a pause. 'He had a beard,' she added.

'Er, yes,' said Mark. 'Yes, he did indeed.'

A clock loudly ticked. Mark picked up his mug and put it down again; the coffee was fairly undrinkable. An occupational hazard; one of Strong's former mistresses had given him food poisoning with take-away kebabs. He gazed at Carrie's odd, rather childish face, and looked away. Green eyes, with little brown flecks. 'It must have been very different here then, with this place in full swing. All those weekend parties. Cary and people. I dare say you sat on his knee.'

'Whose knee?'

'Joyce Cary's.'

'No,' said Carrie.

'You could have done,' said Mark, with faint irritation. 'It's chronologically quite possible, and he was a friend of your grandfather's.'

'Well, I didn't, I'm afraid. Would you like some more coffee?'

'No,' said Mark hastily.

'They had servants and all that then,' Carrie offered. 'Him and Susan. Susan was the person he married after grandmother died.'

Mark sighed. 'Yes. Quite.'

'Actually,' said Carrie, 'I didn't come here all that often because of being with my mother and her not liking England much.'

Mark nodded. He tried to give an impression of sympathy and understanding. The personality of Hermione Summers, Strong's only child, had been explained to him with restraint by Mr Weatherby and rather more colourfully by various other people. 'A little unpredictable and vague' had been Mr Weatherby's phrase, followed by a clearing of the throat. 'Something of a problem to the Trustees, over the years.' Others spoke of her variously as a drunk and a nymphomaniac. '*Louche*,' said the ex-mistress. 'Distinctly *louche*.' She lived, apparently, in the Dordogne and visited London only rarely and in order to try to extract more money from the Strong Trust. Strong, Mr Weatherby hinted, had got the measure of his daughter and her income was accordingly rationed and at the discretion of the Trustees.

Dean Close, since Strong's death, had been owned and administered by the Trust, in conjunction with the Strong Society, an organisation which had been formed some ten years or so later and which while frail in terms of numbers was rich in enthusiasm. Its dozen or so members, several of them associates of Strong's and most of them advanced in years, undertook the preservation of the contents of the house and the arrangements for its opening to the public on the first Wednesday of every month. The public, admittedly, did not flock, but there was, Mark had been told, a respectable trickle of littérateurs and the odd American academic. All this was made possible by the existence of the Strong Trust. Strong's later years had been financially buttressed by, ironically, the one work for which he never made any great claims. Dean Close, the Strong Estate, twenty years' economic peace of mind were founded upon the maverick success of a theatrical piece, tossed off in a winter of desperation and unpaid bills and which, ever since, had been in perpetual production. Somewhere in the world, every night, some company romped its way through *Queen Mab's Island*, that farrago of nonsense history and rumbustious English whimsy – 'a play for children and the young in spirit'. Few people, nowadays, could readily name its author. Barrie, was it? De la Mare? Good heavens – Gilbert Strong! Or, simply – who? Its title was a household name; its author irrelevant. And Strong, frankly, had preferred it that way, while pocketing the royalties with appreciation. And the play had begotten the New York production which in turn had begotten the film musical starring Julie Andrews, on the credit list of which Strong's name rolled up in rather small letters somewhere at the bottom but which nevertheless nicely paid the salary of Mr Weatherby's junior typist, financed various whims of Hermione's and dealt with the nasty outbreak of dry rot at Dean Close in the 1970s. So far as Mark was concerned, *Queen Mab's Island* did not bear too much examination; a glib and arch but adroit enough medley of sentiment, swashbuckle and fantasy, it was variously indebted to Carroll, Thackeray, Peacock, T. H. White and Barrie – a ladleful of theatrical soup in other words and of no great significance, least of all perhaps in the context of Strong's own *oeuvres*. A piece of professional luck, simply, and one of which Strong himself, to give him credit, was always slightly ashamed. It was to be regretted that it was for that that he was, today, chiefly remembered. The biography might, if it did nothing else, correct this.

'Would you like to see the house now?' said Carrie.

'I'm longing to.'

He had considered, several times, coming down unheralded on one of the Wednesday openings but something, an inborn sense of occasion perhaps, had restrained him: he had wanted to see the house and the granddaughter all at once, and alone. He was not, after all, some passing literary dabbler. He was the biographer.

They went through a green baize door and into, immediately, the 1930s. There were cracking parquet floors and carpets with lozenge and diamond patterns and Knole settees and many small wobbly tables and glass-fronted bookcases. It must at the time have been a fairly chic set-up. Mark, recognising the hand of Susan, the energetic and sociable former mistress Strong had married in 1939 after the death of his wife Violet, toured the rooms with fascination, almost forgetting Carrie, who trailed behind him. Strong's study, however, wonderfully intact, was stuck firmly at about 1918. There were a couple of big leather chairs and a fire-place with a brass fender and a huge and frayed Turkish carpet. Mark, more filled with emotion than he would have expected, stood in the middle of it, looking at the desk. He said, 'He wrote the whole of *Disraeli* in here. And most of the Peacock and Thackeray books. And of course the essays which are what I suppose I most admire.' He moved closer to the desk. 'Even the blotting-paper . . . Goodness. Yes, that's his writing all right – I'd know it anywhere.'

'The people from the Society come and sort of go over everything,' said Carrie. 'I don't really come through all that often. Bill's mum sometimes stays in the guest room upstairs because there isn't anywhere through in our bit.'

'Ah,' said Mark. He touched the inkstand with the tip of a finger. '*Disraeli*, of course, isn't to everyone's taste, nowadays. There's rather a turn against that kind of biographical writing, but I'm intending to argue a strong case for it. Get it more widely read again, for a start. What's your feeling about *Disraeli*?'

Carrie gazed at him. 'Actually, I haven't ever quite finished it.'

'Ah,' said Mark again. Silence fell. A different clock ticked; a more sombre and portentous clock.

'I s'pose it takes ages to write a book?' said Carrie politely. 'I mean, it'll take you ages to write this one.'

Mark, briefly, outlined his intended schedule.

'Goodness,' said Carrie. 'Gardening's much easier. At least you know exactly what there is to do every year and then you just get on and do it.'

They continued to stand there in the middle of Strong's study. Dirt from Carrie's boots had made a trail across the carpet, which she appeared not to have noticed. There was a provoking passivity about her; the next move, Mark felt, was always up to him. This was inducing a kind of conversational hysteria on his part. The more Carrie expectantly stood, the more he uttered.

'Let me make one thing clear,' he said. 'I'm not the Did-Byron-sleep-with-his-sister school of biographer. Don't think that.'

'Oh,' said Carrie. 'I see,' and then, after a moment, 'Did he? Sorry – I s'pose that's irritating. I just wondered.'

'Opinions differ,' said Mark crisply. 'The point is, so far as I'm concerned the life is relevant only in so far as it illuminates the work.'

'Grandfather seems to have slept with dozens of people,' said Carrie. 'Is that going to be relevant?'

He laughed, and then realised that she had not been trying to be funny. 'It's something I'm thinking about.'

'I expect you'd like to see the bedrooms,' said Carrie. It was clear that she was being purely logical, rather than arch. They climbed the stairs. Here, again, little had been touched. Susan Strong had died three years before her husband, although considerably younger. Her bedroom bloomed still with chintz; Strong's, next door, was mahogany and linoleum, with some of his clothes still hanging in the wardrobe, just as, in the hall, a hairy tweed hat hung on the hatstand. 'The people who come on Wednesdays like it,' said Carrie.

On the landing she paused. 'What you were saying just now – you really have to read everything he wrote?'

'Yes,' said Mark. 'Everything.'

'Oh dear,' said Carrie. 'Then I s'pose you really ought to look at the stuff up in the attic.'

He stared at her. 'Stuff?'

'Letters and things.'

'I didn't know there were any letters here.'

'Oh yes. Two trunks.'

He swallowed. 'No one ever told me.'

'Oh,' said Carrie. 'Didn't they? I expect they forgot. I almost had. I know Mr Crampton had a look at them two or three years ago and he thought perhaps they ought to go to that place where the other ones are and I said I'd rather we left them here.'

Nigel Crampton, President of the Strong Society and aged eighty-seven, rose before Mark's eyes, going on and on interminably about his own easily forgettable and largely forgotten *oeuvre*, going on in fact about anything and everything, in letters and over the phone till, well, till frankly one had learned to run a mile. Unfortunately, it now seemed.

'Yes,' said Mark. 'I'd better have a look.'

The attic was full of the kind of thing that attics harbour: a trestle table with a shattered leg, bundles of magazines, old table lamps, a gas mask, a paraffin stove, a wicker chair. And two large cabin trunks with frayed labels saying 'P & O', 'Not Wanted on Voyage' and so forth.

Carrie opened the lid of one of these. Mark bent over it. Within was a soup of documents, all jumbled together: wads of manuscripts, exercise books, batches of letters bound with tape. He lifted some of these out at random; they were all addressed to Strong – he recognised the handwriting of various friends and associates. There was a huge bundle from his publisher. No wonder the stuff in the Bodleian had seemed curiously deficient. He delved among the manuscripts; there was what appeared to be an early draft of part of *Disraeli*, and a whole lot of lecture notes, and something he couldn't identify that seemed to be an abandoned novel. All this went right down to the bottom of the trunk.

Carrie said, 'Shall I open the other one?'

He nodded.

And there was the same kind of thing over again. More letters. More manuscripts. A stack of books, annotated in Strong's handwriting.

'Gosh,' said Carrie. 'I'd forgotten there was so much.'

Mark stared at the trunks. Thoughts and emotions hurtled through him in confusing succession: excitement and horror and curiosity and an awful weariness and a whole series of realisations that begat other realisations. That the book would not be finished according to his schedule. That hence he was in for what Diana called a cash-flow problem. That he would be in breach of contract; that his publishers would probably be reasonable about that; that the book would be much longer than he thought; that it would be better; that he felt exhausted already.

Carrie picked up a bundle of letters and put it down again. 'Will you need to look at all this?'

'Yes. All of it.' After a moment he went on, 'Has anyone else?'
'Only Mr Crampton really.'
'Why did you want to keep it all here?'
Carrie fidgeted uncomfortably. 'I'm not sure, really. I thought I might read some of it sometime. I don't expect I ever would have really. And Mr Crampton kept coming and fussing around when I was busy. I wanted to get rid of him really.'
'That I can understand. No one else, then?'
Carrie reflected. 'There was someone else like you, ages ago. Another person who wanted to write a book about him. He hadn't quite decided whether to or not. An American. He looked for a bit.'
'What happened to him?'
Carrie shrugged. 'He never came back. I think he was sort of put off.'
'Yes,' said Mark grimly. 'That too I can understand. Up to a point.'
They closed the trunks and descended the ladder that led to the hatch in the attic floor. Carrie went first. Mark, looking down at the top of her head, was filled with what seemed to him the most extraordinary desire to reach out and touch it; there it was, with grains of dust spinning around it in the shaft of sunshine that came down through a skylight, and the sight of it unsteadied him. He felt as though he were a different person from the one who had risen from his bed that morning; it was as though, in the interim, he had received violent news of some kind, but he could not, at this moment, tell if it was good or bad.

'Well, what's she like, then?'
'Fine.'
'What on earth does that mean?'
'Fine. Very helpful.'
'Aren't you alone?' said Diana. 'Is she in the room?'
'Yes. I mean, yes I'm alone. They're outside.'
'They?'
'Her and um, the chap who's her partner.'
'Aha,' said Diana.
'Not necessarily,' snapped Mark.

There was a fractional pause. 'Well,' said Diana. 'I'll see you tomorrow. What are you going to do about pyjamas and toothbrush, then?'

'I hadn't thought.' Although, in that very instant, the rather fearful notion struck him that, given the state of things at Dean Close, there might well be a pair of Strong's around somewhere. No, that would never do.

'What are you going to do now?'

'Go through this stuff. Get an idea of just what there is.'

'And then what?'

'Eat, I suppose. Converse a bit.'

'Is she,' enquired Diana, 'a mine of information?'

'Hard to say. At this stage. Could be, in time. A pleasant enough girl, anyway.'

'Well, darling, I'll say goodnight, then.'

'Goodnight, darling.'

He lay, not in Strong's bed, but in the one in the guest room across the landing, which was none too comfortable and furnished with sheets of quite stunning coldness. Carrie must have made it up at some point. Probably after supper when he had sat at the kitchen table with another mug of that vile Nescafé, talking to Bill. It had been a strained conversation, even for Mark who considered himself perhaps a little better than most at finding points of contact with a wide variety of people. It was necessary, in his trade. Bill, though, had a quality of amused tolerance that was distinctly off-putting; he waited for you to say something and then when you had said it made you feel inappropriate in some way. Too much enquiry about the business of running a Garden Centre began to seem patronising; too frequent mentions of Strong were somehow pretentious. And yet he was patently an amiable fellow. Trained, evidently, at some horticultural college, like Carrie; good at his job, hard-working, short on intellectual interests but with that capacity to make others feel insufferably highbrow. Mark had floundered eventually into a description of a television situation comedy he had happened to watch, to which Bill listened with tolerant attention. When Mark finished he said kindly, 'We don't watch the box here. Haven't got one, in fact.' He began to roll a cigarette. Carrie came back into the room and Mark said he would go up to the attic if that was all right and continue looking through the trunks. When he came down at half-past ten Bill was nowhere to be seen and Carrie was doing things to the Rayburn. Where they both slept, and under what arrangement, was unclear. Mark had thanked Carrie again for her offer to put him up for the night, rather too fulsomely, it now seemed to him, and gone alone through the green baize door into the empty house, which smelt of damp and books published before 1930.

After an hour he was still not asleep. Anticipating this, he had brought down a pile of Strong's notebooks from the attic; they contained, he had recognised, a lot of draft material for the 'Essay on Fiction'. He switched on the bedside lamp (of which the bulb was not strong enough) and opened the top one. Strong's loopy handwriting, faded to a delicate fawn, flickered across the page. 'The novelist has an infinity of choices,' Mark read. 'He chooses what is to happen, to whom it happens, and in what way he will relate what happens. The picture he constructs is complete in its own terms. When he says "This is the story and the whole story" we must accept it. Perhaps novelists are the only people who do tell the truth.'

2

'AND THERE WON'T,' said Diana, 'be any men from Sotheby's this time.'

Mark sat up in bed, reached for his glasses, and looked at her. 'What are men from Sotheby's to me?'

'Last time we had a private view you had a row with one.'

'I remember having an amiable disagreement with a chap from the Tate wearing, I recall, a pink shirt. He thought Augustus John as good a painter as his sister, which of course is nonsense.'

'Whistler,' said Diana. 'And Sotheby's, not the Tate. But never mind. Anyway, you're coming?'

'I'm looking forward to it. And which of us is right we shall never know, there being no arbitrator. A problem I come up against a lot.'

'As it happens I've got an excellent memory.'

'I wasn't talking about you,' said Mark mildly. 'I was thinking about the book. Balancing what one person says against what another says.'

He was not, in fact, looking forward to this private view and would have conveniently forgotten it if not thus outmanoeuvred at a moment neatly selected to be not so far away that he could plead subsequent forgetfulness nor so close that he could say he couldn't get there in time.

'You can come straight there from the library.'

'Yes,' he said. 'So I can.'

Diana worked in an art gallery. The gallery sold prints and lithographs and a chaste selection of pottery, jewellery and glass. It had exhibitions which changed every two months or so. Diana, in imitation of her employer, Mrs Handley-Cox, had perfected a manner which made it clear that one was not in trade but a patron of the arts. She seldom addressed or, apparently, noticed people who wandered into the showroom; if they wanted to ask a price or to buy something they were obliged to interrupt her in some task to do with catalogues or lists, so that they felt importunate. On the other hand, those who lingered too long (sheltering from the rain) or looked scruffy rather than interestingly eccentric (poor, in other words) were made to feel unwelcome by means of a skillful blend of cool glances and murmured 'excuse me's' as she crossed their paths carrying a picture or stepladder. Suzanne Handley-Cox, fiftyish and of lacquered appearance, remained for the most part in her office where she intimidated young artists.

Diana got out of bed and went through into the bathroom, from whence came brisk sounds of washing. The door was open and Mark could see from time to time the flash of a neat pale limb or the back of her small cropped head. '. . . tie, not shirt,' she said, over the noise of a running tap.

'Sorry?'

'It was his tie that was pink, not his shirt.'

Diana went through life in a state of furious alertness. It seemed to her that she had been cursed with some diseased enhancement of the senses. Everything clamoured equally for her attention: the clothing of people who sat opposite her in the tube, the text of newspapers, every word spoken to her by everyone with whom she was in contact. It was not so much a question of being interested as being seized. She would recount overheard conversations to Mark, who would say, 'Why did you listen?' She could explain only that she was compelled to. She commanded great deposits of useless information; she would have been unbeatable in those television games in which people compete with one another to answer obscure questions. She never forgot a name or a face; an exasperating accomplishment since the names and faces concerned had usually all too evidently forgotten hers. She knew the telephone numbers of most of her friends off by heart; she could recite verse learned as a schoolgirl. Her claim, hence, to have a good memory would seem to have some justification.

In fact, the totally unselective nature of Diana's attention was indeed, as she sensed, a disability and would have made it impossible for her to have a career that was in any way exacting. The gallery, which demanded rather less by way of application than, say, the hosiery counter of a busy department store was ideal. Mark, continuing to lie in bed, abandoned with irritation a train of thought about Strong's fiction essay, for which he had set aside this uncluttered and often rather productive before breakfast period, and thought of his wife instead, which he had not intended to do until later. He thought about the gallery, and her role there; he was aware that this was convenient and why, though Suzanne Handley-Cox, each time he was obliged to consort with her, aroused in him a suppressed fury that was like a sudden onset of fever. Diana's hyperconscious condition was apparent to him, though mysterious since it was in such colossal contrast to his own tendency towards almost exclusive concentration on one thing. It was this capacity that enabled him to chop his time up into systematic thinking bouts, an invaluable ability. Diana, who was incapable of mislaying a glove or forgetting the date, called him absent-minded. Stupid, when she was in a bad temper. Which, of course, she knew quite well he was not. She was herself, Mark considered, well above average intelligence but without powers of elimination she was unable to concentrate this intelligence. She must, he sometimes reflected, have been an unmanageable girl.

Diana came padding from the bathroom with a towel round her. 'Suzanne wants us to go round for a drink next Thursday to meet this Japanese girl we're going to exhibit.'

'Presumably you mean her works, rather than the girl. That you intend to exhibit. I'm afraid, though, I'll be at Dean Close then. I'm going down for three days next week.'

'Three days! I thought it was so uncomfortable.'

'It is. At least the bed is. But what else can I do? This stuff has got to be gone through.'

'Couldn't you bring it back here? In batches.'

'I don't think she'd be very keen on that,' said Mark after a moment's hesitation.

'Or get it photocopied?'

Mark pulled a face. 'Far too expensive. There's so much.'

'And how long will it take? Going through it all?'

He sighed. 'I don't know.'

In fact, six to eight months, he reckoned, depending on how often and for how long he went down. There would have to be some arrangement about food. He would have to get her to let him pay her something. The alternative would be to go along to the pub in the village, which had the usual kind of pub thing, but he didn't fancy the idea of that and it seemed positively unfriendly. She had said, in her vague and slightly off-hand way, admittedly, that it would be quite O.K. for him to have something with her and Bill at lunch-time and in the evenings. She had also said, previously and that also without absolute conviction, or so he decided to think, that she supposed it might be simpler if he took some of the stuff away with him.

Diana, now, was dressed. She wore a cream linen skirt and a green silk shirt and was putting into a carrier bag the dress into which she would change for the private view. She went down to the kitchen and Mark got up. By the time he too came down she was ready to leave; this, in fact, was the usual pattern of their mornings when Mark was going to the library. On some days he worked at home.

'I'll see you at the gallery, then. Six o'clock.'

'Yes,' he said. 'Bye, darling.'

She went. The front door banged and as soon as she was gone he had a vision of her, quite extraordinarily vivid, walking down the street with her quick impatient strides, a vision so forceful that he had to rush to the window and there indeed she was, at exactly the point he had imagined, by the lamp-post on the corner, slowing down to cross the road. He went back to the kitchen to finish his coffee, a little embarrassed by his own impulse but thinking that such certainties of prediction were one of the rewards of intimacy with a person. He did not always know precisely what Diana was likely to say or how she might respond to something, but her physical appearance was like some natural law: unwavering and immutable.

Interestingly, Strong was becoming somewhat like this. One of the oddities of intimacy with Strong, though, was that Mark could never pin any particular age on him. One's friends and relations, after all, were rooted in their familiar appearance of now, today, even if one had known them for long enough to retain images of their younger selves. But Strong he knew over a lifetime and all of him at once: there was schoolboy Strong, writing those creaking letters to his mother, and the young Strong, living it up in the early 1900s, and ebullient Strong as a man about town in his thirties, and Strong at fifty beginning to pontificate and Strong the sage, surveying the world from behind the Niagara Fall of his beard. The man had mutated from a cherubic creature in billowing white dress seated on his mother's knee to the well-known whiskered face that gazed from the Cecil Beaton photograph. It was all very confusing; these figures reared up on top of one another so that he could never see any of them in isolation. Twenty-five-year-old Strong sheltered the sage, and Mark could not split them apart. He contemplated Strong all the time with the wisdom of foresight; it struck him at wild moments that a revealing new approach to biography would be to take a chap whose fate you did not know and move onwards year by year, as innocent as in life itself. 'Ignorant of our ends,' Strong had written somewhere, 'we endure our present. I may be knocked down by a bus tomorrow, which distresses me a great deal less than the fact that my tooth aches today.' Mark, possessed of knowledge that Strong did not have, could read these words with a certain furtive superiority, knowing that the man would die in his bed aged eighty, complaining that the tea he had been brought lacked sugar. On a day of rain and wind, when the first daffodils were out in the garden at Dean Close and Mark was seventeen and had never heard of Gilbert Strong.

When Strong was fifty-five and beginning to pontificate, encouraged by the acclaim for *Disraeli*, he had published the *Memoir*, whose opening words were 'I am, I believe, a reasonably honest man.' One of the more disturbing processes of Mark's growing intimacy with Strong had been the gradual erosion of his faith in the memoir. The alternative versions that he had now read or been related of various events or relationships recounted in it had made him realise that that limpid, slightly self-mocking document was as unreliable as . . . well, as unreliable as most testimony by anyone about anything. He had become aware – uncomfortably aware – of the unreliability of one's own testimony; sometimes he listened to his own edited or amended accounts of things, as related to Diana or to friends. He remembered, as a small boy, being exhorted to tell the truth; at that point one had been given the impression that this was a perfectly simple matter – you did not say that things had happened which had not, neither did you say that things which had not happened had. What was not explained was the wealth of complexity surrounding this basic maxim. It made you wonder how children ever learned to cope; in a sense, of course, they didn't – they merely grew up.

The memoir, then, was no longer the same document as the one he had read first some two years ago; it was coloured now by the wisdoms of his knowledge of Strong. For instance, Strong's picture of his first marriage as of such basic solidity as to be unshaken by his occasional weaknesses for other women was not endorsed by the recollections of others. For them, Mrs Strong was much put-upon and Strong distinctly callous; but then, unsettlingly, there were one or two who described her as drab and obstinate and Strong as patient under fairly unendurable circumstances. It was rather like friendship; that unclouded vision of a person only partly known vanishes behind the turbulence of the whole being.

He left the house and set off for the tube station. The Lammings, mainly because of Mark's choice of a financially insecure career, lived in an even smaller and even more uncentral house than those of most of the people they knew. It was the existence of a very small income from money inherited from an aunt that made things possible; there was always that to fall back on if absolutely nothing else was coming in from advances, royalties, reviewing, the odd lecture and so forth, plus Diana's earnings from the gallery. Mark had contemplated, in his last year at Cambridge, an academic career. He could probably, he reckoned, achieve it; he was not regarded as an outstanding student but an extremely able one and lesser men than he got research grants and subsequent lectureships. There would be competition, but the odds were that he would be up to it. Indeed, if the aunt had not died just then and provided that disproportionately significant little economic cushion he would probably have become an academic, willy-nilly. But he would prefer – oh, he knew that he would infinitely prefer – to be that old-fashioned and indeed barely surviving figure, a man of letters. He wanted to live by writing, to live by literature, indeed. He knew, even at that stage, what he wanted to write: not the novels that so many of his friends had up their sleeves, but substantial books about other books. Biographies. Criticism. Essays, if such a word might be uttered nowadays. But not from the confines of an Eng. Lit. department. From the market place, fair and square, as was done in more spacious times.

'It's going to be hard going,' said Diana, shrewdly, at twenty-six. 'But it's stylish. If you're going to be poor it's not a bad thing to be poor doing.' She was not, then, employed by Suzanne Handley-Cox but this line of thinking was one, Mark subsequently noted, favoured in a rather different sense at the gallery, where the line was that artists expect, after all, to be disadvantaged as the price of doing what they want to do, thus making it all right to require very large commissions for selling their work.

It had been hard going. Grub Street, he had realised during his first few years, is still alive and well. He had gone whoring after literary editors and written copiously on almost anything. He had even been a television critic for a while – he who detested that medium. He had been writer in residence at anything that would have him – libraries, polytechnics, universities. His nerve, from time to time, had wavered; he had cast an envious eye at the cosy nursery world of the institutional salary with index-linked pension scheme. So, presumably, had Diana. But Diana, despite her taste for a way of life that included at least a bare minimum of cultural comforts by way of theatres, concerts, travel and nice clothes, was possessed of an interesting tenacity. If Mark had set out to live by books, then live by books was what he should do. When his resolution faltered, it was Diana's that kept him going.

And initial small successes had been followed by larger ones, culminating in the Wilkie Collins biography which had had a highly satisfactory reception and got him an Arts Council bursary which had made one year at least free from a financial crisis and the favours of literary editors. People knew his name; Diana, especially, appreciated this. Things were not too bad at all, in fact as good as could ever have been expected. What disconcerted was the rapid dash of time and the hardening thereby of certain circumstances: Mark, catching sight of himself in mirrors, was always taken aback by that receding hairline; and the decision whether or not to have a baby, postponed year after year had become, tacitly, a condition of childlessness that would not, now, be altered. Or, rather, not altered deliberately.

His destination, today, was the London Library. He was at that stage in the total assimilation of Strong and all that pertained to him which necessitated scanning innumerable minor works of minor contemporaries of Strong's in order to complete the picture of the period. The major stuff he already knew, of course, but the book was planned not just as a discussion of Strong's life and work but of these in relation to their setting, and the truthful account of a time includes that which perishes as well as that which survives. Indeed, reading some of these almost forgotten names, the foundering of reputations seemed to Mark a very haphazard business. Several of these people read just as well as early De la Mare, say, and a darn sight better than Galsworthy, and compared not at all badly with Strong himself.

At five-thirty he packed up and set off on foot for the gallery, which lay on the outer edges of the West End gallery circuit. The private view, when he arrived, was in full swing. Diana was circulating briskly with a tray of glasses and greeted him with a quick kiss and a look of approval; presumably she had been thinking he might yet chicken out. Suzanne Handley-Cox was standing at the door to her office with an expression of alert aggression, like a traffic-warden about to strike. The exhibitor was the wife of a young poet and the room was stiff with his cronies, all drinking more than the gallery budgeted for on these occasions. Several of them were already well away and furthermore it was abundantly clear that they were not the kind of people who were going to buy pictures, nor indeed were in any position to do so. There was an atmosphere of genial impecuniousness, which presumably accounted for Suzanne's grim expression just as much as the dwindling row of wine bottles.

Diana, whisking past, hissed, 'Go and break up the guy in the thermal vest and Rosburg.'

David Rosburg, an influential art critic, if you thought about such people in such terms, was cornered between a large piece of sculpture (not part of the exhibition) and a young man dressed in check sponge-bag trousers and a thermal vest worn over a T-shirt. Mark said, 'Who is he?'

'One of these damn poets.'

Mark joined the group, of which the sculpture, a glowering bronze head, seemed an integral part. He had nothing against poets; he had written a bit of poetry himself in his time, though his assessment of its quality had prevented him from ever trying to get any published. That was the trouble with an education in literary criticism; it induced a chilling candour about your own efforts. The two of them were maintaining a spasmodic conversation about the exhibition, into which Mark helpfully insinuated himself, which had the effect of drying it up altogether. Rosburg explained to the poet that Mark was writing the official biography of er, Gosse; Mark set this right as briefly as possible while staring furtively at the poet's upper half, fascinated by the concept of the vest on top of the T-shirt, which seemed to imply either great sartorial originality or desperation of some kind. The poet remained basically silent, except for occasional sounds of acquiescence; Rosburg, finishing his glass and beaming a glance over Mark's shoulder in search of further supplies, launched suddenly into an attack on a fellow critic's account of another exhibition. Mark, listening just sufficiently to be able to interpose reasonably anodyne comments at appropriate moments, continued to ponder the poet, who continued to stand there. It was interesting, he thought, how the interpretation of appearances was a skill – or mechanism – acquired as unconsciously and undeliberately as children acquire language. You simply, over the years, adjust the eye and the expectations in tune with what they are offered. You learn your own society without really setting out to, which is one of the reasons it is so extraordinarily difficult to penetrate others. This chap, for instance, with his gear and his rather butch appearance (crew-cut, last shave yesterday) would be one of these performance poets or whatever they call themselves, based in the north somewhere, with a cheery contempt for this kind of scene. Diana, at that moment, hove within reach bearing a tray of filled glasses towards which Rosburg canted himself, still talking; someone stepped sharply backwards into Diana's path, the tray wavered and in distressingly slow motion tipped sideways, the glasses avalanching to the floor quite silently amid the remorseless clatter of conversation. Diana, grim-faced, sped in search of clearing-up equipment; Rosburg, twittering, began to pick up such glasses as had survived.

The poet said, 'Hadn't one better help?'

'No,' said Mark. 'It's the kind of thing my wife prefers to see to herself.' He turned his back on the commotion. 'You . . . write?'

'Not in the sense you probably mean. I'm doing research in early Elizabethan verse. For a PhD.' He smiled kindly. 'I'm really here under false pretences. Fiona's a sort of cousin of mine, and said come along, anyone can.'

'Ah,' said Mark. After a moment he asked, 'Where do you come from?'

'Brighton,' said the not-poet, now evidently puzzled.

Mark sighed. The other thing one learns, or at any rate should bear in mind, is that nothing is ever quite as it seems. There was a flurry around them now as Diana returned with dustpan, brush and cloths. He took the opportunity to move out into the room. A man in a leather coat and peaked cap was pushing his way around selling copies of a poetry magazine from a large canvas shoulder-bag of the kind that postmen carry. He did indeed look vaguely official, as though he might have strayed in from the street, which was perhaps why it took Suzanne Handley-Cox some while to cotton on to what he was up to. When she did her expression became even more aggressive; clearly she considered that if any business was being done around here it should be done by her. Eventually she forged her way across the room towards him and invited him to leave the bag by the coat-stand on the grounds that it was causing an obstruction. Indeed, it was hardly possible to move in the room now. Diana, passing Mark, muttered indignantly, 'Top limit of forty, Suzanne said, and look at them!'

But the cohesive force of any gathering has its point of disintegration, arrived at tonight some fifteen minutes or so after Suzanne had pointedly removed the last of the bottles from the side-table. The gallery emptied, as though the street had acquired some power of suction. Mark, Diana and Suzanne were left alone. Suzanne said merely, '*Christ*...' and disappeared into the little pantry next to her office.

Mark said gloomily, 'Do we have to wash up?'

Suzanne re-emerged, a plum-coloured apron in some rather expensive-looking material tied round her middle. 'I say it every time, and I'll say it again, that's the last private view I'm doing.' She cast an eye on Mark. 'You were a tower of strength, my dear.'

Mark inclined his head graciously.

'Go,' said Suzanne. 'Simply go. Leave all this. I have the most fearful headache. I'm too savage for anyone to be with.'

'Right,' said Mark with alacrity, at the same moment as Diana began to say that they couldn't possibly. Suzanne simply waved a hand with a gesture that implied suffering stoically endured and disappeared again into the pantry. The Lammings gathered their coats and went out into the city.

They headed for the tube, having both separately considered suggesting a taxi and resisted the extravagance. In the train, while subterranean London flicked past, Diana told Mark the names of various people she had spoken to or recognised at the party. Mark said, 'That chap you said was one of the damn poets wasn't.'

'What was he, then?'

'He was somebody doing research on something.'

Diana looked for a moment as though about to argue and then said, 'What did you talk to Rosburg about?'

'Pictures.'

Diana, familiar with the kind of reply that is an evasion while being at the same time superficially true, gave her husband a sharp look. 'Well,' she said. 'At least you came. Did you get much done today?'

'Not too bad.'

They surfaced, into the leafier and less prosperous part of London in which they lived. People were walking dogs on the common in the twilight; aeroplanes twinkled downwards to Heathrow; a covey of youths on motorbikes crashed past. Mark, reflecting on the ten years that they had lived here, thought of the innumerable small and barely perceived changes that fuse together into galloping reconstructions of landscape. That block of flats, for instance, had not existed when they came; the row of shops had been a derelict warehouse; the pub had undergone a face-lift. And above and beyond all that governments had fallen, unknown politicians had become familiar faces, issues undreamed of had become matters of discussion. One's own life, running parallel to public matters, became – even for a person living out, so far, his adult life in a politically and socially stable country in peacetime – hitched at points to these things. So that, for ever, Vietnam would be the nagging background to the years spent working on Wilkie Collins, and Strong would be inappropriately associated with the predatory profile of Mrs Thatcher rearing from the front pages of newspapers. Your own doings were interwoven with the coarser and more indestructible fabric of history, to give the movement of time a grander name than it seems to deserve when one is part of it.

And yet how unspeakably much more so it might be – had been indeed for countless millions of people in this century. Mark, like any normally imaginative person with a grasp of world events, was frequently humbled by the fact that few demands of any significance had ever been made on him. He had never been required to fight in a war, suffer for his beliefs, suffer for the beliefs of others, or show the courage of his convictions. He had lived an essentially private life. Things might have been very different had one been South African, Argentinian, Vietnamese or a resident of Belfast. As it was, you could only feel a curious and humbling mixture of gratitude and inadequacy.

Feelings which extended now to contemplation of Strong's life. There were times when, deep as was Mark's commitment to books and all they stood for, he wished he was writing this time about someone whose occupation had been quite otherwise. A man of action: a soldier, a politician. Strong's lifetime covered the most cataclysmic years of the century and he had stood on the side-lines, commenting. He had fought in neither war – exonerated by age from the second and by his recurrent glandular fever from the first. No action or decision of his had ever, in any practical sense, affected the course of history. Which of course was precisely Mark's own situation. He was, he considered, probably more deficient than most people in what you might call a power lust but nevertheless he did sometimes feel a twinge of envy for friends of his who had entered the Civil Service or vast industrial concerns and whose judgements and opinions could be said, in however small a way, to make a difference to what happened in the world. The influence of books is a great deal more sluggish and less easily perceived.

They had arrived at their front door; Diana was rummaging in her bag for the key. The house was one of a terrace of two up and two down cottages in a cul-de-sac that still retained hints of the rural cosiness it must have had when built in the late eighteenth century. There were picket fences to the little front gardens and roses over every porch. The thunder of traffic from the main arterial road at the end was not as evident as you would expect; the bingo hall on the corner was out of view and only suggested by the glimmer of its neon sign, pulsing over the roof-tops.

Mark said, 'What's our rose called?'

'What do you mean, what's it called? It's a yellow climbing rose. It came from Woolworth's.'

'Roses all have different names. They're called Madam something or other, or Glory of something.'

'Well, this one wasn't.' Diana, now, was in the tiny hall of the cottage. 'I'll do us an omelette. O.K.?'

'Fine.'

The rose, Mark saw, had brown spots all over its leaves which looked as though they shouldn't be there. He closed the front door and went through into the kitchen.

'Anything I can do?'

'Table,' said Diana. 'And you could wash the lettuce.'

The Lammings, presently, sat at either side of the round table that just fitted into the dining end of the living-room and ate their supper. They ate it to the accompaniment of that spasmodic conversation which is a feature of marriage and curiously restful: interludes imply not uneasiness or tension or inability to think of something to say but merely retreats into privacy. Mark thought about Dean Close, about his income tax return, and about an article on Conrad he had been reading. There flickered in his head, as a backdrop, images of Strong's study – its murky furnishings, the ghost of his handwriting on the blotter – and of Carrie.

Diana thought of things she had to do over the next few days and of various arrangements she intended to make, some of which would require Mark's co-operation. Mark disliked forward planning; Diana was addicted to it. She had learned, accordingly, to employ strategies of great subtlety. Reaching a decision to postpone discussion of a possible summer holiday until the weekend, she sat observing her husband. She had caught sight of him earlier, at the gallery, in an unguarded moment across the roomful of strangers and been struck by the curious way in which the sight of those known intimately induces a mixture of tenderness and faint irritation. She had wanted to signal affection but had also wanted to smooth that strand of hair that hung backwards from the parting that he always put too low. When they had first met and set about the interesting and provoking process of courtship, Diana had recognised a person who required management. Since she was herself perfectly prepared to offer this, the recognition was stimulating, rather than daunting. The only difficulty, since, had been definitions of areas within which Mark was prepared and even willing to be managed and those in which he was not. Mistakes – or deliberate transgressions – prompted their dissensions. She, too, thought about Dean Close, which she intended, before very long, to visit.

'What are you thinking about?' she said.

'Nothing, really.'

Diana rose, and began to clear the table.

'And you?' enquired Mark.

'Ditto,' she replied, promptly.

3

CARRIE SUMMERS and Bill Stevenson ate their breakfast while listening to the farming news on the radio. This, of course, was because they needed to know the more technical and precise weather forecast that is provided for those seriously involved with the outdoor world. They ate bacon and eggs and the fried-up remains of last night's potatoes, with a great deal of tea. They, too, enjoyed conversation laced with silences: the fruit of long intimacy. The intimacy in their case, though, was not sexual since Bill was homosexual and had a more potent relationship with a man in the nearby market town, whom he saw at weekends. It was based, rather, on shared interests – both actual and economic – and a basic amiability on both sides. They had never, or hardly ever, exchanged a cross word.

Bill said, 'That delivery of conifers is due today. I'll deal with it if you get on with the geraniums, O.K.?'

'O.K.,' said Carrie. 'That man's coming back, by the way.'

'Man?'

'The one who's writing a book about grandfather. With long legs and specs. Mark something.'

'Yup. I remember.'

'He's going to stay two or three nights.'

'Poor guy,' said Bill, rising. 'It's fish fingers tonight. I'm off. See you later.'

Household management, in so far as there was any, was

shared between them. Since neither particularly cared what they ate and in what manner, no problems arose over catering. Equally, cleaning was a simple matter since they lived entirely in the kitchen. The main part of the house was looked after by a woman from the village who came in twice a week. Carrie, when she remembered, went through and had a look round to see that all was well; the house was still technically administered by the Strong Society but Carrie, since her occupancy of it six years ago, had taken over the office of caretaker.

It had all happened when she was twenty-six. She had woken up one morning and the whole impossible adventurous idea had come into her head complete and impregnable. She had gone to the lawyers the very next day and laid it all before them and they had considered and consulted and within six months she had moved in to Dean Close, taken Bill, whom she had known at Pershore College of Horticulture, into partnership and set about mastering the intricacies of stock-taking, invoicing, tax and VAT. The actual stock was no problem at all. They grew the annuals and the greenhouse stuff, most of the shrubs and herbaceous, and bought in what it was not possible to grow themselves.

It was, everyone had agreed, something of a solution. There Dean Close had been, for over twenty years, empty, ravenous of upkeep, with its grounds mouldering away. The house was managed in a somewhat haphazard manner by the committee of the Strong Society, who arranged and administered the opening days. If Carrie moved in the caretaker would no longer be necessary. The house could still be opened, and the grounds would become fruitful instead of unkempt. The lawyers, without much hesitation, agreed to release sufficient capital from the Trust to set up the Garden Centre. Carrie's mother, Hermione, said she didn't give a damn who lived there so long as she didn't have to. One or two of the Strong Society, on respectful annual pilgrimages, winced a little as they made their way past the piled sacks of peat and fertiliser, the garden fencing and the displays of fibre-glass urns that were a necessary side-line to the main business of the Centre but cheered up when they got inside the house and found everything as it had been: Strong's pipe-rack still in the study, his hat hanging in the hall, his books on the shelves. Carrie and Bill lived cosily in the old servants' quarters and on the rare occasions when she received visitors Carrie opened up the old guest room. In what little spare time they had she and Bill rescued the rose garden at the back of the house and retained it as a private area where Carrie indulged a penchant for lilies: the rest of the grounds – the long walk and the huge herbaceous borders and the tennis court and the wild garden and the canal garden – were taken over by the Garden Centre. 'Ruined,' said ageing members of the Strong Society. 'Tragic, really.' But in truth they had vanished long before, weeded over in the long years of non-occupancy.

The house, with its veranda and rustic stone pillars and gables and silvery shingling had a flavour that made people who were architecturally well-informed assume it to be by Lutyens. In fact it was not, any more than the garden had owed anything to Gertrude Jekyll beyond a tendency towards paving and masses of lavender and senecio and cineraria maritima. Both were simply tethered to a period, doggedly reflecting it thereafter. These *cognoscenti*, meeting Bill in the rose garden on open days and passing informed comments, were liable to find themselves genially put down: 'Gertrude flipping Jekyll, love, is out nowadays: we're into the *nouvelle* gardening down here. Like the *nouvelle cuisine*, right? Simplicity and prime ingredients.' The visitors, who had probably taken Bill, in his jeans and lumber-jacket, for one of the Centre's workers (which of course he was) would move onwards, disconcerted.

The old stable block had become the sales area and three huge glasshouses had been built where once had been the kitchen garden. The rest was filled with aisle upon aisle of container-grown plants and trees, each area labelled with markers in elegant lettering designed by an art-school friend of Bill's: Shrub Roses, Fuchsias, Fruit Trees, Buddleias and so forth. Carrie, sometimes, would stand gazing with wordless pride at this landscape of her creation, these ranks of healthy growth that would root and bloom and furnish the gardens for forty miles around. Both Bill and Carrie would have preferred plant nursery to dominate over Garden Centre, but economic considerations forced them into buying in most of their produce. Nevertheless, they did as much growing as they could, both in the greenhouses and the two acres of stock beds beyond. This primary production was Carrie's especial pride.

She was profoundly content, being a person capable of contentment but for many years denied it. She had, during her childhood, come to realise with a glum and silent precocity that she was disastrously misplaced. Trailed by Hermione from Tossa to Spetsai to Marrakesh to Gozo, she had grown from infancy to adolescence in a state of perplexity that gave way to resignation. When for brief spells she attended schools she plunged blissfully into this halcyon world of predictability, conformity and instruction. Even now the smell of chalk and poor quality soap induced a *frisson* – a whiff of tantalising paradises from which she had been plucked each time Hermione got bored with Spain or Greece or France or her current gang of associates and decided to move on. Carrie became a silent docile little girl occupying herself with elaborately constructed private gardens made out of driftwood, gravel, prickly pears or whatever the local landscape provided. She did not do amusing and precocious paintings like the children of Hermione's artist friends; she was freckled and victim to appalling sunburn and insect bites and not at all pretty. Since Hermione was only intermittently aware of her this last point did not matter all that much. When she was small she was looked after by a succession of slatternly Greek, Spanish and French girls and when she was older she remained roughly in Hermione's vicinity and put up with having lunch at three or four o'clock or whenever Hermione and her friends had finished their morning drink. She went to bed every night at eight, not because Hermione told her to but because she thought this sensible. When she was nine she still could not read; eventually an amiable out-of-work actor who was part of Hermione's entourage at the time noticed this and taught her.

At fourteen and fifteen and sixteen she perceived that not everyone lived in this way. When Hermione made forays to England to have rows with the lawyers about money, Carrie gazed longingly at suburban streets and school playgrounds and the purposeful disciplined English-speaking crowds at Victoria and Charing Cross. Hermione huddled under layers of woollies and moaned about the cold and the damp and the beastly drabness. Carrie wandered fascinated around Woolworth's and Marks and Spencer's; she ate chips in cafés and furtively bought copies of *Women's Own*. And finally, when she was eighteen, on one of these trips she walked out of the Bayswater Hotel at nine o'clock one morning while Hermione was still asleep, took herself to the office of an educational advisory establishment whose advertisement she had seen in the *Evening Standard* and returned at lunch-time with the prospectuses of three colleges of horticulture. Hermione was too astounded to produce much by way of protest. She said, 'But, darling, if you want to learn about flowers and things we could have found some heavenly place in Tuscany or somewhere.' Carrie, wearing under her French raincoat an Aertex shirt and Harris tweed skirt she had bought from Selfridges, gazed at her mother without expression: 'I'll need some money for the fees.' 'Ring up Weatherby's,' said Hermione petulantly. 'Tell them to take it out of the Trust.' She flew back to Corfu the next week and Carrie took the train to Worcestershire; she was not to cross the channel again for ten years. She and Hermione met for tea at Harvey Nichols on Hermione's visits to London, and found less to say each time.

Carrie was the product of Hermione's brief and only marriage to an American painter called Jim Summers. The marriage disintegrated when Carrie was eighteen months old and Summers returned to California, whence he sent Carrie Christmas and birthday cards which, when she was older, said, 'We must get together one of these days.' Recently he had sent a photograph of himself, grey-bearded and naked except for a pair of faded shorts, standing outside a low-slung house that curiously combined echoes of Seville, log cabins and cuckoo clocks all at once. The accompanying card said, 'Be sure to stop by and visit whenever you're in LA.' Carrie put the photograph on the kitchen dresser where it remained until she was obliged to use the back of it to take down an order over the phone, after which she threw it away.

When Mark arrived at midday Carrie had forgotten all about him. She was in the big greenhouse, potting up fuschia cuttings, a transistor radio contentedly buzzing so that she did not hear him until he was standing beside her. She jumped and went pink. 'Oh!' she said. And then, 'Goodness, I'd . . . No, I haven't. I did make up the spare bed last night.'

'Look,' said Mark. 'I don't want any kind of bother. I just thought I'd better let you know I'd come. I'll go in and get to work. I wonder . . . Is there a table I could use to spread things out on?' He had to raise his voice slightly; the transistor, bubbling Radio One, seemed to have turned itself up a notch. He thought of Strong's fastidious musical tastes – the essay on Mozart, the interest in Bartok.

Carrie switched it off. 'Sorry. Yes, there's a sort of collapsible table somewhere, I know. You could put it up in your room. I'll come in and find it.'

'I'm being a nuisance, I'm afraid.'

She brushed dirt off her hands. 'It's O.K. – I was coming in soon anyway to have something to eat. Bill's gone to Stanwick to get some plastic sheeting.'

The table, when eventually located in a cavernous cupboard beneath the stairs, turned out to be a card-table, its baize top faded to a light ochre colour and ravaged by moths. Mark, delighted, exclaimed, 'This is the one that crops up in letters.' He opened it up. 'Yes, it's got a wonky leg. He and Susan used to play bezique on it in the evenings by the fire. I can't think of anything I'd rather work on.' They carried it to the guest room and set it up under the window. 'D'you want something to eat?' enquired Carrie.

Mark, awkwardly, launched into the delicate business of paying his way. Carrie, somewhat unhelpfully, allowed him to flounder. Finally she said, 'We have rather awful food, actually. It doesn't cost much anyway. I should think if you gave us a pound a day that would do.'

Mark, reflecting upon Diana's housekeeping bills, said, 'I don't think that's nearly enough.'

'Oh well, two, then.'

They went through into the kitchen. Bread was produced,

and cheese and fruit. They sat opposite each other, in an uneasy domesticity. Mark commented on the table covering. 'I haven't seen a piece of real old-fashioned oilcloth since I was about six.'

'It's always been here,' said Carrie. 'Ought we to have something else?'

'No. It's splendid. Like . . . Like – well – everything here.' That, he thought, sounded absurdly gushing. He glanced furtively at Carrie, who looked quite blank.

There was a silence, with which Mark decided not to interfere. Carrie, at last, said politely, 'Have you written lots of books?'

'Three. Well, two proper ones and one that's an edition of someone's letters. Somerset Maugham's. Not so many but . . .' Mark looked modestly down at the oilcloth, '. . . but people have been fairly kind about them which is more or less what has led to my taking on this.'

'I'm afraid I don't read very much.'

Mark tried to look at the same time sympathetic and understanding and imply that who cared, anyway. Mr Weatherby had hinted something of Carrie's less than adequate upbringing when hinting rather more positively of Hermione's life-style: '. . . Rather intermittent schooling . . . Done awfully well to set herself up as she has . . . Not really what you could call a chip off the old block.'

'In fact,' Carrie amended, 'I don't really read at all.'

Mark cleared his throat. None of the things that he normally said or felt like saying in response to this and similar statements rose to the lips. A long time ago when he and Diana were courting they had had an embittered argument about Diana's response, or rather lack of response, to the Russian novelists. Diana, in fact, read a lot but that particular taste of his he had not been able to transmit. He had said, in a fit of annoyance in a pub in Charlotte Street, 'If you want to go through life as a person who's never read *The Possessed* then that's your problem.' Diana, quite justifiably as he now considered, had got up and walked out and he had had to pursue her into Tottenham Court Road and embark on a reconciliation outside Goodge Street station.

'Jean Plaidy,' offered Carrie. 'I did read two books by her. And that man who's a vet somewhere. I don't expect those are much good, are they?'

'Well . . .' said Mark. He helped himself, briskly, to some more cheese. Carrie's arm, which was very lightly furred with pale gilt hairs, lay on the oilcloth close to his hand. He had, again, that unsteadying and baffling feeling he had had in the attic the week before. Rubbish, he told himself. For Christ's sake, Lamming.

'I've never really read any of the sort of books you write. Books about real people's lives. I should think it must be awfully difficult to do.'

'It is,' said Mark fervently.

'I mean, everyone seems different to different people. So you've got to sort out what they were really like.'

'That's just it!' cried Mark excitedly.

Carrie's involvement, at this point, seemed to flag. She got up and wandered to the sink, stared at the pin-board for a moment, scribbled something on a sheet of paper stuck there and then asked Mark if he wanted some coffee. When he declined she sat down again.

'Who are the people who do what you do well, then? Write biographies.'

'Um . . . Let's see . . . There's Bernard Crick on Orwell. Highly thought of. Holroyd on Lytton Strachey. Several people like that. Then there are the exhaustive American academics – Walter Jackson Bate on Johnson, Ellmann on Joyce, Edel on Henry James.'

'I'm afraid I haven't heard of any of them.'

'Not even Henry James?' enquired Mark, after a moment.

'No,' said Carrie.

Again, Mark experienced none of the feelings that such an announcement would normally have provoked. No advancing tide of boredom; no urge to bring the conversation to a close as soon as decently possible. So she hadn't heard of Henry James. So what? Nor have lots of people. Nor have most people.

'The thing is,' he said, 'to combine involvement and scepticism. I mean, that is, to be involved with your subject and at the same time be able to stand back and receive information with absolute detachment. Evidence.'

'I see,' said Carrie politely.

'I'm an admirer of your grandfather's, as it happens – or I wouldn't be doing this. But this won't be a hagiography, in any sense at all.'

'A what?'

'I'll show him warts and all. And he had warts all right' – Mark laughed – 'I've come across a good deal of conflicting evidence already. About his row with Shaw and about the publication of the *Essays* and, well, about the marriage.' His tone became, now, a little concerned. And more diffident. 'It does look as though, well, he and your grandmother didn't always . . . um, get on.'

'Oh,' said Carrie. 'I don't know anything about that. Maybe Ma would.'

'I'm very anxious, of course, to meet your mother at some point.'

Carrie gazed, blankly. 'I thought you said the sort of books you wrote only had that sort of thing in them if it was to do with what the person they're about was writing.'

Mark, for a moment, struggled with this. 'Oh, I see what you mean. The life as relevant to the works. Oh, absolutely. Don't get me wrong. There's no way in which I shall be prurient about the marriage, but the trouble is that it is relevant to the kind of man he was. And I have to write about that. I have to try to arrive at some kind of truth. In so far as that is possible.'

'I see,' said Carrie again. She was sitting, Mark realised, with the resigned expectancy of a child waiting to be told that it may leave the table. He pushed his chair back: 'Well, I'm sure you're busy, and I must get down to work.'

Carrie shot to her feet: 'See you later, then.'

Mark went through the green baize door. He unpacked his overnight bag, opened a window in the room, and climbed the ladder to the attic. He did some further sorting out of the contents of the trunks, and then, according to a scheme he had already worked out, selected various items, which he carried down to his room.

There, he sat at the window in the afternoon sunshine. He opened up his card-index and his notebooks and set about the task of transcription and description. He read from a bundle of loose-leaf manuscript what was evidently an early draft of the 'Essay on Fiction', with many crossings-out and additions, and doodles in the margin: ink blots that had been turned into spidery creatures and that rear-view of a bun-like seated cat that was a favourite of Strong's and one of those small idiosyncratic touches that somehow made the man more real than any photograph or written word. 'The novelist,' he read, 'recounts as much of what happened as is appropriate or pertinent. He leaves out what is either unnecessary (to the plot and to the theme) or what would distract. In other words, the silences of the novel are not lies but rejection of extraneous matter. Only those conversations are reported which are relevant; only those actions that have some bearing on what is going on. The characters, presumably, have a whole other life as well, off the pages of the book; they eat and sleep and talk to people who never feature.'

He raised his eyes from the page and saw Carrie walk across the gravelled circle in front of the house. From behind the hedge which screened off the stable-yard Bill appeared, carrying a bale of black plastic; the two of them stood talking and Mark, at the window, sat watching. He noted Carrie's short blue boots with yellow tops, and Bill's green sweater with a hole in the elbow. He saw Carrie laugh, which gave him a feeling of exclusion, and saw Bill, for an instant, lay a hand on her arm, perhaps to emphasize a point he was making, perhaps for some other reason. Bill glanced up in Mark's direction and so, after a moment, did Carrie; undoubtedly they were talking about him. Mark's feeling of exclusion intensified.

With a frown he turned back to Strong: 'The biographer does something entirely different. He is aware of the existence of a "true" account of what happened to his subject; everything conspires to conceal this from him. His job is to pursue this so-called "truth" – which is itself unattainable. His lies and silences are therefore his areas of failure, the points at which he is obliged either to speculate or simply to omit. All he can produce is an account which is dependent upon the energy with which he has pursued his researches and the manner in which he has chosen to interpret what he has learned. He is, of course, in his fashion, a historian, and we all know that history can give no final truth.'

'You know something?' said Bill. 'The guy at Hammonds fancies you. His face fell something awful when he saw it was me this time. He said "Oh, it's – er – your partner who usually collects the order." '

Carrie blushed. 'Don't be silly.'

Bill patted her on the arm. 'There you go again. Ticklish as a sixteen-year-old. I never knew a girl so lacking in feminine guile. What you need, duckie, is the love of a good man. What's happened to him down the road, by the way? Steven whatsit.' The reference was to a new neighbour, a journalist who had bought a nearby cottage as a weekend place and had spent much time and money at Dean Close stocking up his garden.

'He came in on Saturday,' said Carrie, 'and bought an acer and some bedding plants.'

'Ah,' said Bill. 'Bedding plants, eh? I told you he had his eye on you.'

Carrie giggled. 'And he had a girl with him. She was really nice. She works in television.'

'Come now,' said Bill. 'You can deal with the competition.'

This kind of exchange was an amiable feature of their relationship, though Carrie sometimes wondered why she was not allowed to tease Bill in the same way about his encounters, which were a matter for a great deal more intensity and usually engendered long muttered telephone calls during which Carrie had tactfully to leave the kitchen.

Bill, now, had turned and was looking up at the house. 'That guttering needs renewing, you know. You'd better get the builders round before any of the guys from your grandfather's admiration club come down again. You haven't finished moving those petunia seedlings, have you? I'll be getting on with that.'

He departed, and Carrie stood for a moment looking with a frown at the shabby façade of the house. Her feelings about it were very similar to her feelings about her grandfather: respectful without any emotional commitment or, indeed, a great deal of interest. Indeed, the resemblance went even further: both were edifices which for reasons that always faintly puzzled her had public significance and of which she was a somewhat unwilling custodian. The question of the literary executorship had been a tricky one. When the problem had arisen, with the death of Strong's old friend, she had been summoned by Mr Weatherby to his office and the matter had been discussed. Hermione, clearly, would not do: 'Your mother's, er, itinerant life-style . . . certain resistance to answering letters . . . need for someone with, um well, a basic sound judgement.'

'She wouldn't want to, anyway,' said Carrie.

Mr Weatherby sighed. A sigh of relief, not of frustration. 'As I rather imagined. In which case we have to think further.' There was a pause. Mr Weatherby, whom Carrie had known since she was about eight and had never seen in anything but his dark suit, discreetly patterned tie, seated behind the big desk in his office, contemplated Carrie. Carrie, who was wearing a tweed jacket, Marks and Spencer's blouse and the only skirt she had which she kept specially for visiting Mr Weatherby, gazed back. She said, 'Have I got basic sound judgement?'

Mr Weatherby cleared his throat. After a moment he said, 'Frankly, yes.'

'I'll do it if you like. The trouble would be me not being the sort of person who knows about books.'

Mr Weatherby looked down at the desk and realigned some already tidy papers. 'Well . . . The task of a literary executor, as I've already said, requires capacities of judgement rather than – what shall we say – vast erudition. I myself, representing the firm as co-executor, am not . . . well, I like to think I read as much as the next man, but not, shall we say, excessively. And it is appropriate and indeed usual practice for executorship to be taken on by a member of the family where possible.'

'O.K., then,' said Carrie.

She hoped, when she thought about the matter, that her grandfather would have felt that this was all right. Since she could barely remember him anyway there was no recollected relationship on which to base any speculations. Her only memories were trivial: once, aged about seven, she had come out of the lavatory at Dean Close still pulling up her knickers, and had bumped into Strong on the landing – a moment of painful embarrassment. Another time she had been taken for a walk by him in the nearby woods and had been surprised to realise that adults, also, suffer from not being able to think of anything to say. They had walked in silence, mainly; the only remembered point of communication had been when she asked him the name of a flower. 'That,' he had said, 'is a foxglove.' The name, to one raised amid prickly pears and tamarisk and oleanders, had been entrancing.

So, when decisions of one kind or another were required of her, she apologised to his spirit and acted to the best of her abilities and according to the guidance of Mr Weatherby. Though she would have been quite prepared to go against this if it seemed to her necessary. She had read with great care his letter recommending that Mark be allowed access to all papers and had reflected on it for several days. She had considered visiting the public library and asking for his previous books (listed for her by Mr Weatherby – her question to Mark had in fact been formal politeness rather than a search for information); but what, she asked herself, would be the point of this? She was in no position to come to any conclusion about their merits. It was more sensible to be guided by what Mr Weatherby called 'my discreet enquires as to Mr Lamming's literary standing'. Which, apparently, was considered excellent.

She thought about Mark as she went into the kitchen to telephone the builders. It might be a bit awkward having him staying at Dean Close so much, but she couldn't see what else was to be done, and in any case presumably he wasn't going to want to spend much or any time with her, or with her and Bill, since obviously they weren't his kind of person. He'd have to eat with them, and that would be that. They wouldn't be likely to bother each other.

She was therefore rather surprised when, that evening, Mark did not return to his papers immediately after the meal but continued to sit on in the kitchen. He had insisted on doing the washing-up. Bill, who was going over to see his friend, grinned: 'Well, I'll leave you two to amuse each other, then.' Carrie threw him a look of appeal; he put on his anorak and went out, whistling.

'What do you usually do in the evening?' said Mark, after a moment.

'Well . . . If it's fine I often go out and do some work till it's dark,' – they both glanced at the window; it was pouring with rain – 'otherwise I do office stuff. Orders and whatnot.'

'Ah,' said Mark. 'Perhaps I could add things up for you?'

'Actually I've got a calculator. Thanks very much, though.'

'I suppose you and Bill have known one another for a long time?'

'Oh yes, ages.'

'I see. Lucky that you both are . . . well, have the same interests.'

'It wouldn't really work otherwise,' said Carrie.

Mark gazed out of the window. 'What wouldn't?'

'Well, running the Garden Centre together.'

'No. Quite.'

Silence. The telephone rang. Carrie leaped at it, held out the receiver to Mark. 'It's your wife.'

'You're not alone,' said Diana.

'No.'

'The lass?'

'Yes.'

'How's it going?'

'Fine.'

'Hard day's work?'

'So so.'

'All right,' said Diana, 'don't chat, then. Listen, I've had a thought. Early closing tomorrow. Why don't I hop on a train and come down? Then I could come back with you the next day.'

She stood in the hall and watched the shadowy heads of the yellow climbing rose bounce on the other side of the fan-light. 'Mark? Are you still there?' That inhabited silence of a telephone into which the other does not speak; behind it the scrape of a chair on a stone floor.

'Yes. Um. Well.'

'It's a double bed, didn't you say?'

'Mm.'

'Well, then . . .'

'Look,' said Mark. 'Why don't I call you back a bit later?'

'You need to sound out?'

'Up to a point.'

'O.K., then. 'Bye.'

She hesitated, for perhaps three seconds, then whisked into the kitchen. There, she set about cooking in advance a meal for the following Sunday evening, to be put into the freezer. At the same time, she made a shopping list and two telephone calls and she thought. Thoughts, of course, cannot be set down like conversations, being processes that defy description, areas that demand from the novelist not silence but transcription. Diana had never read Strong's essay on fiction; if she had she would have known that he, addressing himself to this subject, had compared the novelist's attempt to extract coherence from formlessness to a cook's translation of an individually meaningless assortment of flour, eggs, sugar and so forth into the recognisable entity of cake or pudding. Strong, of course, had never in his life laid hands on mixing bowl or rolling pin; the homeliness of the example appealed to him – he liked juxtapositions of intellectual rhetoric and bluff English commonsense. He had spoken of thought as the individual's attempt to impose order upon chaos – 'the churning waters of the mind from which flash, from time to time, clear bright messages in words . . . That flickering erratic progress which, every now and then, we wrench into a deliberate sequence: we work out a problem, make a decision, pursue a memory.'

So, the churning waters of Diana's mind, an impressionistic torrent which includes references to Hungary (she is cooking a goulash, and tries to remember from whence this dish emanates), her mother (whom she must telephone), a blue dress with white collar (which she saw in a window this week and considers buying), Welsh slate (a builder has called with estimate for the repair of their roof) and Mark. It is at this point that the darting track of images assumes a steadier path, and the clear bright messages flash.

There's something up. Only ever so slightly up, but up all the same. I can always tell – that fidget in his voice, silences, not wanting to say yes or no. Something about the Strong stuff? Some project? Or difficulty with this girl? More likely that. She's being awkward. Wants to look over his shoulder. May be going to interfere. Or . . .? Or what?

Which is why I need to go down and have a look.

Mark said, 'Would it be a nuisance if Diana came down tomorrow? For the night – I'm going back on Friday, anyway. She's rather longing to see it all. And, um, to meet you.'

'That's O.K.'

'It won't,' continued Mark, 'be often. Just this once.'

Carrie, who had put on a pair of National Health service wire-rimmed spectacles and was sorting through a pile of invoices, looked across the table at him. 'I don't mind people coming. It's boring for them, that's all, here. If they're used to London.'

'I don't think it's boring at all.'

'Oh.'

'I didn't realise you were short-sighted.'

'It's only when I have to do this kind of thing. Sorry – they look ghastly, I know. Bill's always saying.'

'Is he?' said Mark, in a rather tense tone that made Carrie look at him again. She wondered why he didn't go off and do whatever it was he was doing. She had a vague feeling of guilt. Probably she ought to entertain him in some way. But how? she wondered – I can't talk about the sort of things he's interested in and I don't know anybody else like him I could ask round to do it. Actually it wouldn't help all that much if Bill were here. So there isn't really anything to be done. An idea struck her. 'There are lots of books in grandfather's study, you know.'

'Yes,' said Mark, perplexed. 'I saw.'

'I just thought you might like to borrow one.'

'Oh, I see – in case I want something to read. No, thanks. The last thing I want at the moment is a book. In any case,' he added gloomily, 'I've probably read them all.'

'Goodness,' said Carrie. 'There are hundreds.'

Mark, who had not meant to brag but merely to state what suddenly seemed to him a rather dispiriting fact, was silent. He was thinking of a passage in one of Strong's essays in which he called books one of the greatest divisive forces in society. Something about being distanced from one's neighbour as much by what you have both read or not read as by circumstances of birth or economic status. Quite so. At this point an immense jumbled heap of books – the contents of a moderate-sized public library in a small market town – seemed to come between him and Carrie. He could see another reason why people burn books, apart from the historically conventional ones.

'I'm not boasting,' he said. 'It's just the way it is. It's what I've spent most of my life doing.'

Carrie pushed the spectacles up onto her nose with one finger. 'Yes. I see. Actually, I didn't think you were.'

Outside, the rain continued to fall. Somewhere a blackbird sang ripely in the twilight. Mark said, 'I don't think those glasses are ghastly. They suit you, somehow.'

4

DIANA, PREPARING herself to visit Dean Close, put on quite different clothes from those she would have selected for a day at the gallery, or even for any day in London. She retained, in fact, though she was not aware of this, an outdated sense – product of the more affluent days of the middle class – that one dresses in one way for town and in another for the country. Her parents, who lived in Somerset, would have had special equipment for their twice yearly visits to London: a dark suit for her father, as opposed to his tweed ones; a little black dress for her mother, and a navy outfit with matching accessories. It is odd that cities seem to require a form of mourning, not quite banished even with the passing of the Clean Air Act and the consequent lightening of the atmosphere. At any rate, Diana, clad for Dorset, wore a pair of neatly fitting cord jeans normally kept for holidays or occasional weekends at home, a T-shirt which had cost more than T-shirts usually cost, and a blazer. She had put into her overnight bag a warm sweater, since it is known that the country is several degrees colder than London, even in May. Thus equipped, she stepped into the train and, eventually, out of the station taxi into the drive at Dean Close. Where, like Mark, she stood for a moment gazing up at the house.

Needs a coat of paint. And one or two repairs. Lutyens? Could be. Nice, if you like that sort of thing. Freezing cold, I bet. Should have put in a hot water bottle too.

At this point Carrie appeared from the stable-yard. Diana, whose instincts were neat, knew at once who this was.

She's not attractive. At least I'm almost sure she's not. She can't be – that fuzzy gingery hair, all those freckles, funny white skin, awful clothes. She obviously doesn't give a damn what she looks like – scruffy shirt, dungarees.

Carrie said, 'Oh – hello.'

Diana advanced, briskly smiling. 'I'm Diana Lamming. How nice to meet you.' Having noted Carrie's generally earthy appearance she did not hold out a hand.

'Mark's somewhere,' said Carrie. 'I'll go and . . .'

'Don't bother. I'll find him. I'd adore to see the house, if you've got a moment.'

They toured the ground floor. 'Good grief!' said Diana, looking round Strong's study. 'It stopped dead in 1920, didn't it?'

Mark came into the room. Husband and wife discreetly embraced. Mark turned to Carrie. 'I was up in the attic – I hadn't realised Diana was here. Anyway, you've introduced yourselves.'

Carrie, who was thinking about *Botrytis* and wondering if it would be all right to go now, said yes they had. Diana continued to comment on the furnishings. Mark watched Carrie.

Carrie, as was usual for her, had paid only superficial attention to Diana. During her years with Hermione she had met so many people that she had almost ceased to notice them. Hermione's associates had swirled around her, talking and drinking and having rows with each other and changing from month to month and place to place so that they had in fact become interchangeable: they all seemed much the same anyway. When at last she reached college and embarked upon a life of her own she had acquired such a habit of self-sufficiency that her contemporaries and instructors continued to have little impact on her. She was politely responsive but more interested in soil types and grafting and mist propagation: learning about things she found positively entrancing. Her first job was in a big nursery in Hertfordshire where she quickly rose in status, being good at everything and hard-working. Here, she became connected with one of the two sons of the proprietor – the more usual term 'involved with' is inappropriate since, as the young man complained, involvement was outside Carrie's range. 'I'm never sure,' he said, 'if you even *like* me.' Carrie, frowning in concentration and scanning her feelings as she would a sickly plant, assured him that she did. The young man, eventually, took up with a new Austrian apprentice and Carrie left for Dean Close. She had by now had three lovers (the other two had been fellow students) and had come to the conclusion that she was not like other people, who always seemed to be in a state about these things. She had been exposed to the anguish of the lovelorn and the howling grief of the jilted and wondered at these things rather like some unlettered peasant might marvel at the complexities of a dictionary. She saw that she must be flawed in some way and could not make out if this was a good thing or a bad thing. It was difficult to be envious of all those hours that other people seemed to spend weeping into their pillows, on the other hand whatever it was that generated it must be in some way interesting. Sex she found rather fun.

'We mustn't hold Carrie up,' said Mark. 'She has work to do.' Carrie, gratefully, began to sidle towards the door. 'Tell you what,' he continued, 'why don't we take you for supper at the pub later? And Bill if he's around.'

'Lovely!' beamed Diana.

'O.K.' said Carrie, with doubt. A meal out she had no objection to at all, but it would mean clean clothes and, ideally, washing her hair. She glanced uneasily at Diana's outfit, which struck her as extremely chic.

Diana, upstairs, dumped her bag on the floor and bounced on the bed.

'Jesus – this is a *hair* mattress! I didn't know they existed outside of folk museums. Have you slept a wink?'

'One gets used to it,' said Mark.

Diana grunted.

'You needn't have come,' he added. Mildly.

'Didn't you want me to?'

'Of course I did.'

'Is this all the stuff you've got to read?'

'Some of it. There's another trunkful and a half upstairs.'

'Lor!' said Diana.

Mark, after two days' work at Dean Close, saw where he was going and it seemed immeasurably far off. He had scrapped one outlined schedule of advance and adopted another. He would return now to the chronological approach, abandoning for the time being his previous system of scrutiny of all material regardless of sequence. The diaries and letters in the attic could be sorted into five-year parcels and looked at in order, each lot endorsing (or not, as the case might be) the other. Different themes – money, health, family, friends and so forth – would be entered, as before, in the card-index which provided a system of cross-reference independent of chronology. Thus, he was building up two separate sources of information – Strong's life as it was lived, year by year, and Strong's life according to various subjects. This latter division, while useful, struck him as peculiarly artificial, something like the slicing up of history by historians into different areas of study: social or economic or political. Strong suffering from jaundice (1932) was after all the same Strong as was at the same moment negotiating with his publisher for a substantially higher advance and embarking upon a liaison with a young woman working in Hatchards (she who some fifty years later was to give Mark food poisoning with take-away kebabs). Life like history is one and indivisible. That, of course, is the nature of its complexity and the reason why those brave enough to embark upon analyses thereof are obliged to chop it up into more manageable segments.

'Anything I can do to help?' enquired Diana.

'Well, yes, actually there is.'

And so the Lammings spent the afternoon side by side in the attic of Dean Close arranging upon the floor in as orderly a manner as possible the contents of the cabin trunks: pile upon pile of shabby paper staked out by Diana with card markers – 1920–25, 1925–30 and so on. The bundles of letters had to be undone and carefully redivided according to period (none of these were from Strong himself, but included all or many of those written to him by both wives, and by various editors and literary associates); the diaries and draft manuscripts had equally to be allocated; miscellanea like photographs and books and newspaper cuttings had to be identified and put in the right place. Diana was good at this, methodically beavering away; Mark tended to be led astray by detail, poring over a snapshot or flipping through a notebook. The sun began to go down and the light leaked from the attic. Diana complained about how dirty she was getting and speculated on the hot water supply.

'I feel nosy, too. I wouldn't like the idea of someone rummaging around *my* things. Don't you feel like that sometimes?'

'Frequently,' said Mark.

'It's like marching into someone's bathroom while they're out and having a look at what kind of deodorant and laxative they use.'

'Is that something you've done?'

'Only inadvertently.'

This subject arose once more when, a couple of hours later, the Lammings, Bill and Carrie were seated around one of the saloon bar tables in the Horse and Jockey eating steak, chips and salad off enormous oblong platters which Diana had criticised as more suitable for carving on than eating off. Music leaked from the walls; the sporting prints and hunting horns displayed around the room all had the sparkle of recent production. You could, Mark thought, have been anywhere; in Yorkshire, Somerset or mid-Manchester. An image, sepia-tinted of course, drifted into his head of some pub patronised and described by Strong, with tankards (really?) and sawdust and colourfully spoken yokels. The clientele here, from snatches of overheard conversation, seemed to consist mainly of commercial travellers.

'Well,' said Diana. 'It's food, I suppose. Of a kind.' She lifted three discs of cucumber and some cogwheels of radish from the large and dry leaf of lettuce upon which they lay.

'The chips are super,' said Carrie. 'We never have chips because they're always either soggy or the oil catches fire.'

Diana, who had in her eye a glitter of interest familiar to Mark that meant she was at work diagnosing the nature of a relationship, had turned to Bill and was questioning him on his past. 'I'm fascinated,' Mark heard her say, 'about the Garden

Centre. Tell me all about how you organise things.' Bill, tucking heartily into his own meal and a half-plateful of Diana's with which she declared herself unable to cope, supplied bits and pieces of matter-of-fact information about wholesalers and the demand for conifers, all of which Mark knew that Diana would store away in her system of instant mental retrieval and produce possibly in five or ten years time, correct to the last detail. He allowed himself to study Carrie. She was wearing a pair of quite clean-looking jeans and a plaid shirt. He was seeing, for the first time, her natural waistline and the size of her hips, unshrouded by the dungarees. She was thinner than he had expected. He described to her the afternoon's progress in the attic.

'There are quite a lot of letters from your mother when she was young. Would you like me to put them aside for you to read?'

'Well . . .' said Carrie. And then, after a moment, 'Thanks, but actually I don't think I really want to.'

It occurred to him that perhaps her reluctance stemmed from delicacy. His own role looked immediately distasteful. Gloom seized him. 'I don't blame you,' he said.

'Oh, we sort of get on all right now, but I just wouldn't be terribly interested.'

He had been on the wrong track, he realised. 'I meant that I feel . . . well – intrusive – sometimes. After all, reading other people's letters was one of the things one was brought up never to do. And here am I earning my living by it.'

Carrie reflected. 'I suppose it's a bit like doctors having to look at people with no clothes on. I mean, they don't exactly want to but they couldn't do their job properly if they didn't.'

Mark beamed. How extraordinarily direct and perceptive she was, like a child. An instance, it struck him, of the value of natural responses, uncontaminated by the wisdoms of acquired knowledge. This was not a quality that normally appealed to him, so that the warm glow she induced was mixed with faint perplexity as to why he should feel like this. You could also call it naïve, and he didn't usually care for naïvety.

'That's exactly it,' he said. 'So one has to swallow one's scruples and soldier on. In the interests of the end product.'

Diana swung round, having finished for the time being with Bill. 'What's all this about scruples?'

'I was complaining,' said Mark, 'about having to spend a lifetime reading other people's letters.'

'Nonsense, darling – you love it. He revels in it,' she continued, addressing Carrie, as though she might not have caught on. 'He has all the instincts of some bloke in the CID. He likes ferreting away and filing it all up and then coming out with the answers. For Wilkie Collins he read mountains and mountains of stuff, in the BL and the Bodleian and over in Texas and goodness knows where. I hardly ever saw him. He'll do the same this time. He'll turn up everything there is to turn up.'

Carrie and Bill, throughout this, gazed at her. Bill began furtively to gather glasses. When she had finished he turned to Mark, 'Drink?'

'Nonsense,' said Mark. 'This is on me.' They wrangled briefly; Mark won and went across to the bar. Glancing over his shoulder while he waited he saw Diana in full flow once more, while Carrie and Bill sat politely attending. He wished the evening was over. He wished he were back in London and then immediately knew that he didn't really. He wished it was next week and he were back here again. There really wasn't a lot of point in Diana coming down like this often, it wasn't as though there was anything for her to do here, or as though she was going to get on particularly well with Carrie. Or with Stevenson.

The Lammings lay side by side on the hair mattress. 'God,' said Diana. 'It's even harder than I thought it would be.'

'Susan Strong spent twenty years on one. So did Gilbert, come to that.'

'They didn't know any better in those days.' There was a pause, during which Mark and Diana drew closer to one another, ending up thigh to thigh, not out of lust or a sudden access of affection but because both were cold. 'And it's damp, too,' said Diana. 'You know something – that fellow's gay.'

'Who?' said Mark, suddenly alert.

'Bill.'

Diana's instinct in these matters was usually infallible. Mark was seized with a sense of wild exhilaration, which he instantly tried to tamp down. 'I shouldn't think so.'

'Yes,' said Diana. 'You mark my words. Odd set-up, I must say. And she's a funny little thing. Not exactly an intellectual front-runner. When you were talking about Strong visiting Conrad it was obvious she didn't even know who Conrad was.'

Mark, who had been regretting that reference ever since, grunted.

'Though she must have a certain amount of natural nous of some kind or she wouldn't be running this place.'

'Mmn,' said Mark.

'But stylish she is not. One labours a bit, keeping up a conversation.'

Silence. Darkness. Outside the window, the rustle of a car on the road, then more silence. Within, the instinctive perceptions of those who know one another through and through.

'Don't you find?' said Diana, an edge to her voice.

'A bit, I suppose.'

They lay without speaking. Mark, who felt a mixture of apprehension and mysterious satisfaction and did not wish to talk, pretended to fall asleep. Diana dwelt upon a small, disquieting seed of speculation. Both found the mattress excruciating but decided to say no more about it.

Diana recounted her experiences to Suzanne Handley-Cox.

'Dorset,' pronounced Suzanne, 'is very pretty. I'm always meaning to find time to go there. And it's the place Hardy is all about, isn't it?'

'Right,' said Diana, from the top of a step-ladder. They were engaged in hanging the Japanese girl's silk-screen prints for the new exhibition.

'I simply adored that film *Tess*. Move it a fraction left, darling. O.K. – that's fine.'

Diana had not seen the film because Mark considered cinematic renderings of great books an abuse, after a bad experience with *Pride and Prejudice* many years ago. So she passed this over and went on. 'And I can't tell you the amount of stuff there is there that Mark will have to look at. He'll be going up and down for months to come.'

'Poor old Mark,' said Suzanne. After a moment she enquired, 'And what's this girl like?'

Diana climbed down from the step-ladder and contemplated the row of prints. 'Fairly ordinary, really.'

'Just as well,' said Suzanne. 'Not of course that Mark's the type that strays, bless him.' She sighed. 'You're *so* lucky, my dear.'

Suzanne's marital history remained unrevealed to the Lammings, even after five years' association with her. It was rumoured that she had had two husbands; Mark's view was that she had probably eaten them.

Diana shot her a look. 'When Mark's on a book he's completely involved in that. He hardly even notices *me*.'

'Is that man who made that film *Tess* the one that gets into trouble over little girls?' said Suzanne. 'Polsky or something.'

'Polanski. Yes.'

'You're so clever – you always know about everything. Incidentally, if Ivan comes in at any point today I'm not here.'

'Right,' said Diana. Suzanne's trains of thought, if you could call them that, were familiar to her. In this case the connection would be Russian-sounding names, rather than cinema or dubious sexual inclinations. Ivan was, in fact, a young sculptor from Birmingham whom the gallery had once or twice exhibited and who continued to press his luck.

'Anyway,' continued Suzanne. 'I envy you having this foothold in Dorset. I yearn for the country, at this time of year. I'll leave you to finish off, darling, I've got to do some phoning.' She retired into her office, from whence Diana heard, at once, the fruity but chilling voice that had blighted the career of many a young artist.

Diana continued to put finishing touches to the display of prints. She then sat down at her desk to type up the descriptive labels and the price list. This she was able to do while keeping a surreptitious eye on three people who wandered into the gallery, and disconcerting a woman who wanted some pottery for a wedding present and had been under the impression that the piece in the window was priced at eight pounds rather than the eighty shown on the not-quite-visible sticker. Meanwhile she was concentrating upon other matters.

Principally upon how she was to nail Mark down to a specific week, and ideally to a specific destination, for a holiday later in the summer. Mark detested holidays; Diana had the atavistic English taste for foreign travel. The budget, she had reckoned, would stretch to a packaged fortnight somewhere. The time and the money and the organisation were not the problem; such things are simple compared with the slipperiness of people. People, Diana had long realised, are what you are up against in life, especially those nearest and dearest to you. The material world had never seemed to her a problem: heat and cold and blown fuses and recalcitrant cars and even shortage of cash were all things she could deal with. People were another matter. They are inconsistent and unreliable and apt to shoot off in unexpected directions.

She liked, for instance, to know where Mark was at any given time. At a desk in a specific library, or making a specific visit, or sitting at home. Which was where he should be now. She picked up the phone and dialled. There was no reply. Unsettled, she returned to the price list.

Theoretically the biographer, unlike the novelist, should not suffer from writer's block. He knows, after all, what the plot is; he has not got to make it up. In practice, of course, he is equally subject to crises of inspiration or onsets of lassitude. Which was what had happened to Mark today; he had tried to read and he had tried to write and was aware that he was unable to do either with any degree of efficiency. He tidied his desk, answered a couple of letters, sat down once more at his planned task for the day and gave it up as a bad job. He decided, on the spur of the moment, to go off and look at the house in north London in which Strong had had lodgings when first he came to the capital as a young man. Mark knew the name of the street, but it was in an area unfamiliar to him. He checked the notes filed under his 'Housing' subject entry, and set off.

To drive from south-west to north-east London is not just to spend a lot of time sitting in traffic-jams but also, for a certain kind of person, to pass through a system of references and allusions that ought to be more dizzying than it actually is. Mark, during the next hour and a quarter, found himself reflecting – in quick succession – upon Roman Britain, Whistler, Daniel Defoe, Harrison Ainsworth, Virginia Woolf, Isambard Kingdom Brunel, and various other matters, all of these prompted by fleeting glimpses of the silvery glitter of the river, the dome of St Paul's, a railway station or street name. The city, indeed, seemed to exist not just on an obvious, physical and visual plane but in a secondary and more mysterious way as a card-index system to an inexhaustible set of topics which in turn spawned other topics. The river always made him think of the Romans, because of some oddly luminous book on Roman London, author and title long since forgotten but whose insights lay around still in the head. But then it made him think of Whistler also; you took your pick. And then Tavistock Square and St Pancras station . . . And all these references coexist in the landscape even though separated from one another by decades and centuries; the mind has no problem in latching onto each in turn, switching obediently from one level to another, providing without effort the appropriate furnishings by way of costume and language and action. The head should be spinning, and yet it isn't; it accepts quite calmly the promptings of what is seen and what is known.

A West Indian conductor, laconically manning the platform of the bus ahead, and whose set of references must be assumed to be utterly different, set Mark thinking further about this. They were passing Liberty's at the time; *art nouveau* presumably meant nothing to the conductor (an advantage, Mark considered). What we see and what we know about what we see not only liberates the imagination but furnishes also a kind of strait-jacket; associations are also inescapable. The bus lurched across Oxford Circus in the direction of the BBC and Mark instantly forgot it, off on another tack.

A more practical one, in this instance. A programme was being planned in which the survivors of various bookish figures of the twenties and thirties – friends and relatives – were interviewed on their memories of these people. Mark had been acting in an advisory capacity to the programme producer: he had been wondering who should be asked to speak about Strong. His thoughts homed suddenly on Carrie. Would she want to? Would she like it? He could put it to her, at any rate.

He found the street for which he was looking, which was composed of late nineteenth-century double-fronted houses, many of them in the process of what estate agents politely refer to as 'reclamation'. Cement mixers and heaps of sand were much in evidence. Façades yawned windowless. Others had their brickwork picked out in the exuberant colours that indicate West Indian occupation. Mark parked the car and wandered in search of number seventy-two, in which Strong had briefly lodged as an ambitious and slightly brash young man from the provinces seeking a niche in cultural life. He had described it in the memoirs as 'A neighbourhood of tired respectability, in which the aspidistra flourishes alongside the bicycle and the Church of England'. Religion, indeed, in the form of a landlady who insisted on grace being said at breakfast, had caused him to move after a few months to more liberal-minded surroundings in Chelsea. Strong's agnosticism had been an early intellectual development.

So the undistinguished Victorian villa in front of which Mark eventually found himself was never going to qualify for a blue plaque. All the same, there was the usual *frisson* of interest in reflecting that Strong once walked (no, bounded probably, in his early twenties) up those steps, and passed through the door with its garish panels of stained glass. Mark contemplated the house for a minute or two and decided to explore the neighbourhood a little.

There was a church at one end of the street (attended, no doubt, by that officious landlady of Strong's) and a row of shops at the other. The church, though uncompromisingly plain, looked on the whole the more interesting destination. It turned out to be locked. Mark wandered round into the churchyard and patrolled the graves. There was not a lot to engage the attention here, either, except for a nauseous marble cherub which would have entertained Diana.

It was warm. Mark sat down on the grass and removed his jacket. A woman stared at him from the window of one of the neighbouring houses. As well she might, he thought; no able-bodied man should be sitting in a peculiarly prosaic north London graveyard in the middle of a Friday morning. Embarrassed, he took his notepad out of his pocket and made some unnecessary jottings. Neither the house nor the neighbourhood, so far as he could see, would merit more than a mention in the book.

So what was he doing here? Well, leaving no stone unturned, as Diana would say. Something might have caught his eye which would have provided some insight, linked up in some way with another aspect or stage of Strong. Nothing had, but never mind. And at least one was in the open air for once, instead of behind a desk. He thought, not for the first time, that this obsessive shadowing of another man's life was one of the more bizarre ways to spend one's own. Strong, of course – trust him – had had a word or two to say on this theme: 'Biography is one of the oldest and the most widespread of literary forms; a person decides, for a variety of reasons, to recount the life of another person. Note, please, the qualifying phrase, for the resulting efforts will be themselves qualified by those reasons. Consider, in this light, the following works; Asser's *Life of Alfred*, the Gospels, Johnson's *Lives of the Poets*, Morley's *Life of Gladstone*.'

And Lamming's *Life of Strong*, or whatever in the fullness of time it would be called. A far cry, both in intention and in execution from any of the above. A good read, one hoped, enlightening both about the man, his times and his works. Price fifteen pounds or thereabouts. And four years of Mark Lamming's life.

'Would you know him if you met him?' Diana had once asked. 'If he appeared, walking towards you in the street.' And Mark had replied, after consideration that yes, he was pretty sure he would. 'And how would you describe him, as a person?' she continued. Well, he had said, um, let's see now . . . Aggressive, opinionated, lusty, emotional, hard-working, inquisitive.

'Describe me,' said Diana. 'Beautiful,' he offered, promptly. She watched him through narrowed eyes: 'And?' 'Efficient. Vivacious. Energetic. Occasionally dogmatic.' 'No, I'm not,' snapped Diana. 'That's just you never admitting you're wrong.' 'I don't imagine Strong considered himself aggressive and opinionated,' said Mark, amiably, 'but collective evidence suggests it.' 'You think people know less about themselves than other people do?' 'On the whole, yes.' 'You,' said Diana sweetly, 'think you're tolerant. But you're not. You have an irrational prejudice against journalists, dons and waiters.' 'Rubbish!' exclaimed Mark. 'Some of my best friends are . . .' 'Waiters?' Mark glared. 'Anyway, all prejudices could be described as irrational, I should have thought.' 'And you're sometimes pedantic, too.'

Let's describe, he said to himself now, sitting in the May sunshine on this patch of frayed London grass, Carrie. Just for an exercise, as it were. Well . . . Elusive, somehow. No, not elusive – reserved. Honest. Yes, definitely honest. Direct. Innocent? A word debased by overuse – but yes, innocent. Not exactly pretty but quite extraordinarily . . . Well, you want to keep on looking at her. That nice curly gingery hair, the way she sits down with her legs curled up underneath her, her eyes, her voice, the way she says 'Sorry' all the time, the guilelessness of her (anyone else would have *pretended* they'd heard of Henry James), the way she scowls when she's adding things up, the way she . . .

He got up abruptly and headed for the car. Enough time had been spent on this trip. He could still get in an afternoon's work back at home and in any case, while it was in his mind, he really ought to give them a ring at Dean Close, just to check arrangements for going down there next week.

Diana, dialling Mark again, got this time the engaged signal. Satisfied, she did not try again. There he was, anyway, where he ought to be.

'It's Mark.'

'Oh,' said Carrie. 'Hello.'

'You sound out of breath.'

'I was outside.'

'Oh dear – I'm sorry – you were busy.'

'Well,' said Carrie, 'sort of. Yes.'

'I only wanted to say, if it's all right with you I'll be down again on Tuesday. Through till Friday. Is that O.K.?'

'Yes. Actually you said that before you went.'

'Did I?' said Mark. 'How stupid – I'd quite forgotten.'

There was a pause. 'Well,' said Carrie. 'I'd better . . .'

'Did I by any chance leave a blue pen on the kitchen table?'

Carrie stared round the room. 'No. At least I can't see it anywhere.'

'Never mind. I mustn't keep you. Gorgeous day here. A waste, one feels, in London. What are you doing?'

'Potting up begonias,' said Carrie, puzzled.

Mark was silent for a moment. Better not ask what a begonia was. 'I'm looking forward to getting down to Dean Close again very much.'

'Oh. Good.'

'And seeing you.'

'What?' said Carrie.

'I said "And seeing you".'

'Oh. Sorry. I didn't hear properly.'

'Anyway . . . I won't keep you.'

'No,' said Carrie. 'Goodbye, then.'

'Goodbye,' said Mark. 'It's nice hearing you,' he added, but the line was already dead.

5

MARK'S LIFE now divided itself between London and Dean Close. There were London days, which were much as London days had ever been, and Dean Close days, which were something entirely different. There, he existed in a curious state that was a marriage of energy, exaltation and anxiety. He became acclimatised to the hair mattress and the crudities of the cooking; he achieved some kind of relationship with Bill, based on breezy comments about items on the news (the radio was seldom off, in the Dean Close kitchen) and jokes about Mark's mechanical ineptitude. Bill fixed the rattle in Mark's car engine (an embarrassingly simple matter, apparently). During the day Mark worked in his room and in the evenings – the long light evenings of early summer – he drifted outside to where Bill and Carrie were usually still engaged in mysterious jobs in the greenhouses or out on the nursery beds, where the new stock was grown. He asked if there wasn't something he could do to help. Bill and Carrie looked at him doubtfully. 'Something simple and untechnical,' he added, with humility. He was allowed to hump hoses and cans of water around; at least it was a way of staying within Carrie's orbit.

He observed visitors with suspicion. There was a man from the village, some fellow who worked on the *Guardian* and had bought a weekend cottage there, who dropped in twice and stood chatting to Carrie for half an hour or so. Her giggle kept reaching Mark through the open kitchen window or across the garden wall and he was driven eventually into Strong's study out of earshot and sight. He prowled up and down the bookcases, reading titles without registering them and bewildered by the ferocity of his feelings. Diana, ringing up, said, 'What's the matter?' 'Nothing,' he muttered. 'What do you mean "What's the matter?"' 'You don't fool me.' said Diana. 'Why don't you come home? That place doesn't seem to be agreeing with you.'

On the London days he continued to work according to the old system, pursuing various lines of enquiry in libraries and collections. He telephoned an acquaintance, a woman who shared his trade and was working on a book about Sybil Forrest, a minor poet of the twenties with whom Strong had had a brief amorous skirmish.

'My chap,' he said, 'appears to have dined with your lady on – let's see – 27 January 1928.'

'Is this a statement of fact or are you seeking confirmation?'

'There's that letter in the Bodleian.'

'I've seen it. In point of fact they subsequently spent a weekend together in Aberystwyth three weeks later. Carnal, I assume.'

There was a pause. 'That I can't accept,' said Mark. 'Strong had better taste than to go to Aberystwyth in February. Or any other time, probably. Where do you get that from?'

'The diary.'

'Oh, come now,' said Mark. 'The reference is entirely ambiguous. She never names Strong. It could have been anyone.'

'Are you implying,' enquired the acquaintance huffily, 'promiscuity?'

'I just think that to infer it must have been Strong is pushing it a bit.'

'None the less, I think I may push. A measure of intuition is permitted in our line of business. Yes?'

'Hmn,' said Mark. 'Up to a point, Lord Copper. How goes it, anyway?'

'It goes. And you?'

'Ditto.' They parted, amicably enough. Mark entered the reference in a file marked 'Unconfirmed matters', beneath which he had scrawled once, in red biro, in a moment of frivolity or frustration, 'Lies and silences'. It was in these terms that he now thought of it, and within the file lay a gradually thickening wad of notes pertaining to things about which he was not sure, or about which there was conflicting evidence. Where exactly was Strong from April 1912 to the end of 1914? What was the real nature of his relationship with Shaw, superficially jocular in the letters but claimed by others to be one of mutual antagonism? Was he a closet Tory, despite his modish socialism? Did he fiddle his income tax in the thirties? Was he allergic to strawberries?

Carrie, who had at first found Mark's presence unsettling, began to get used to him. She did not dislike him – she seldom, in truth, disliked people, having acquired massive powers of tolerance in youth during her exposure to Hermione's friends – but she would have preferred on the whole that he wasn't there. On the other hand she could see that he had to be, so there was nothing to be done about it. She rather wished he didn't feel so obliged to keep offering to help, but couldn't think of any way to deter him. She also felt a bit sorry for him; it couldn't be all that much fun having to spend half the week away from his wife, whom she had thought very dashing. Never having been in close contact with the institution, Carrie had a puzzled respect for matrimony. Everybody seemed to want it, but most people who'd got it seemed to be complaining about it.

She usually got on well enough with people, though often she couldn't think of anything to say to them. If you waited, she had learned, they mostly solved the problem themselves; the ones who didn't went away. She frequently couldn't think of anything to say to Mark, but he didn't seem to mind. He was always asking her questions about plants – what they were called and where they came from – and she couldn't imagine he was really interested in this. Being herself naturally polite, though, she respected what she took to be his motivation and supplied detailed answers. She was surprised when he apparently remembered all this information and came out with quite informed remarks. On several occasions he was able to answer queries from customers who came across him around the place and took him for one of the Garden Centre's staff. Amused by this, she said, 'You'll have to watch out or you'll find yourself becoming one of us.' Mark looked smug; she was again surprised, and rather touched. Several times, though, she found him gazing at her in a way that was vaguely disconcerting; for some reason it reminded her of her old boyfriend, the proprietor's son at the nursery where she had once worked, and anyone more different to Mark than him it would be difficult to imagine. He had been a motorbike enthusiast, and went on scrambles at the weekends; once he had persuaded her to ride pillion while he did a ton round a disused aerodrome, an experience she had not enjoyed. The involuntary association with Mark perplexed and embarrassed her. She was plagued with an uncomfortable feeling that others can guess what you are thinking – probably induced by cohabitation with Bill, who often did, and delighted in making her blush.

Carrie never minded being alone: another attribute gained in childhood. In fact she preferred it, in many ways. The passive and undemanding company of plants and birds was much more restful and in many ways more interesting. What she spent her days doing now was an adult and more purposeful extension of the way she had spent many days during her childhood, constructing small fantasy landscapes, making order out of chaos. Growing things, and then selling them, was much the same thing. She left most of the dealing with customers to Bill, who was better at it; her idea of bliss was to potter alone and uninterrupted among plants from morning to night. Her particular indulgence was alpines, a private sideline of which Bill mildly disapproved on the grounds that it was time-consuming and uneconomic. Carrie, though, persisted – a little guiltily – and got a great deal of quiet pleasure from her trays of Primula species and saxifrage, delicate infants thriving at her behest. She set out the mature plants herself on a special trestle table, arranging them with the seductive intent of a window dresser, and observed purchases with a glow of satisfaction. Much more fun than the purveying of some other grower's hybrid teas or floribundas.

She was responsive also to birds and animals, especially birds. This of course set up problems, since for a gardener, and especially a professional gardener, birds are the natural enemy and should logically be exterminated or at least rigidly deterred. Carrie fed them, which made Bill cross. She also allowed weeds to flourish here and there: sheets of the blue speedwell that will cover waste tracts of ground, ground ivy and herb robert and clumps of mallow and purple loosestrife. She was, in fact, environmentally minded but since she rarely read newspapers or watched the television she had no idea that what she felt was ideologically bang up to date: it was simply the way she had always been, and the kind of thing she had always done.

Mark, deeply urban, was ignorant of these things, though appropriately respectful. He could name few birds and even fewer wild flowers. He kept asking Carrie what things were called, which she found surprising and faintly irritating: she wasn't certain that his interest was serious. Also, it frequently referred back in some way to Strong.

'Your grandfather,' he said, 'had a feeling for nature. One would expect that, of course, there was always an undercurrent of that around. The Georgian poets, and Hardy and the Mary Webb school, though of course he'd have been pretty dismissive of that. Lawrence he never had much time for – dark forces and so forth – too mystical for him. His line was more a good long hike and bluff appreciation of the beauties of the landscape.'

'Mmn,' murmured Carrie, intent on pricking out primula seedlings.

'And the travel books have a lot about flora and fauna. Not as much as about people, of course, which was what really obsessed him, but digressions on lesser egrets and pomegranates or whatever. Maybe that's where you get it from.'

'Oh, I shouldn't think so,' said Carrie.

'You should read *The Road to Anatolia*. That's particularly – visual.'

'Mmn.'

There was a pause. Carrie set aside a tray of seedlings and started on another.

'You aren't really interested in him,' said Mark.

'No,' she agreed.

'What are you interested in?'

Carrie pondered. 'Lilies. Clematis. Species roses – though not quite as much as I used to be. Sorry,' she added.

'I'll stop talking about him,' said Mark.

'I don't mind a bit. Just so long as it doesn't make you cross me not saying anything much back.'

'Would it,' Mark enquired, 'matter to you if I was cross?'

Carrie pondered again. 'Oh yes. I mean, it's much nicer if you're getting on with someone than if you're not, isn't it?'

Mark strode to the other end of the greenhouse and back again. 'Anyone?'

'Yes, of course.'

'You just like to get along with everyone, regardless?'

Carrie wriggled, uncomfortable at the turn this conversation was taking. 'Well sort of.'

'Some people,' said Mark, 'are much more important to one than others.'

'Oh yes.'

'I won't ask who's important to you.'

'No,' said Carrie gratefully.

It was conversations of this kind – and there had been several – that reduced Mark to a state of mild frenzy. He was not at all sure whether she even liked him. Was she just enduring him? What *was* her relationship with Bill? What about that journalist fellow? And how, above all, did it come to be a matter of such intense importance to him? 'How are you getting on with the lass?' Diana had asked, and he had mumbled, 'O.K.' 'Of course,' she pursued, 'there's no need to consort more than good manners requires.' To which Mark retorted, with a note of irritation, that she was after all the granddaughter and hence a somewhat central figure. 'I thought she hardly remembered him?' 'That's not entirely the point,' said Mark. 'Oh?' persisted Diana. 'In that case it must be a bit of a chore, with her being somewhat dim.' When Mark had snapped that Carrie was not dim Diana had gazed thoughtfully at him.

He should have pointed out, he thought afterwards, that nobody dim could be running a successful business. Indeed, a conversation along these lines took place only a few days later in the Dean Close kitchen. Bill and Carrie were sorting out their papers prior to the accountant's visit for the annual audit. Mark was drawn in, allowed to sort invoices into chronological order. They all three sat round the table.

'I'm impressed,' said Mark. 'I couldn't cope with all this. It's much as I can do to get through my income tax return.'

'Lack of too much formal education's a great help in these matters, mate,' said Bill. 'It's a known fact.'

Mark, always distracted by information, scanned a piece of paper which said that someone had bought two dozen silver birches and nine copper beeches. An afforestation maniac? 'Well, Johnson of course held much the same view – "Trade could not be managed by those who manage it, if it were difficult."' The remark, as soon as it was out, struck him as appallingly inept on at least two counts. 'Admittedly that was in the eighteenth century, and it was brewing he had in mind.'

'Ah, is that so?' said Bill. It was impossible to tell if he was being sardonic or not. Mark sweltered with embarrassment. To his relief the telephone rang. Bill, answering it, said 'Yes' and 'Will do' two or three times in a low voice. He shrugged on his anorak and said to Carrie, 'Just nipping out for a jar. O.K. if I leave you to it?'

'Fine.'

'That's my girl.' He dropped a kiss on top of her head. 'See you, then.' He left.

There was a silence. Mark's emotions had now switched tack. Unable to help himself, he plunged. 'I suppose you and Bill will think of getting married one of these days?'

Carrie pushed her spectacles further up her nose and gazed at him. 'Oh goodness, no. Bill's gay. That was Ron, I expect. His friend.'

The kitchen, which had been seeming rather dark and oppressive, became suddenly lighter. 'Oh,' said Mark, airily. 'Good Lord – I hadn't realised. I'm never very good at these things. Well, well. Fancy that, then.' He returned to the invoices, with renewed energy. After a moment he looked across at her again. 'Of course, some people are both.'

'Are they?' said Carrie. 'I didn't know that. Do you think Bill is?' she continued, with apparent interest.

'I've no idea,' said Mark stiffly.

Carrie reflected. 'I don't think so. He's awfully fond of Ron.'

'Why doesn't he live with him?'

'Ron lives with his mum,' said Carrie, as though this explained all. They continued to sort papers, in silence. Carrie, once, put out a hand and switched on the radio. Muzak chattered. She turned it off again, with a guilty look: 'Sorry – you don't like that sort of thing.'

Mark opened his mouth to prevaricate, and decided not to. 'No, I don't, I'm afraid. But it won't bother me.' Carrie, though, fiddled with the knobs. 'Is this better?'

'Well, yes, in my view. It's Beethoven. One of the quartets.'

'O.K,' said Carrie. 'Let's have that then.'

And so they sat together in Gilbert Strong's house, listening – or not listening – to Beethoven.

Mark, back in London, went through the mail. There was a note from Stella Bruce, Strong's one-time mistress, asking him to call her. When he did so she said, obscurely, 'I've been thinking, Mr Lamming.'

'Ah?' said Mark. She was in her eighties: as soft and pastel as a powder-puff, glittering with paste and pearls, lipstick and nail-varnish, relentlessly feminine but, you sensed, as tough as old boots.

'I enjoyed our little talk. I hope it was a help.'

'Invaluable,' said Mark. He expanded on this. She heard him out, with little deprecating noises, and then went on.

'One is so anxious that you should really get to the bottom of Gil. He was a very, very complicated person, you realise.'

Mark acquiesced.

'Probably I know that better than anyone. So I've been having a little think.' There was a pause. 'Come and have lunch with me one day this week.'

Mark hesitated, remembering the take-away kebabs. 'Well, I don't want to put you to any trouble. Perhaps a cup of tea . . .'

They arranged that he should call round the next day. Diana said, 'What does she want, do you imagine?'

Mark shrugged. 'Just attention, I rather fear. She talked for three-and-a-half hours last time. Mostly about herself.'

'Well, at least don't eat anything this time.'

'I shall plead indispostion,' said Mark.

Stella Bruce lived in a flat overlooking the river at Putney Bridge. The windows were tight shut; the room smelled of flowers and chocolate; the furnishings were all padded and gilded and swagged and fringed. Two walls were lined with mirrors; a fashion magazine lay on the coffee table. Stella, when Strong knew her in the thirties, had been one of those young women of uncertain occupation who hung around the edges of the book world, picking up parties, and from time to time, literary gentlemen. Their association, Mark now knew from other sources, had lasted for two or three years, on and off, while Violet Strong was still alive.

She ran, for a while, over familiar ground. 'Sure you won't have some coffee? I'm frightfully domesticated nowadays, one has to be. As I was saying last time, Gil relied on me for that stimulus he wasn't really getting at home and I don't mean just . . .' – her eyelashes fluttered – '. . . just the physical side. Mental things too. I used to *listen* to him. He knew he could come to me and relax and talk and be ministered to. Like those sweet girls in Japanese pictures – what d'you call them?'

'Geishas?'

'That's it. Of course, I was terribly young. And not awfully *au fait*. I adored Gil. But I have to say that he was not always . . . absolutely straightfoward.' She gazed at Mark, who nodded, implying understanding or connivance or whatever seemed appropriate. 'He wanted to marry me, you know, after Violet died, but some sort of instinct told me it would be the most ghastly mistake. No, I said. Friends, Gil, always, but not marriage.' Mark, who had other evidence that in fact Stella had been supplanted by Susan some years before this, nodded again. 'So there it was . . .' she sighed. 'And anyway by then,' – delicately – 'there was, well, another gentleman.' Mark nodded again, suggesting respect for such range of emotional experience.

Boredom, in fact, was setting in; the flat was unbearably hot and stuffy; it seemed unlikely that he would get away in under a couple of hours; he had probably already got all that could usefully be had from Stella Bruce, who was a pretty peripheral figure in Strong's long life anyway.

'He was, to be frank, a bit of a liar.'

Mark perked up. 'Really?'

'I don't know if I should tell you this or not.'

He gazed at her, with an expression of attentive sympathy.

'It seems, well, slightly disloyal.'

He inclined his head, ambiguously.

'But the vital thing is that you should have the truth, for this book.'

He nodded, with gravity.

There was a pause. She leaned forward. 'The Russia book – you know the one I mean?'

'Of course.'

'The one that was so well written up at the time. Everybody saying how super it was.'

'Yes – *Long Weekend in the Caucasus.*' Strong, naturally, had latched on to the period vogue for travel writing. The *Road to Anatolia* had been followed only a couple of years later by the more ambitious *Long Weekend* – a considerable bestseller.

'Gil never went anywhere near the place.'

'Then . . .' said Mark, after a moment's digestion of this. 'How . . .? I mean, it's full of the most graphic stuff.'

'He bought it,' said Stella. She eyed him smugly from her nest of pale blue satin cushions, pleased with the effect she was having.

'*Bought it*? But how on earth . . .?

'Do you know about someone called Hugo Flack?'

Mark shook his head.

'Well, he was a kind of crazy layabout who was around then – everyone sort of knew him vaguely, you ran into him at parties, he wrote a bit of poetry but he never really got anywhere and he was always broke, borrowing money right and left. You know the type . . . Anyway, he was going to do this travel book on the Caucasus, he somehow got the cash to go there and he looked around and came back with stacks of notes and then he never got around to writing it up. He couldn't write for toffee, anyway. He got ill – he'd been drinking like a fish for years – and he came to Gil sponging as usual, and Gil gave him a fiver to get rid of him and then he started talking about the Caucasus stuff. Gil asked to have a look at it and Hugo brought it along and Gil offered him a hundred quid for it. That's how Gil wrote *Long Weekend*.'

Mark considered. There was, one had to admit, a certain plausability to it all. 'Why did he do it?'

'Because he'd promised the publishers a travel book and he needed the cash and he knew it would sell if it was right and he loathed travelling.'

'How did he know this fellow – Flack – wouldn't go round telling people?'

'He didn't. He took a risk. He couldn't trust him, of course, but Hugo was a frightful story-teller, he was known for it, no one ever believed anything he said. It would be his word against Gil's. And in fact Hugo died only a few months after the book came out so Gil was in the clear. No one else knew. Except,' – coyly – 'me.'

'How did, er . . .'

'Because Hugo came to see Gil to sponge money at my flat. He knew better than to go to Dean Close – Violet would have chucked him out straight away.'

'Does Flack have any relations still alive, do you know?'

Stella made a little moue. 'Now you're not telling me you don't believe me?'

Mark looked determinedly over the top of her head. 'Simply one has to check and double-check. Everything.'

'Well, you won't be able to this time,' she said petulantly. 'I shouldn't think there's a soul. He never married and God only knows where he came from. From under a stone, I should think. And it's no good asking Hermione, she doesn't know a thing.'

A change of subject seemed expeditious. 'I've been spending quite a lot of time at Dean Close,' said Mark. 'Miss Summers has a lot of papers down there, it turns out.'

'Are there any letters of mine?' asked Stella avidly.

'Not that I've come across so far.'

'Do tell me if there are. That'll be Hermione's girl, of course. I remember seeing her when she was about two. Johnny and I called at Dean Close once after we were married and Hermione was there. *Louche* as ever. And the child. What's she like now?'

'She runs a Garden Centre,' said Mark.

'What a shame. Of course Hermione never seemed to have the vaguest connection with Gil either. If Violet hadn't been the type she was one would almost have wondered . . .'

Mark, with distaste, contemplated a rococo cherub dangling its foot above a mirror. Stella chuntered on. He thought about her allegation. Hmn. Possibly. But equally possibly not. Without some other conveniently corroborating piece of evidence, such as the survival of this bloke Flack's notes among the stuff at Dean Close, it was dubious material. Boredom returned. When Stella paused, momentarily, for breath, he seized his opportunity and rose to leave.

At the door he said, 'By the way, how did Strong spend the time he was thought to be in the Caucasus?'

She smiled, archly, 'With me, of course. In the south of France. It was heavenly, the mimosa was out and we had a delicious little villa near Antibes.'

'He wasn't totally averse to travel, then?'

'The south of France wasn't travel. It was simply the place people like us went to, in those days.'

Mark, released, stopped in the middle of Putney Bridge for a few minutes' appreciation of the river. Gulls bobbed on the water like bath-toys; a solitary oarsman flashed deftly beneath him; the sky was pale turquoise ribbed with dove-grey cloud. Everything seemed very clean and neat: white buildings and paint-box red buses and seal-black taxis. He found London inexhaustibly satisfying, even in its less agreeable manifestations. He liked Tottenham Court Road and Battersea and the wastelands of St Pancras, for complex reasons that would not have been understood by environmentalists. He shared, fervently, Gilbert Strong's feeling about travel. On the occasions when Diana succeeded in getting him out of the country a weary longing to get back to normal life conflicted uncomfortably with a dutiful interest in what he was seeing that was more the product of training than the emotions. One ought to know about other places; one didn't necessarily want to. The difference between him and Strong in this, of course, was that nowadays you could more easily get away with it; Strong, in the age when no self-respecting intellectual could be seen to be untravelled, had had to grit his teeth and put up with it. He had been at one time or another to Morocco and Anatolia and Serbia and Spain. He had turned out his quota of articles that were the required combination of erudition and wit. He could keep his end up with the Harold Nicholsons and the Norman Douglases; indeed, his style in the travel book was a ramshackle marriage of the two. All the same, Mark was not surprised to be told that he didn't really care for it; that part at least of Stella's story was probably true. It was borne out by certain cultural complacencies of Strong's and a detectable fidgetiness, sometimes, in the face of Bloomsbury and others of his contemporaries. He could well have been a closet Georgian, in some respects.

In the tube, these thoughts gave way to others. The others, in fact, had been there all the time, lurking in the background like a toothache. Now, they surfaced with full force and he sat glumly in the Piccadilly Line, confronting them. There was no evading it; self-deception got you nowhere; he knew what had happened to him.

6

A MINOR IRRITATION of working life at the Garden Centre was the need to pander to popular taste. Bill and Carrie were united in their dislike of French marigolds, calceolarias, berberis, begonias, salvia, and most of the varieties of rose requested by their clientele. Nevertheless commercial common sense required that they should supply these. 'I'd like to infect them all with black spot,' said Carrie, trundling a new delivery of 'Peace' and 'Queen Elizabeth' to the rose section.

'They'd only be back for more, duckie. They know what they like.'

Occasionally they cherished thoughts of retreating into the esoteric world of specialisation. No more bedding plants or peat or bulbs or fibre-glass urns or ranks of forsythia and 'Frensham'; just a chaste line in irises or hellebores or peonies. It could be done; others did it. But in fact both also took an unstated pride in their own success, the product of efficiency and sheer hard work. Carrie derived, daily, a quiet satisfaction from the sight of the crowded greenhouses, the well-tended stock beds. Bill liked the idea of being able to supply anyone with anything, even if you sometimes despised their requirements. Neither was financially ambitious: indeed as the Centre prospered and they were able to pay themselves higher salaries they experienced a slight embarrassment. Carrie could never think of anything at all to spend money on. Bill gave a good deal of his to his mother.

The point was not the money but to do what you did as well as it could be done.

'It's them that balances the books,' Bill added, 'not your poncing around with *Sedum* and *Gentiana*.' Carrie, unruffled, continued to heave roses into position. The jibe at her alpines was not all that seriously meant. The great thing about Bill was that he was hardly ever cross – genuinely cross. Carrie was made anxious by disapproval and preferred tranquillity in her relationships. All of which, as she herself vaguely realised, no doubt stemmed from the hurly-burly of her childhood. Hermione was famous for the extravagance of her temper and while Carrie herself had learned to avoid trouble by being as self-effacing as possible, she nevertheless had numerous distasteful memories of Hermione having hysterics at Rome station or in the market at Marrakesh, throwing things at her current lover or indulging in outbursts of maudlin weeping. The merest suggestion of a scene, nowadays, or even raised voices or signs of impending disagreement, sent her racing for cover. Once she had observed a woman pocket a pair of Wilkinson secateurs in the sales office and had cravenly done nothing rather than face the ensuing commotion. When aggressive customers complained about the demise of plants that they had clearly murdered through neglect or ignorance, she hastily gave them replacements, behind Bill's back.

This inclination to please people if you possibly could and to back away from raised emotional temperatures had, of course, complicated the few more intense relationships she had had. Being obliging had got her into bed with people she hadn't really wanted to get into bed with, whereas trying to avoid scenes had got her even further embroiled with her boyfriend at the plant nursery. When he asked her if she loved him she went on saying yes (while futilely crossing her fingers) long after she knew she didn't. Eventually, of course, there had been the most dreadful scene which had raged all over the dwarf conifers (to this day the sight of a juniper gave her a nervous twinge) and ended up with him weeping. Carrie hadn't realised that men could, or did, and had been appalled. She had resolved never again to get enmeshed in saying things she wasn't absolutely sure that she meant, and so far this had worked. She didn't, in fact, have very many relationships; the closest was with Bill and was based on compatibility, mutual interests and the amiability of both. The emotional temperature had always been comfortably low.

Bill, dumping another insensitively thriving 'Peace' alongside its mates, said, 'When's your boyfriend coming back?'

'What on earth are you talking about?'

'Our Mark.'

'Today, I think. And he's not my boyfriend. He's married, anyway.'

Bill laughed.

'You are *silly*,' said Carrie vaguely. 'Oh dear – we're out of "Albertine" again. And "Etoile d'Hollande".'

'He's taken a great shine to you, married or not.'

'Oh, for goodness *sake* . . .' said Carrie. Quite irritably, for her.

When Mark arrived, that afternoon, he parked the car in his usual place slightly to the right of the front door and took his things up to his room. There, everything was just as he had left it, except that a fly had died on the open pages of Strong's 1937 diary. He put down his briefcase and stood for a moment, looking out of the window. Then he went downstairs again and outside. He walked round into the Garden Centre. The girl who looked after the sales office was talking to a customer; Bill, in the distance, was doing something with plastic sheeting. Mark stood there, chewing his lip.

Carrie came out of one of the greenhouses, caught sight of him, waved, and went into the other greenhouse.

Mark returned to his room and worked. Several times he ceased to read or take notes but sat staring at the line of trees beyond the window, which were shaggy with rooks' nests. Strong, in fact, had had a thing or two to say about rooks in his time; the noise they made woke him in the mornings. Mark, though, was not at these points thinking either about Strong or about the rooks.

At six o'clock he came downstairs and went through into the kitchen. Bill was doing a fry-up; Carrie was laying the table, an uncomplicated process. Everyone said 'Hello' at the same moment. Bill added, 'Two eggs or three?'

'One, please.'

'We manual workers,' said Bill, 'see things different.' Mark smiled, half-heartedly.

They ate. Mark and Bill had a conversation about dentists. Bill and Carrie discussed, in a desultory way, the terms offered by a new supplier of fertiliser. Mark asked Carrie what he should put in the window boxes of his London house. Someone telephoned. Bill said he'd push off over to see Ron for an hour or two. Mark and Carrie began to wash up.

Mark said, 'What are you going to do now?'

'Do things outside, I s'pose,' said Carrie, glancing at the window. It was a fine, warm evening.

'Can I help?'

'Well . . .' Carrie, who was heading for the greenhouses, hesitated. There wasn't, to be frank, a thing he could do without getting in the way. Charity prevailed: 'O.K.'

In the event, he sat down on the low stone wall by the stock beds while Carrie inspected plants and hoed.

'What are they?'

'Syringa and viburnum, mostly.'

'Why are they in those tormented attitudes?'

'It's called layering,' said Carrie patiently. 'It's the way you propagate them. There, that'll do. I'm going to the compost shed now.'

'Could you come and sit down for a moment,' said Mark. 'There's something I want to say.'

Carrie looked at him in surprise.

'It won't take all that long.' He sounded somewhat terse. She wondered if she'd done something wrong. Placatingly, she sat.

He turned and looked at her. 'I'm afraid I've fallen in love with you.'

There was a long silence, during which he continued to gaze at her and Carrie looked first down at her feet and then began to nibble at a finger-nail. Eventually she said, 'Oh dear.' Then she added, 'Are you sure?'

'Of course I'm sure. I'd hardly be saying it if I wasn't, would I?'

Carrie abandoned the finger-nail and took her boot off. She shook out a pebble and set the boot down on the path. She was wearing bright orange socks into which her dungarees were tucked. She said, 'I shouldn't think Diana's awfully pleased, is she?'

'Diana doesn't *know*,' replied Mark violently.

'Oh.' There was a further silence. At last Carrie continued, in a rather bright voice, 'Some people fall in love a lot, don't they? I expect you're one of them. I knew someone once like that. She said it was the most awful bother.'

'I am not,' said Mark, 'like that.' He took her hand and sat looking at it, stroking the fingers. Carrie too stared down. She said, 'I'm afraid my nails are filthy. They always are, however much I try to remember to clean them.'

Exasperation and passion were now so fused that Mark felt as though he might explode. He let go of Carrie's hand and she slipped it hastily under her thigh. He said, 'What do *you* feel about *me*?'

'Oh, I'm awfully glad you came. I don't meet people all that much or at least only people to do with gardening. The only thing is you being so much better educated than me and all that.'

'Don't be so damned humble.'

'Sorry. I didn't exactly mean you're *better* than me. Just different. Good at different things. I mean, I don't read books. I've really hardly read anything very much.'

'You don't fall in love with people because of what they've read.' Unfortunately, he thought with bitterness.

'I s'pose not,' said Carrie. She put her boots on again. 'I should think Diana must have lots of people in love with her, hasn't she? I mean before she married you. She's so beautiful and good at conversation.'

'I'd really rather not talk about Diana.'

'Sorry.'

Mark said, 'I don't know at all what you feel about me. I don't know if you even like me.'

Carrie looked desperately towards the house, as though willing it to burst into flames. 'Is that the phone ringing?'

'No.'

'Oh. Sometimes you can't quite hear it out here.'

'Do you like me, Carrie?'

She stared firmly down at the boots. 'Oh goodness yes, I like you very much.'

'Good,' said Mark grimly.

'You know,' said Carrie with a rush. 'I expect it must be to do with me being his granddaughter, don't you?'

'Frankly, no. I don't think that's got anything to do with it.'

'Oh, well . . . People don't usually fall in love with me, that's all.'

'And I don't make a practice of falling in love.'

'Then it really isn't anyone's fault, is it?' she said brightly.

Mark sighed. 'Such situations seldom are. It doesn't improve matters.'

'Perhaps it'll sort of go away when you get to know me better.'

'Perhaps. Or equally well perhaps not. In the meantime it's generally agreed to be one of the more exacting experiences in life.' He looked at her. Carrie looked back – with a small propitiating smile. Mark yanked the hand from under her thigh and took it firmly in his. At that moment the telephone, unmistakably, began to ring from within the house. Carrie leaped to her feet. 'Oh dear – I'd better dash . . .' She raced away.

Mark, pole-axed by emotion, stared after her. What he was going through or enduring or enjoying or whatever it might be was, he realised, something entirely new to him. The process of becoming involved with Diana had not been at all the same; there had been initial attraction which had bloomed into very definite desire and alongside that a gathering compatibility stemming from shared opinions and tastes and acquaintances, all of which had ultimately coalesced into what was apparently love. Yes, what was definitely love. This Carrie business was another matter altogether: some kind of awful involuntary seizure. Compatibility and all that simply did not come into it. Desire most certainly did. As did exasperation and something like despair and also the most extraordinary elation.

He took his glasses off and scrubbed them furiously with his handkerchief. Last month, time before Dean Close, seemed now like another era, as glassy and detached as the various decades through which Strong had tramped: irretrievable and vaguely nostalgic.

Thus passed Monday. Mark, waking on Tuesday, was aware first of the steely inhospitality of the mattress on the Dean Close spare bed, then of rooks, raucously clamouring, and finally of the events of yesterday. He travelled over exactly what had been said, by him and by her; it didn't help much.

When he got down to the kitchen neither Bill nor Carrie was there – already out at work, presumably. He made himself tea and toast and withdrew to his room, where he worked steadily through until lunch-time. He was reading a batch of Strong's diaries, a curious hotch-potch of jottings which combined a record – clearly incomplete – of what he had been doing and who he had been seeing with random reflections on this and that and occasional drafts of future works, in this case, notably, the 'Essay on Fiction'. One had to assume that the diaries were intended for eventual publication – Strong was far too professional a writer to put pen to paper on any scale without purpose – though in fact none had ever appeared. Nevertheless much of the material they included had, in the form of essays, articles and so forth; Strong had clearly pillaged them whenever short of an idea. It was the tone, and the extent of the omissions, that convinced Mark that they were meant for the general reader: all mention of Strong's private life, except for suitably uxorious or fatherly references, was left out and there was a great deal of genial reflection larded with the kind of gentle self-deprecation that is meant to indicate to the reader what an honest, unassuming chap the writer is. There were deliberately literary passages from time to time, dealing with places seen or people discussed, and these periodic excursions into a draft of some kind, usually unheralded, so that you lurched from a run-of-the-mill account of a dinner with Shaw at the Garrick to a passage like this: 'In life, the nature of a relationship is known only to two people: those at either end of it. All else is idle speculation, however much you and I may pride ourselves on our unerring perception and judgement of the feelings of others. The novelist is another matter; he or she really is omniscient. The relationship now is three-sided; there are the participants and there is also this god-like figure who knows it in its entirety, knows it indeed even better than those involved, who can slip from the one skin into the other.'

True, Mark thought, if a little obvious. That was the trouble with Strong; he had a knack of hitting nails on the head with such a flourish as to claim total originality. It gave one a good idea of what he must have been like in the flesh: pontificating away, banging his points home on the table, chucking home-made aphorisms around. Mark looked, guiltily, at his watch; the morning continued to crawl onwards. It would, eventually, be one o'clock and he could decently go down to the kitchen.

And, eventually, it was and he did and there she was sitting at the table eating bread and cheese, the orange socks on her feet and a streak of dirt down one cheek. At the same moment as Mark entered the room, saw her and experienced that universal thrill that is compounded of panic and exhilaration in equal proportions, it came to him that he was, quite simply, suffering a form of illness. He was temporarily disabled; there should be some kind of treatment for men of his age and situation thus stricken. It should be possible to go along to some professional but understanding bloke in a consulting-room and say, 'Look, I have this tiresome problem; I'm a busy man and I've fallen in love with a girl with whom I have nothing whatsoever in common and I happen to love my wife anyway and I can't afford the expenditure of time or emotion.' And the chap would nod and reach for a prescription pad and say, 'There's a lot of it around at the moment. Take these three times a day – they usually do the trick.' And that would be that.

She avoided his eyes. She said, 'Oh gosh, I hope there's some more bread. I expect there's some in the bin. Bill's just coming. D'you want some coffee?'

Mark sat down. 'I thought,' he said, 'I'd go for a drive this evening. Explore the local scenery. I'm beginning to feel desk-bound. Will you come with me?'

Carrie became very involved with the arrangement of cheese on bread. 'Well . . .'

Bill came in.

'I was just suggesting to Carrie,' said Mark, 'that she treats me to a tour of the local beauty-spots this evening. Seeing as it's such a nice day. What about you?'

Bill, washing his hands at the sink, thought that this was a good idea. Give the girl an evening off. Count him out though – one or two things he had to see to.

'Ah . . .' said Mark, in tones of regret. 'O.K., then, Carrie?'

'Well . . .' said Carrie, squirming.

'Sixish, then. I'll stand you a pub supper somewhere.'

'There,' said Bill. 'Say thank you to the gentleman.'

Mark cut himself another hunk of cheese. 'Terrible racket the rooks make in the mornings. What's it all about?'

'Sex,' said Bill.

'Really?' Mark pondered this with the air of one receiving interesting but possibly debatable information.

'They're nesting,' said Carrie, and went pink.

'Your grandfather disliked them. He organised shoots from time to time.'

'How horrid.'

'Live and let live is her line,' said Bill. 'Regardless. Universal tolerance, eh? She hasn't got it in for anything. Or anyone.'

Carrie, pinker still, muttered, 'Oh, don't be stupid.' Mark, covertly, beamed upon her. Bill, ignoring them both, picked up the local paper.

When at last he had got her into the car Mark said, 'I had in mind the Sturminster direction, if that's all right by you? A general potter round the area and stop for anything interesting.'

Carrie, it turned out, was a good deal less familiar with the locality than one might have expected. She knew this place or that because it was where she went for supplies of one kind or another, or because she had delivered things to customers there, but that was the extent of her knowledge. For Mark, on the other hand, this lush emotive landscape had two dimensions – what it was and what it suggested. It was peopled twice over, both by the mundane matter-of-fact figures of the transistor-playing girl who filled the car with petrol for him or the pseudo-military landlord of the pub at which they stopped and those other presences, in many ways more powerful: Tess and Angel Clare and Bathsheba and Henchard and the rest of them. The names signalled on road signs – Dorchester and Blandford Forum and Shaftesbury – had also these inescapable reflections. The whole place was both what it was and what one knew it to be. This preoccupied him so much, despite everything else, that once he said, 'I must go to Casterbridge at some point – I've never even been there.'

'Where?'

Mark, put out, crashed a gear. 'Damn. Dorchester, I mean. Dorchester is really Casterbridge, in Hardy's novel. The Mayor of, and all that.'

Carrie considered this for a moment and said, reasonably enough, 'Then it isn't really Casterbridge, if it's in a book, it's really Dorchester.'

'Well, yes, I see what you mean. But if you know the books very well it all gets a bit confused.' Hell – one didn't want to start going on about books again, the damn things seem to crop up all the time, whatever you did.

'Are they good books?' enquired Carrie. She sounded quite dispassionate; on the other hand she might just be making conversation.

'Well . . .' said Mark. He decided against an in-depth literary consideration of Hardy. 'There's one I'm rather fond of about a girl who is seduced and has a baby and then meets the man she really loves and marries him and when she tells him about the baby he walks out on her, more or less, and eventually she's driven to live with the man who seduced her and when her husband comes back she kills him.'

'The husband?'

'No. The seducer. And in the end she's hanged. At Winchester.'

There was a pause. 'It sounds like one I read once – Bill's mum left it in the bathroom after she'd been staying. I can't remember what it was called. It was that kind with pink covers and a picture that you see lots of in corner shops.'

'Mills and Boon,' said Mark after a moment.

'They come in Gothic or Historical or Hospital Romance. This was Historical, I think.'

Mark was silent. They passed a row of beetle-browed cottages and a pub festooned with floral hanging baskets. 'Actually that wouldn't really be very like the book I'm talking about. There's a lot more to it than what I said. It's a question of how you tell a story, really, as well as what the story is.'

'Mmn,' said Carrie, and then, 'Could we stop for a moment?'

He pulled into the verge. Carrie hopped out and vanished behind the hedge. Mark, tactfully, stared in the opposite direction. After a few moments she called out, 'Don't you want to come?' Perplexed, he scrambled through the hedge to find her half-way up a hill-side, on her hands and knees.

'Orchids.'

Mark inspected. They looked, to the untutored eye, rather scruffy little flowers, but he made noises of appreciation. 'How did you know they'd be here?'

'It just looked an orchidy sort of field,' said Carrie vaguely. She sat down on the grass. It was an evening of blue and green and gold: sky and grass and warm thick air that seemed, in the fading sunlight, as though it were slightly tinted. Carrie glittered all over in its rays – her sandy lashes and brows, the hairs on her bare arms. Mark sat down beside her and watched her out of the corner of one eye. He wanted desperately to touch her.

She picked a buttercup and took it to pieces. 'What you said yesterday – is it any different today?'

'No. Frankly.'

'Oh. I thought perhaps it might be sort of getting better.'

'Well, it isn't,' said Mark irritably. 'The condition tends to be a bit more enduring than that. At least at my age. Perhaps,' he added, 'it would have been better if I'd never told you.'

'Oh, I expect you should have. I mean if it was bothering you.'

Exasperation seized him. He had to wait until it subsided a

bit before he could speak. 'Haven't you ever felt like this about anyone?'

'Actually I'm afraid I haven't.'

He was about to say, 'But you must have read about it,' and checked himself. Instead he said with determined lightness, 'Well, we'll just have to hope for a rapid recovery,' glancing sideways at Carrie to see how she took this. You couldn't tell. She was now making a buttercup chain. He laid a hand on her knee. Carrie did not shift the knee but continued to fish in the grass for more buttercups. Mark, gazing into the blue wastes of Dorset, was quite unable to decide if he was extremely happy or much disturbed.

'Out *where*?'

'Driving around. It was a nice evening. Not raining.'

'All on your own?'

'Carrie came with me,' he said. 'She was at a loose end.'

In London traffic rumbled beyond the open window and someone was whistling. 'And how was that?' enquired Diana.

'Oh – fine.'

'Given the weather, I thought why don't I come down on Friday instead of you coming back. Then you could work through the weekend and come back with me on Monday. I take it they wouldn't mind?'

At Dean Close the hall clock thrummed and the rooks raged in the elms. 'Well. Yes. No, I'm sure they wouldn't. Yes, well, why not? On Friday, then?'

'Tomorrow. Suzanne can do without me for a day.'

'Tomorrow,' said Mark. 'I see.'

'Tomorrow. The ten-thirty train, if you could meet me.'

'Right,' he said.

'Diana rang. She'd like to come down for the weekend, if it's all right.'

'Oh, good,' said Carrie enthusiastically.

'Tomorrow. Till Monday, when I'll have to go back with her. I've got to do things in London next week.'

'I'd better see if there are any clean sheets for the bed.'

'So we won't get much more time alone together.'

'I s'pose we won't.'

'Tuesday evening was wonderful.'

'Yes,' said Carrie. 'I'm glad I found that orchid place.'

'I shall think about it when I'm back in London.'

'The orchid place?'

'Up to a point the orchid place,' he said.

'D'you think Diana would like to go there?'

'No.'

'Doesn't she like the country?'

'Up to a point, again. In moderation and largely through the windows of cars.'

'Well,' said Carrie, fidgeting. 'I must get on . . .'

'I'll see you this evening.'

'Yes.'

'If you're not busy.'

'Yes.'

'I'm not sure if that means you will be busy or you won't.'

'Nor am I,' said Carrie, after a moment's reflection.

He looked at her with despair. He could not recall ever having known anyone before with whom conversation took this disconcerting elastic course. Except, it occurred to him, children. Carrie went out into the garden and he climbed the stairs to his room where, festering with various emotions, he opened the next of Strong's diaries. It occurred to him also and for the first time that Strong was personally responsible for his present situation: if he, Strong, had not perpetrated – indirectly – Carrie he, Mark, would not be feeling like this. His attitude towards Strong underwent another subtle adjustment.

7

DIANA WAS afflicted not only with an indiscriminately recording eye but also with an unstoppable urge to improve. She had long since learned that on the whole this could not be indulged, but there was still nothing she could do about it. On the brief train journey from London to Dorset she redesigned some British Rail posters, reconstructed the train compartment, re-dressed the girl opposite and gave her a new hair-do, and thought for a while about her own kitchen, which could do with an uplift. That, at least, was a possibility. When she saw Mark at the station barrier she noted that he needed a clean shirt and that his shoes would soon be past redemption, but, with the wisdom of experience, forebore mentioning either of these things.

In the car she set about assessing the next three days.

'What do they do at the weekends?'

'Work. It's when the Garden Centre gets most customers.'

'What are the eating arrangements?'

'Haphazard,' said Mark.

'Would it be taken amiss if I suggested doing the cooking?'

'It would be taken with a sigh of relief, I should imagine.'

Diana, who disliked inaction as much as she disliked indifferent food, looked satisfied. 'Shops?'

'The village. Or Winterbury for anything ambitious.'

When they arrived at Dean Close Diana strode straight into

the Garden Centre to find Carrie. Mark saw her briskly greeting and proposing. Carrie shifted from foot to foot, smiling. For some reason, the whole exchange made him uncomfortable. He retreated upstairs where, after a few minutes, Diana joined him.

'She seems to like the idea. I'll go down and suss out the kitchen and then take the car to Winterbury.' She stood behind Mark's shoulder, looking down at the desk. 'What awful scrawly handwriting he had. These people should think of others.'

'Yes,' said Mark. 'They should.'

'Odd girl, that. Slightly fey, one feels.'

Mark made a note and turned the page; he wore a frown of concentration.

'I'll leave you to it, then. See you later.'

He nodded, and made another note.

Thus it was, that evening, that the inmates of Dean Close ate, for supper, not the usual fry-up but chilled cucumber soup followed by a prawn quiche and interestingly eclectic salad, ending with a lemon sorbet and cheese. There was a bottle of wine. Diana whisked from stove to sink to fridge, explaining how her menu had had to be adapted to the shortcomings of the kitchen.

'No,' said Bill. 'A garlic press is not known here, I'm afraid. Now I know what to give Carrie for her birthday.'

Carrie said little and ate enormously. Bill was evidently concealing amusement. Mark, tense with various reactions, made some conversational efforts of which, later, he had no recollection whatsoever. Diana, apparently impervious, presided.

The ghost of Gilbert Strong, were he looking on, would have been hard put to it to know what to make of them. He would probably have paid most attention to Diana, as a man with an eye for an attractive and vivacious woman. Mark he would have registered – a mite wearily perhaps – as a type he knew only too well, a bird of a feather, a book man, a tribal associate. Carrie he would probably have passed over, unless he happened to get a whiff of that faint, oh very faint, family resemblance. Bill would have mystified him, his dress and accent being too difficult to define; he would probably have taken him for the chauffeur or handyman, though in that case his presence at the table would be puzzling. But the whole set-up would have baffled: what had these people to do one with another?

When Mark and Diana were courting he had realised one day that she was literal-minded. He had said, in a rather uncharacteristic moment of sentiment, 'Just think, we might never have met. That I should have met you, out of all the people in the world . . .' And Diana had replied, after a moment's consideration, 'Oh, but we were bound to. I mean, we both know Peter Jamison and his friends all meet each other.' Speculation, for her, was confined to thinking about the various different outcomes suggested by alternative courses of action. She was more interested in the future than the past. It was a habit of mind that affected her attitude to literature, naturally enough. Fantasy maddened her, for obvious reasons. Equally, deviousness or obscurity of purpose irritated her; she insisted on discussing the motivation of, say, Dorothea or Anna Karenina or Catherine Earnshaw as though they were acquaintances faced with tiresome but soluble practical difficulties. Henry James, as you would expect, infuriated her. 'I simply do not understand what these people are trying to say. Have you ever heard anyone talk like that?' And when Mark would begin, cautiously, 'Well, no, but that isn't entirely the point, it's a question of style and . . .' she would interrupt, triumphantly, 'Exactly!' Back then, in the courting period, which now had a fictional character of its own, he had been unwilling to be too contentious. Nowadays, they had rather ceased to talk about that kind of thing. Nevertheless, Diana continued to read a great deal, though what she derived was slightly mysterious to Mark; people who are unable to suspend disbelief, he reckoned, are difficult both to entertain and to enlighten.

'One sometimes wonders,' said Diana, 'how on earth one fetches up with particular people. I mean, these two aren't really potential soul-mates, from our point of view.'

Mark glanced warily at her along the bedclothes; the first half of the remark was uncharacteristic. Outside, the rooks were into their morning round of contention. Diana was wearing a sweater over her night-dress.

'He is gay. I'm sure of it.'

Mark grunted.

'I froze, all night. Of course in this case it's him who has to be held responsible. Old Gilbert S.'

Mark, discomfited to hear his own sentiments quite so accurately voiced, said, 'Well . . . somewhat indirectly.'

'Have you found anything on this travel book he's supposed to have lifted off someone else?'

'Not so far. I'm not sure that I really expect to. If there's anything in the story the first thing he'd have done, I assume, would be to make sure no one was going to find out accidentally.'

'You, in other words.'

'I suppose so.' This, Mark realised, led you off into a really rather odd line of thought. He lay in Gilbert Strong's spare room bed and pursued it while Diana, huddled into a winter dressing-gown, went off to the bathroom. Here you were, tethered for a period of your life in this curious intimate fashion to a man you never knew. And all the while he, too, in his way had had to make allowances for you, admit you into his life as it were. When you were still in the cradle, or not even in existence. Strong had known all too well that people would be writing his biography. He had stashed away letters and diaries and manuscripts in the full knowledge that at some point a faceless man or woman would pore over them, speculating. What did that feel like? 'Jake Balokowsky, my biographer . . . "I'm stuck with this old fart at least a year." ' Well, no – dry detachment of that kind wasn't really Strong's line. He would have been more inclined to do a bit of interfering or even manipulating. How far was it accidental, for instance, that certain volumes of the diaries survived but others didn't? That whole chunks of correspondence had disappeared? The memoir was clearly designed as a piece of special pleading. By which, said Mark sternly, to the shade of Gilbert Strong, I am not taken in. I cannot see you as an exemplary husband nor indeed as a tolerant and accommodating friend. I think you probably did rather badly by Violet and there is incontrovertible evidence that you were a difficult bloke to deal with in many of your more impersonal relationships. You undoubtedly went in for a good deal of shameless literary politicking to get yourself reviewing and to push your own works. You buttered people up when it suited you and gently shed them when they weren't useful any more. I doubt if your published judgements were always quite as detached as they ought to have been (but, he uncomfortably reflected, which of us has not occasionally bent with the wind, however mildly . . .). I don't care for the way you conducted that campaign against De la Mare. You were overbearing towards those you regarded as your inferiors, by several accounts, and dismissive of those who bored you. On the other hand, you wrote some interesting books, some of your insights are penetrating and thought-provoking, and you were undoubtedly extremely good company, or people would not have sought you out as they did. Your second wife certainly loved you; two of your servants stayed with you for thirty years; you maintained your daughter's ex-governess in a nursing home until she died.

I am not to be fooled, he said, or at least only up to a point. Gilbert Strong's house creaked around him. Downstairs Gilbert Strong's granddaughter would be making (and probably burning) the breakfast toast.

Carrie was doing her best to put the matter of Mark and his condition out of her mind, in the hope that it would thus disappear. This had worked occasionally in the past with unwelcome situations. If she pretended it hadn't happened and wasn't happening, then perhaps that would turn out to be the case. She found it rather hard to believe in anyway, especially on seeing Diana again, who was so obviously more interesting in every respect to a person like Mark. She felt uncomfortable with Diana, but that was nothing to do with what Mark had said; it was simply that Diana was everything that she wasn't, and she really couldn't find anything to say to her. Not that that mattered all that much, since Diana did the talking in any case. Mark, on the other hand, was quite easy to talk to; she wasn't uncomfortable with him, even now, though she was beginning to have this feeling of guilt. You really couldn't be unpleasant to someone who liked you; if a person announced that they were in love with you it was even more difficult. They acquired, like it or not, a claim on you.

She chewed her lip, unwillingly pondering this. The click of Diana's heels could be heard in the stone passage beyond the kitchen door. Carrie jumped up. Blue smoke fumed from the toaster.

Diana said, 'Good morning. Mark's on his way.' She reached for the toaster and switched it off. 'And I think we all deserve an outing tomorrow.' Carrie looked at her in alarm.

The car park was crowded. Diana had laddered her tights and wished she had brought a sweater as well as her jacket. It was freezing. Typical English summer day – well, early summer. May. She thought fleetingly of her holiday scheme: Tunisia would be lovely, if Mark could be persuaded. She said, 'There are hundreds of people. Pity. I suppose we climb this thing? What did you say it was, darling?'

Two Frenchmen, in pointedly English clothes, stood at the start of the track, looking up the hill. Diana said, 'Excuse me,' swinging past them. She glanced back; Mark was just behind, looking morose. Carrie had paused and was staring at something in the grass. She had taken off the denim jacket that Diana had persuaded her to buy from the boutique in Dorchester and left it in the car; her T-shirt was frayed at the neck and the colour clashed with her dungarees. Well, Diana thought, I've tried. That jacket did something for her. One of these days, by hook or by crook, I'll get her to a hairdresser.

The path was coated with thin creamy mud. She picked her way from one dry place to another. This camp or fortress or whatever was a series of turfy hillsides enfolding one another. Diana began determinedly to climb the first ridge. From there you could see the next, and then a plateau dotted with people. She went on. When she got to the top of the second ridge she saw that Mark had sat down and was staring out into the landscape. Carrie drew level with him and paused. It had taken quite a bit of persuasion to get her to come – presumably shy or diffident or feeling she'd be in the way. And now she trailed rather like a child: biddable but not contributing much. Nevertheless, Diana thought, it's what she needs – some company a bit more stimulating than the live-in gay, not that he isn't nice enough but far from one of the world's most scintillating characters, and what an odd set-up, incidentally, if they weren't the types they are you'd think it distinctly liberated. She looked at her watch, and waved. If all was to be done that apparently Mark wished done then they must get on. Mark had stood up. He gestured at the interior of the camp or fortress or whatever; Carrie gazed in response. Diana, faintly unsettled, thought: it's funny, he's not as irritated by her as he ought to be by a girl like that. As he normally is.

In the car she saw to her hair, with the aid of the driving-mirror. 'They certainly picked windy residential sites, in the Stone Age. I'm borrowing your sweater, Mark, I'm perished.' She caught Carrie's eye in the mirror, and smiled. 'All right, back there?' Carrie said, 'Yes, thank you.'

'Iron, not Stone. And it was a defensive site rather than somewhere they lived.' He put up his hand to straighten the mirror.

'Don't. I haven't finished. He hustles one,' she said to Carrie. 'You have to resist. All right, now we'll go to this museum of yours. And then I want a cup of tea. Does Dorchester rise to your good old-fashioned tea shop?'

'I don't know,' said Carrie. 'I've never looked.'

'Then we shall find out.'

They stood and gazed into Hardy's petrified study: book-lined walls, desk, chair, lamp. Diana said, 'Now that I find quite extraordinarily creepy.' She looked at Carrie. 'Don't you?'

'Is he the one who . . .?'

'Yes,' said Mark abruptly. 'He is.'

'Is what?' enquired Diana.

'Wrote *Tess*.'

'The one that got hanged?' said Carrie.

'Mmn.'

Diana looked from one to the other of them. She said to Carrie, 'You've been given his Hardy lecture, have you?'

Carrie went bright pink.

'Not at all,' said Mark. 'I merely . . .'

Carrie broke in. 'Why,' – brightly – 'is it creepy?'

'A *study* in a glass case?' said Diana. 'Like a doll's house. Of course it's creepy.' She turned away. 'Come on. Time to look for this tea shop.'

She strode off through the museum, past the fossils and the displays of agricultural implements and the stuffed animals, without looking to see if they were following. They would be. Presumably.

He stood beside the car staring up at Maiden Castle and shed, for a few moments, the presences of both Diana and Carrie. It was larger than you expected, billowing away there, and somehow wilder despite the trail of people on the path and climbing the turf ramparts. He kept seeing, also, some eighteenth-century print of it, neater and tamer with statutory gesticulating frock-coated picturesque figure in the foreground. Since then, the Ministry of the Environment had done its stuff with fences and notices and the cars glittered in the sun and there was a strident ice-cream van doing good business, but even so . . .

Diana said, 'There are hundreds of people. Well, I warned you. Tourist site on a Saturday afternoon.' She marched off up the path. Mark locked the car and looked round for Carrie: 'All right?' She nodded. He wasn't sure if she was hating the afternoon or not. Diana had bulldozed her into coming, disregarding her excuses; he had stood by, embarrassed, both wanting her to come and not wanting her to. Wanting her to, on the whole. And then there had been a business of Diana hauling her into a shop and making her buy a coat thing which admittedly suited her rather well but with which she was clearly uncomfortable. She had taken it off again now, he noticed.

They passed two Frenchmen, one saying to the other with precise, upper-class diction, 'Voilà – le ciel tourmenté des peintres anglais . . .' Mark looked up and there indeed was a Constable sky with great swags of pewter-bellied clouds sweeping down to the tops of the hills. And below, in a shaft of light, were feathery grey splodges of Cotman trees and a great glowing Constable cornfield and a sweep of Paul Nash plough and the distant silvery white tower of a John Piper church. He stood for a moment, concurrent speculations showering through the mind: did the pleasure derived from landscape come from what you saw or what was prompted by what you saw? Did children find the world beautiful before people told them it was, or only after? Was it ever possible to look at anything, after the age of about four, without what you knew interfering with what you saw?

He glanced back. Carrie appeared to be investigating a discarded cigarette packet beside the path. He loitered for a moment, and went on. When he reached the top of the first rampart he sat down. Diana was now in the central enclosure. Carrie, dawdling, was on her way up. When she drew level he said, 'It's odd you've never been here before.' He pointed out the concealed entrance and told her what he could remember of the last Celtic stand against the Romans; he thought she seemed interested, but you couldn't be sure. Above them, Diana was waving impatiently.

In the museum, he was beset by the gloom such places sometimes engendered. All this information, all this evidence of the past, labelled and pinned down and marshalled into glass cases. How much more interesting, in the last resort, was that small child swinging on a balustrade, having discovered suddenly the charms of centrifugal force, or that man and woman in the doorway, frozen in a moment's unheard talk, both faces dark with anger. Discontentedly, he moved past medieval pottery and indigenous reptiles; maybe I am not at heart a fact man, he thought, maybe I have spent my life doing the wrong thing. Sometimes I don't give a damn about truth.

And then there was the ultimate mockery of Hardy's enshrined study. He stood alongside Diana and Carrie and inspected it. One was viewing, he supposed, one of those interesting points at which history ceases and mythology is born. Certainly the effect of this curious construction was to make you wonder if Hardy ever actually existed. Diana was going on about something. She said to Carrie, 'You've been given his Hardy lecture, have you?' Carrie went bright pink and he felt simultaneously protective and defensive; the orchid evening came sweeping back, and with it his present adolescently diseased state. 'Not at all,' he protested, and then Diana was waving a dismissive hand at the displayed study and comparing it to a doll's house. And marching off.

They followed, he and Carrie. He said, 'I hope this hasn't been an awful afternoon for you. I didn't know if you really wanted to come or not.'

Carrie considered. 'I didn't, really. But it's been quite nice. There've been . . . things.'

'What things?'

'Oh – just things.'

I am temporarily unbalanced, he thought, that is how I shall have to look at it. I am having a middle-aged literary hallucination. Company executives get coronaries; those of us who are in the book business get a bad attack of life.

As soon as Diana turned her back Carrie wriggled out of the denim jacket and left it on the seat. She felt all wrong in it and anyway it was a hot afternoon. She had had to wait until Diana wasn't looking before she could do this because, as she now realised, she was definitely somewhat frightened of Diana. It was fear combined with her usual tendency to oblige that had forced her to buy the jacket in the first place; it seemed so much simpler than annoying Diana.

And then she spotted the harebell at the side of the path and forgot for an instant both Diana and the jacket. And Mark. And there were clumps of eyebright, too, and a kind of saxifrage that she would have to look up later on. She squatted down to study it. Then she got up and moved on, eyes down so as not to miss anything. She could still experience that heady feeling of discovery that she used to get as a child, finding different plants, poring over French meadows or scratchy Spanish hillsides, isolating a tendril or a seed-pod. She was so intent on scanning the turf that she almost walked past Mark, sitting on the crest of a ridge. He said something about her not having been here before so she had to ask what the place had been for and he began to tell her; she could not follow, though, who had been fighting whom and over what and when it had all been and didn't like to ask. Diana was waving, higher up, and she said nervously, 'Hadn't we better go on?' Diana was beginning to have much the same effect on her as a sharp-eyed and hyper-critical French governess whom Hermione had once hired for a few weeks until the woman's horror at the *ménage* had made her hand in her notice, tight-lipped. As then, Carrie found herself trying to anticipate what you might be about to do wrong, and keep as unobtrusive as possible.

When they were in the car again she folded the jacket and stuffed it into the corner of the seat, twitching guiltily when she suddenly caught Diana's eye in the driving-mirror. They were to go to Dorchester now, apparently. She felt uncomfortably trapped, sitting there in the back seat behind them, without even a door through which you could leap if desperate. She retreated, as she had so often done in youth, into the privacy of her own concerns; she thought of the greenhouses and the stock beds, where she would much rather have been, pottering around cherishing and observing. ('You can't work *all* the time,' Diana had said, sweepingly. 'It's frightfully bad for people, they get atrophy of the soul. Of course you must come.') Indeed, she became so absorbed by this (the question of *Trillium* and low germination, whether or not to persist with some of the more flighty primula species or concentrate on the obliging ones) that without having noticed how they had got there she found they were standing in the museum in front of what seemed to be somebody's study set up inside a glass case. She looked, obediently; it reminded her somewhat of the study at Dean Close, at which people also respectfully gazed. If you took the glass away it would probably have that same peculiar smell – 'The actual smell of the 1930s' she had once heard a visitor to Dean Close declare. She remembered suddenly her conversation with Mark the other evening. 'Oh.' she said. 'Is he the one who . . .'

'Yes,' said Mark abruptly. 'He is.' He sounded cross. With her, she wondered, or with Diana? Married people, she knew, got extremely cross with each other, that one couldn't fail to observe; it had always seemed one very good reason for not being married.

And then Diana said something sharp about giving people lectures and it did sound as though they might be about to have an argument so she asked Mark a question hastily to try to stop it developing. Diana walked off and she followed with Mark. He said, 'I hope this hasn't been an awful afternoon for you. I didn't know if you really wanted to come or not.'

She wished he wouldn't ask things like that. She had never been any good at telling lies, even innocent little lies; people always knew, at once, she could see them knowing, staring at her. So she told the truth, and felt bad because he looked even more despondent.

It hadn't been a good afternoon at all, really. Except for the saxifrage.

8

CARRIE TURNED on Mark in horror. 'I couldn't possibly. I don't have to, do I?'

'No, no,' he said. 'Of course not. Not if you don't want to. I just thought you might think it fun.'

'I wouldn't. Anyway I wouldn't have anything to say.'

'Forget it. It was a thought, that's all.' A somewhat inept one, clearly. No, you couldn't really see Carrie in a BBC studio chatting to a microphone about her grandfather in response to the tactful promptings of an interviewer. There were plenty of other people he could suggest for the Strong section of the 'Writers Recollected' series. Stella Bruce would love it. Or . . .

'My mother,' said Carrie, 'would like that kind of thing. But she isn't here, of course.'

Hermione had not occurred to him. He considered. He didn't much care for the sound of her, frankly, but she might come up with something interesting. 'The programmes don't go out until the winter. She could be recorded, I suppose, if someone went down there.' An idea unfurled itself, put out a tentative green shoot . . . 'It's worth bearing in mind.'

They were in the kitchen. It was Monday morning. Diana was upstairs packing.

'I've got to be in London all this week,' he said.

'Yes. You told me.'

'I can't get down again till next Wednesday.'

'No.'

'So I won't see you till then.'

Carrie avoided his eye. 'No.'

'I hope,' said Mark bitterly, 'that one day you fall irrevocably for some unresponsive . . . manufacturer of plastic ferns.' He slammed through the green baize door and immediately returned. 'I don't mean that.'

Carrie beamed. 'Oh good.'

The Lammings, back in London, went about their respective business. Diana left for the gallery and Mark shut himself in his study where he contemplated moodily the filing-cabinets and card-index boxes for a few minutes and then set about putting in the right places the notes he had taken at Dean Close. Where work was concerned, his habits were tidy and methodical; it was the one weapon you had against the disorderliness of the subject matter. He then set off for the wine bar at which he was to meet the editor of a journal for which he occasionally wrote articles.

The place, recently established (Mark thought he remembered a delicatessen on the same site only a matter of months earlier), strove after an effect that was not immediately apparent. There was a long mahogany bar, gloomily lit, behind which a dapper but sullen-faced waiter polished glasses. There was a juke-box (silent, to Mark's relief), dark red flooring and walls, frondy plants in ugly china pots and alcoves in which glistening wooden pews for two confronted one another. It wasn't until he had been sitting on an uncomfortable bar-stool for a few minutes feeling as if he had been there for a very long time that he caught sight of a framed reproduction of the Edward Hopper painting of a thirties saloon in night-time New York, with solitary drinkers, and recognised the intention. At that point Paul Stamp arrived. Mark bought two more expensive glasses of wine and agreed to do a piece on twenties and thirties travel writing.

'How's Strong going?'

'He progresses,' said Mark.

'You must come across all sorts of interesting people, as they say, in the process.'

'Some more than others.'

'He was a great lecher, was he not?'

'Not spectacularly so,' said Mark. 'Outstripped by many.' He didn't particularly want to talk about Strong, he found, despite professional compunction. Nor did he particularly want to be in this place; the atmosphere sought after was all too effective: he now felt depressed and as though it might be about two o'clock in the morning.

'We'll do a piece on him when the time comes,' said Stamp. 'Tie it in with the reviews.'

'Good.'

They exchanged book talk for a while; Mark experienced his usual combination of boredom and spasmodic uplift. Books were what you lived for and by, and everything pertaining to them induced a responsive twitch, but conversations of this kind were curiously deadening. Stamp discoursed upon the background to a new series on contemporary poets and speculated about a palace revolution in a leading publishing house. Mark watched a girl who had planted herself further down the bar; she had a white face and much black hair and looked to be contemplating suicide, slumped over an empty glass with a dead cigarette in her hand. Probably she was waiting for her washing load to be done at the launderette next door.

'Ever talked to Edward Curwen?'

'No,' said Mark. Curwen, a young man at the time, was a historian who had had the temerity to attack Strong's *Disraeli* when it came out in 1934.

'Didn't he have some sort of public row with your chap?'

'Very much so. Why – do you know him?'

'He lives in the village where we have our weekend place. Doddery but gregarious. I said something about your forthcoming work the other day and there was a certain display of malice at the mention of Strong's name. You might be interested.'

'I might,' said Mark. He made a note of the address.

Stamp got to his feet. 'Well – good seeing you. I'll look forward to the travel piece.' He left, canted slightly sideways by a briefcase filled with review books destined for the nearby business which conveniently rerouted unread books from the shelves of literary editors to the shelves of public libraries, where they presumably remained unread. Mark, after a few moments' further melancholy contemplation of the wine bar (the black-haired girl had left and was replaced by a couple holding hands in strained silence) went to the British Library where he sat for three hours amid the gentle flutter of paper and the muted footfalls of fellow readers. He had once attempted to estimate the number of hours he had spent in the place and the resulting figure dispirited him. They seemed like a section of a lifetime spent at the coal-face, and while one could hardly complain of uncongenial working conditions there was still a sense of incarceration. When he was a small boy his mother had disapproved of reading in the morning on the grounds that you should be out in the fresh air; she seemed, now, to have had a point.

Diana, arriving late at the gallery, found her employer wrecking the confidence of a young man with a portfolio of lithographs. Suzanne was going through the pictures poker-faced and without uttering, devoting the same three seconds to each one while the young man attempted occasional phrases of expiation. She closed the portfolio, handed it back with her version of a smile, and briskly interrupted him to say that she didn't feel she could do anything to help just at the moment. The young man left and Suzanne raised her eyes with a look of patient suffering. 'Poor things. They never learn. Did you have a lovely weekend, darling?'

'The weather was O.K.'

Suzanne, moving towards her office, stopped and shot a quizzical glance across the magnolia wastes of the gallery's pile carpet. 'Mark being difficult?'

'Not specially,' said Diana evasively. She had once, in a moment of irritation, confided in Suzanne about some of the areas in which she found Mark unbiddable. Difficult was Suzanne's word, not hers, and she had subsequently regretted the confidences, which gave Suzanne a subtle vantage point.

'Mark,' said Suzanne, 'is terribly clever of course and basically a very sweet person but he is vague and frightfully wrapped up in his work which isn't always fair on you.'

'Mmn.' Diana, non-committal, hung up her jacket.

'Intellectuals are wonderful people to have a relationship with but *wearing*, and believe me I *know*.' Suzanne sighed, portentously. 'Anyway, all I'm saying my dear is that you need to be firm when the occasion demands. I suppose he's absolutely immersed in this book about what's his-name?'

'Pretty immersed, yes.'

'I once had a thing with a writer when I was awfully young and what one did feel was that these people are only half in touch with reality. I'm not saying that Mark's like that but he is just a bit other-worldly at times, bless him. Have you fixed up about going abroad yet?'

'I'm working on it.'

'France is the thing now,' said Suzanne. 'Everyone's started going there again since Greece and Portugal got so horrid. I'm going to have a week in the Jura in September. Anyway, let me know as soon as you have dates so that I can get Peggy or someone in to help hold the fort.' She went into her office and Diana set about drafting the catalogue for a forthcoming exhibition. From time to time her thoughts returned to Dean Close. She found it uncomfortable and rather boring there. The girl and her gay chum weren't exactly on one's wavelength and the bed was excruciating. Cooking in that grotty kitchen would soon lose its appeal. She had no particular desire to go there ever again but Mark would be to and fro for months to come, apparently. And there was something puzzling about it all, something she couldn't put a finger on.

Diana scowled, listing Abstract Suites and Mood Pieces and Studies in Blue and Grey.

Carrie, examining some tiresomely unprosperous geranium cuttings, did not hear the telephone ringing in the yard. She couldn't stand geraniums – they were a commercial necessity – and she always had an uncomfortable feeling that they knew this and therefore got *Botrytis* or *Phytophthore* in protest. Bill appeared at the entrance to the greenhouse. 'It's your mum.'

'*Here*?' Carrie, aghast, swung round.

'No, no, you dope – on the blower. From France. Chuntering on about some letter. Hurry up.'

Hermione's phone calls were infrequent and usually meant trouble. Either she was coming to London and required Carrie's presence for a meal or she had had another row with the lawyers and wanted to let off steam or there had been a tiff with whoever she was living with and she needed to complain about how appallingly she had been treated. Her current consort was called Sid; he was twenty years younger than she was, described himself as a painter and had an aggressively well-developed Cockney accent. She had brought him down to Dean Close on a day visit six months ago. He had put his feet up on the sofa in Strong's study, dropped cigarette ends in the greenhouse seedling beds, and got tipsy on a bottle of brandy Hermione had foraged from the old pantry. Even Bill's extensive tolerance had snapped. Accordingly, Carrie picked up the receiver with a sinking heart; whatever this was it wouldn't be agreeable.

She said, 'Hello . . .' and Hermione, unavoidably audible, sprang into instant discourse. She wanted to know who the hell this guy Mark Lamming was.

Carrie shrank. She explained about Mark.

'I should have been told,' said Hermione. 'If he's going to write this book I'm going to be in it, aren't I? I should have been asked if I agreed. Who on earth said it was O.K. for him to do it and what's he been doing rooting around in Daddy's stuff at Dean Close?'

Carrie explained further.

'Why are you this literary whatever and not me?'

'Mr Weatherby and I thought you wouldn't want to be,' said Carrie. 'We thought you'd think it was a nuisance.' It was always simplest, in the end, to be perfectly straightforward with Hermione; her own responses were so irrational and unpredictable that anything else became unnecessarily tortuous and probably wouldn't get you any further.

'Well, it would have been,' said Hermione. 'And I'm frightfully busy. Sid and I are doing up this heavenly old farmhouse near Sarlat. Except that Weatherby as usual is being absolutely foul about money.'

'How did you know about Mark Lamming?' Carrie enquired, cautiously.

'I've had this letter from him, haven't I? About this radio programme. He wants me to talk about Daddy. He says he can have someone come down here and record me. It would be more amusing if it was for television but I suppose I'll do it anyway. He says something about possibly coming himself. What's he like? Is he amusing?'

Carrie said Mark was very nice.

Hermione snorted. 'Whatever that means. You don't change, darling. Like getting blood out of a stone. How are all the flowers and how's thingummy?'

Carrie said that the flowers and Bill were fine.

'Well, I can't go on for ever – this is costing a packet and I'm broke, as usual. Sid thinks we should sue Weatherby if he goes on digging his toes in about the bloody Trust. He knows a frightfully clever lawyer in the East End who can deal with other lawyers. If this Mark whatsit comes down here you'd better come with him.'

'I can't,' said Carrie in a panic. 'Not possibly.'

'Don't be silly. I don't see why I should be expected to cope with him on my own, especially if he isn't particularly amusing.'

Hermione rang off. Carrie went back to the greenhouse where the geraniums looked suddenly more resilient, as though defying her. She wondered uneasily exactly what Mark had said in his letter.

Hermione's prompt response was not the only one produced by Mark's latest round of correspondence. Edward Curwen, the elderly historian, telephoned to say that he would be very pleased to have a chat about Gilbert Strong and as it happened he was making a trip up to town that very week. Mark arranged to meet him for lunch. He turned out to be sprightly, white-haired and sharp-tongued. After his second glass of wine he said, 'He was a bit of a shit, between you and me.'

'In what sense?'

'Devious. Tricky. Not as straightforward as one would expect from a man of letters – hah! – isn't that the expression?' The old man, eighty-three by all accounts, glinted at Mark with very blue eyes. Mark observed that such characteristics were not unknown in literary circles.

'He was referring to himself as an historian in those days, mind. He liked to call *Disraeli* a history, not a biography. You've read the famous row we had in the *TLS*?'

'Of course.'

'Ah,' – Curwen leaned forward cosily – 'but that's only the half of it. There's something that didn't get in there. Want to know what?'

'I'd love to,' said Mark.

Curwen held out his glass for replenishment. 'He tried to buy me off, that's what. Called halt. Couldn't take any more. What d'you make of that, eh?'

'It's very interesting.'

'I went for him, you remember, for trivialising history, for going in for fine writing instead of fine interpretation. Boudoir stuff. I was considered an insolent young pup – there was he, a solid fellow, chum of Wells and Galsworthy and God knows who, and there was I, a lecturer in history at Manchester no one had ever heard of. *Lèse-majesté*. But it got sympathy. The red light was on for that kind of historical biography. And people like a slanging match so the *TLS* let the correspondence run on and old Strong had to keep on defending himself. No good just making Olympian noises. He had to come down and slog it out in the ring, and he didn't like it. That was when he got in touch with me privately and suggested we had a drink one evening.'

Mark refilled their glasses.

'Thanks. Very nice too.' The old man took a swig; little pink horns of wine-stain remained at each corner of his mouth. The great advantage of the living, Mark reflected, is that they can see to it that they have the last word. The silence – the no doubt infuriated silence – of Gilbert Strong was overwhelming.

'Took me to his club. All meant to intimidate, see. Said he wondered if it wasn't time we agreed to disagree and leave it at that. Boring the readership etcetera. I said I thought our discussion was seminal and highly pertinent to the state of historical biography and I'd got plenty still to say. Made noises of deference but I wasn't really feeling them – I could sense he was rattled and wanted to get shot of the whole thing. And I'd been getting a good deal of support; I didn't see what harm he could do me. And then he came out with it. There was a Cambridge Fellowship going and I was in for it. He must have heard this. As it happened, he said, he had a couple of close friends in the college. At that point I got the message.'

'Further intimidation?' said Mark.

'More than that,' Curwen went on, smugly. 'Bribery. If I laid off, he said – all put in a roundabout way, you understand, but clear enough to me – if I laid off he'd have a word with his pals about what a good chap I was basically, over-enthusiasm no bad thing in a young man and so forth, and my chances would shoot up. Alternatively, he implied . . .'

'I see,' said Mark. 'So of course you said you'd have nothing to do with it.'

Those very blue eyes glinted again (was there somewhere, somehow a whiff of unreliability, like the hint of a blocked drain?). The old man hawked noisily and finished his wine.

'Naturally. I blasted off another letter to the *TLS* a few days later. His response was feeble. It's all there, you've seen it.'

'Yes, indeed. What sort of date would this have been – your meeting with Strong? The correspondence, if I remember rightly, runs from around April to June of 1934.'

'For God's sake,' said Curwen, a trifle snappishly. 'It was fifty years ago, dear boy.'

'Quite. And, er . . . the fellowship?'

'I got it. His pals were less influential than he thought, evidently. Or they weren't prepared to meddle. Or he didn't ask them to.' The old man gazed across the table at Mark, with a kind of smug triumph.

They talked of other things. As they parted Curwen said, 'Going to put this in your book?'

Mark spoke of enormous quantities of material, difficulties of assimilation, not yet seeing the wood for the trees. He added, 'By the way, Strong's club . . . It would have been the . . .'

'Garrick,' said Curwen promptly. He gave Mark a sideways look. '*Au revoir* then, dear boy. Nice to talk to you.'

Mark made for home. The Garrick at least was correct. As for the rest . . . Well. Ho, hum. If Curwen hadn't got this fellowship the case would have been stronger. As it was, there were two interpretations to that, even on his own account. A mischievous old man, clearly. But not necessarily an untruthful one. Another item for the 'Lies and silences' file.

He walked across the park, feeling in need of air and exercise. This made him think of a passage in Strong's diary about taking a woman friend out on the Serpentine and as he stood on the bridge the man seemed to materialise, tweeded and hatted, leaning back from the oars, the girl at the other end of the boat, hazier but only too conceivable. It sometimes seemed to Mark impossible that the historic past was extinguished, gone; surely it must simply be somewhere else, shunted into another plane of existence, still peopled and active and available if only one could reach it. Despite such evidence as yellowing letters, disintegrating books, and the decease of almost everyone to do with his researches, he found himself disbelieving in organic decay. Somewhere, Strong was still prowling around in that light green knickerbocker suit, or sitting at his desk writing with the scratchy nib pen, or laughing on the Serpentine with a woman.

He leaned on the parapet, watching a gang of French teenagers with a wailing transistor. Tomorrow he would be going to Dean Close. Tomorrow he would see Carrie.

'I've had a letter from your mother. She seems only too happy to say something about your grandfather for the radio programme. So I shall have to get going on that as quickly as possible.'

Carrie, reading a catalogue from some new rose people in Suffolk, said 'Mmn.'

'In fact, I'm thinking of going down there myself.'

Carrie looked up from the catalogue and said in a rush, 'Yes, that's a good idea, Ma likes visitors. Yes, I'm sure you should.'

'I don't' said Mark, looking fixedly out of the window, 'fancy tackling your mother on my own. What I had in mind was you coming along too.'

'I can't,' said Carrie. 'Not possibly.'

Bill walked into the kitchen. 'Can't what?'

'Come to France for a few days and visit her mother,' said Mark.

'Why not?' said Bill.

'The alpines,' cried Carrie wildly. 'My clematis. The fertiliser people. The soft cuttings.'

'No problem. Ron's got a couple of weeks holiday. He'll pop over and lend a hand.'

'Good,' said Mark easily. 'Maybe next week then. We'll drive down.'

Carrie knocked a mug off the table. Bill knelt to pick up the pieces; 'No need to get over-excited, now.'

'What about Diana?' wailed Carrie.

'Diana might well follow us on down later. Doubt if she could get off from the gallery quite as soon as that.'

Bill dumped the pieces of the mug in the dustbin. 'Good for you to get abroad, dearie. Make the most of it.'

'I hate abroad. I was brought up there.'

'It's improved since then,' said Bill. 'They have proper loos these days. And they're into fast food. You'll love it.'

Carrie, crimson, gabbled of passports and money and a delivery of heathers and her primula seedlings.

'She doesn't get on all that well with her mum,' Bill explained to Mark.

Mark nodded understandingly.

'I'll see to all the bumph. Tickets and stuff. Has she got a passport?'

Bill rummaged in the kitchen drawer. 'Should be here somewhere. Yup. All clear.'

Carrie glared. Outside, tyres scrunched on the gravel. 'That'll be the Taplin lorry,' said Bill. 'Coming, Carrie?' Carrie followed him from the room. At the door she turned and threw Mark a look of appeal. Mark smiled placatingly. When she had gone he picked up the passport. There was a blizzard of frontier stamps until 1970 and then nothing, but it had been renewed. In the photograph she looked about twelve.

For the rest of the day she avoided him. At dinner she refused to say a word to anyone and vanished immediately afterwards. Bill, a note of compunction in his voice, said, 'Carrie does get a bit uptight about her mum. Mind you, she is rather a horror. But it's high time the girl had a holiday.'

'I'm sure it is,' said Mark heartily. 'We needn't stay all that long. Nice break for me too. And Diana,' he added.

When eventually they did come face to face she rounded on him like a small animal, cornered but still showing some fight. 'You planned the whole thing.'

'Planned?' said Mark innocently.

'You didn't have to go yourself. Someone else could have.'

'I have to see your mother at some point. There are things I need to ask her. She is after all Strong's daughter.'

Carrie was silent, exuding truculence. He hadn't realised she could be like this. It was surprising. His elation, suddenly, began to subside.

'All right,' he said. 'If the idea of a few days in France with me is so absolutely appalling, let's forget it. Stay here. I'll go alone.'

'Would you mind?'

'Of course I'd mind.'

Carrie chewed a finger-nail. She blinked. He watched her. 'All right,' she said. 'I'll come. Just for a little while.'

9

DIANA STALKED up and down the room. 'France! Next *week* . . . ! What on earth's got into you? You're immovable, normally. Next *week* . . . Where does she live, did you say?'

'Sarlat-la-Canéda.'

'Dordogne. Lovely. But I can't possibly get away next week. Suzanne'd have a blue fit.'

'Oh dear,' said Mark.

'The week after, possibly, when the exhibition's over. Can't you wait till then?'

'No.'

Diana, disoriented by this waywardness, flung herself into a chair. 'I can't think what's the matter with you.'

'I'm writing a book,' said Mark tranquilly.

'Of course you're writing a book. You're always writing a book. But you don't normally want to go dashing off to France. Is she married?'

'She has some sort of arrangement, I understand.'

'And how on earth are you going to manage without me to navigate? You loathe long-distance driving.'

'Carrie thinks she may be able to come along, actually.'

Diana, disorientation complete, gazed. '*Carrie*?'

'She is Hermione's daughter,' he reminded.

'I thought they didn't get on.'

Mark shrugged.

Diana, silent, gathered all this in and set about sorting it out. After a moment she said, 'I'll ring Suzanne and see if she can get Peggy to come in for a week or two. It'll all be the most terrible rush. The car should be serviced. I haven't got the clothes I'd need. I s'pose I'll get a train down and you'll pick me up at the nearest station?'

'Yes,' said Mark. 'I should think that's the best thing to do.'

Diana, distracted from her earlier consternation by this feast of necessary planning, reached for a notepad and began to make lists. Mark retreated to his study and set about his own projections, which involved sitting at his desk and staring, frequently and for longish periods, out of the window.

He realised that it was a long time since he had experienced the delicious pleasure of looking forward to something. There were small anticipations, of course – seeing a friend, or some outing to a theatre or concert – but this internal glow was a sensation almost forgotten. Tenderly, he let it have its way. He luxuriated in it. For one whose professional concern was the examination of the feelings and motivations of others his own state of mind was curiously unexplored: a foreign country. How all this could end except in tears (his, probably) he had no idea but he simply didn't care. It was enough to sit amid the infinitely familiar but subtly transformed landscape of his study and wallow in it.

'She'll drive you nuts,' said Diana. 'That girl. What on earth will you *talk* to her about?'

He telephoned her to tell her to get travellers' cheques and then he telephoned her to remind her of the time of the ferry and finally he telephoned anyway and got Bill. Carrie was in the greenhouses and Bill didn't reckon she'd take kindly to being called in. Mark said uneasily, 'D'you think she's remembered we must leave at ten sharp?'

'Doubt it. Leave it to me, I'll get her lined up.'

'Thank you, Bill. I'll be down this evening, then.'
'See you later, squire.'

When he reached Dean Close she was nowhere to be found. There was a half-packed grip in the kitchen, which looked encouraging, but no Carrie. He wandered around and eventually found her in Strong's study, standing in front of the bookcase.
'What on earth are you doing?'
She jumped guiltily. 'Oh, hello.'
'Hello.'
This was one of the moments he'd been caressing at his desk in London for the last week. It was indeed rich but oddly the expectation of it now had a nostalgic glow of its own.
'I was looking for something to read,' said Carrie.
'To read this minute?'
'No. In France. You'll be reading sometimes, won't you? In the evenings for instance.'
'Yes,' he said doubtfully. 'I suppose I might be.'
'Well, then . . . I thought I'd better too. I mean, I won't have anything else to do and I'm not used to not having anything to do and it'll be a bit irritating for you if I just sit there doing nothing. What shall I take?'
He stared at the ranks of Gilbert Strong's books. There was the lot there, more or less; just about everything that mattered written over the last two hundred years.
'A novel, were you thinking of?' he enquired, cautiously.
'Oh, I should think so, wouldn't you?'
He scanned the shelves. He hesitated, discarded, scanned again. He took down *Emma*. 'You could try this.'
Carrie gave him a distinctly mischievous look. 'Actually I've heard of Jane Austen. I even know when she lived. O.K., then.'

They emerged from the maw of the car ferry. Carrie wound down the window and slap through it there came a pungent gust of something that made her wince: the smell of abroad. Goodness knows of what it was composed: cigarettes and rubbish and petrol and food or perhaps it just came smoking out of the ground. She would have know it anywhere; this was France smell, but there was also, for her, Greece smell and Italy smell and Spain smell and each summoned separate and on the whole disagreeable sensations. France smell flung her with awful immediacy into the skin of another Carrie, a morose and weary Carrie aged nine or twelve or fifteen, stoically waiting on a bony café chair while Hermione and her friends had yet another glass of something before the lunch or dinner that was already postponed by two hours. She stared with hostility at the French customs officials and the man selling *Figaro* and *Paris-Match* and the line of GB cars snaking ahead of them out of the docks.

As Carrie opened the car window Mark was swamped with a sudden titivating combination of guilt and excitement which he at first attributed to his present state of mind and then realised was nothing to do with it. It was prompted by the whiff of the cigarette held by the official lolling at the barrier, a Gitane or whatever just such as he himself as a schoolboy had furtively smoked with his companions of the Upper Fifth on a French Club outing to Chartres. A feeling of cheery relief took over, succeeded by exhilaration. He decided that he had been underrating travel. Indeed probably he had been passing up much enriching experience. It was partly Diana's fault, of course; one had been pushed into reaction against her pursuit of the latest flea-bitten Turkish town or whatever it was that the Sunday newspapers or the Suzannes of this world were going on about. A couple of dire sessions in Corfu and Gozo in the early days of their marriage had a lot to answer for. And then more distantly there was the remembered foreign fever of his parents' generation just after the war, when everything continental was good and everything British was bad. *Les Enfants du Paradis* and Elizabeth David cookery books and the *toile de Jouy* fabrics with which his mother enveloped the living-room. Sex, in his youth, had been firmly associated with the Continent; the first time he had achieved it what seemed disorienting was that the girl had not spoken in sub-titles. Even at the time it had struck him, looking around the homeland, that all this supercilious dismissal of what on the face of it was an interesting and often spectacularly attractive country was a bit silly. Later, this resistance to fashion had developed into a form of quiet xenophobia.

Nevertheless, he decided, as the line of cars crept forward another few yards, one had ended up victim oneself of a reverse prejudice. It was too long since he had done this kind of thing. Dreamy enticing images swept through his head: poplars flashing past and blinding sweeps of sunflowers and lovely solitary Romanesque churches and glistening mayonnaise and croissants and huge peaches and wine drunk at bosky roadsides. He wanted to transmit this to Carrie but couldn't think how to so began instead to talk about routes. He wondered if she would turn out to be any good at map-reading. She seemed, at this moment, somewhat glum. They were out of the docks and emerging into the town traffic; he applied himself to the matter of staying on the right side of the road and finding which way to go.

'How long is it going to take us to get there?' Carrie enquired. She seemed to have little or no idea of distances or geography.

'Well . . . I thought a couple of nights on the way, possibly three.' Which was about as slowly as you could plausibly do it. 'There are some nice places we could see. Shall we start looking for a hotel soon? I'm beginning to feel I've had enough driving.'

Quite enough. One thing he had forgotten was the potent combination of murderous and suicidal urges with which all French drivers were apparently possessed. It wonderfully concentrated the mind; solitary Romanesque churches, if they were around, went unappreciated.

'O.K., if you want to.'

'That red book on the floor . . . If you look up the next town it'll tell you what hotels there are and what they're like.'

Carrie, intrigued, investigated the complexities of *Michelin*. Mark, distracted now by a further preoccupation, scraped the car against a projecting wall. 'Hell!'

He stopped to size up the damage. Carrie said, 'Will Diana be cross?'

'Yes.'

'Is it more her car than your car?'

'It's both of us's car.' He was snapping, he realised. And pouring with sweat. He got out a handkerchief and wiped his face.

'I've found a hotel with the right knives and forks and what-not.'

'Good.' He continued to sit. Carrie looked at him expectantly.

'Shall we go on, then?'

'Look,' he said. 'There's something I want to say.'

'I s'posed you would. About one room or two.'

He gazed at her, startled. 'Well, yes.'

'I should think,' she said, 'it had better be one because otherwise you'll be driving into things like just now and we can't go on like that all the way to this place Ma's living at if it's going to take three days.' She went richly pink as she spoke and added, 'At least, if that's what you meant.'

'Yes,' he said. 'I did.'

'O.K., then. It's called the Auberge des Fleurs, this place. It's got some sort of garden.'

He started the car. He would have asked if this sternly practical resolution of the problem was her only interest in it, but did not dare; the answer might well be unwelcome. He devoted himself to driving very carefully and deliberately and, in so far as it was possible, to thinking of absolutely nothing at all except Carrie's directions about street names and turning right or left. He parked the car and went into the hotel and yes, they had a double room for the night. He informed Carrie and disembarked the cases and led her into the hotel and up the stairs and into a room in which was a large double bed and, presumably, other appurtenances but that was all he could see. This moment also had been mulled over back in the study in London but now that it had arrived it was entirely different. Carrie walked to the window and looked out of it. 'You can have dinner in the garden. There are tables and chairs.'

'Ah, good.'

She turned round and inspected the room. After a moment she said, 'I s'pose Diana would be even more cross about this.'

When he woke the next morning and had weathered the initial shock of where and with whom he was he thought she had disappeared. The bed felt empty. He turned over, warily, and there she was at the far side sitting bolt upright with her glasses on reading *Emma*.

She looked down at him. 'Sorry. I didn't mean to wake you up.'

There was, he saw, a wodge of read pages. 'How long have you been awake?'

'Ages. I'm not used to being in bed this late.' She turned a page and continued to read.

Mark lay contemplating her for a couple of minutes. Finally he said, 'What do you think of it?'

She considered. 'You feel they all ought to have something to do and then they wouldn't go on so much about money and getting married. But all the same you want to know what's going to happen.'

'Mmn.'

She flipped back a page or two, as though to check something. 'Is Emma meant to be nice or not?'

'Well,' he said. 'I s'pose it's not so much a question of is she nice as how she sees herself.' He stopped. Carrie gazed down at him enquiringly. 'And that the reader is allowed to see what's going on while Emma never does, although she thinks she's so perceptive.'

'I see,' said Carrie. She started to read once more.

God, he thought, this is what people like me come to. Holding forth about 'the reader' at a moment like this. He said, 'I wish you'd stop.'

'Stop what?'

He pointed a dismissive finger at *Emma*. Carrie put the book down. 'Should we go and have breakfast?'

'Do you love me? All right . . . I shouldn't have asked. Do you like me?'

'Usually. Just now I do. Actually, I nearly always do.'

'But not absolutely always?'

She was beginning to slither from the bed, as though hoping he might not notice. He took hold of her arm.

'Not absolutely always, no.'

'Then why are you doing this?'

'Because you'd have kept going on about it otherwise. And it seemed awfully rude to be saying no for ever.'

'Did you enjoy it?'

'Oh yes, thanks. Very much. I nearly always do.'

He let go of her arm. She shot into the bathroom with a backwards glance of apology. Mark continued to lie in the bed. Exasperation and euphoria were now so hideously mixed that he felt slightly ill. One should never, ever ask questions of a person disposed to tell the truth. That last remark, for instance. Who? When? Bloody well don't ask, he told himself savagely.

It was hot. They breakfasted in the garden. Mark was careful to make no comment. Last night, at dinner, he had looked round casually and said, 'Lovely, isn't it?'

'No,' said Carrie. He looked again, puzzled, at what seemed to him an agreeable enough pot-pourri of flowers and plants.

'The geraniums are horrid with the French marigolds and salvia is nasty anyway and everything's in straight lines.'

'Oh,' he said, humbled.

This morning, he treated it with the contempt it evidently deserved. The croissants weren't all that marvellous, either. He drank a great deal of coffee and allowed himself many quick looks at Carrie. She was sitting in a shaft of sunlight that turned her completely golden; ginger-golden curly hair and arms and legs pollened with streaks of gold and glinting eyelashes. He knew now that her pubic hair was sandy-coloured also which admittedly was to be expected but at the time he had been oddly startled.

They bought food and wine for a picnic lunch in a small local supermarket. Carrie said, 'This is just like Tesco's or Fine Fare except that the stuff's French.' She sounded rather cheerful about it. 'They didn't have places like this when I was here with Ma.' Mark, perusing the range of wines (some of them bottled in plastic) observed that you wouldn't be buying pâté or bread like this in Tesco's. 'Wouldn't you?' said Carrie. 'I don't really know about things like that. Diana's very good at food, isn't she?' Mark, picking something he hoped would be drinkable, did not answer. He thought again about bosky roadsides.

In the event, it was extraordinarily difficult to find anywhere to stop it all. They pounded on in rising heat, Mark's nerves jangling from the demands of the constant leap-frog overtaking as he strained for the split-second chance to pass the lorry ahead before the blaring Citröen behind rode up his back. There was nowhere to turn off the road, or if there was it was gone before the decision could be made. Carrie said she wanted to go to the lavatory. Eventually, in desperation, he pulled into a lay-by. Carrie slithered down into some adjacent scrub. Mark got out the food and a rug and arranged it as far from the road as possible; even so each passing car sent a swirl of dust over the rug. Carrie was gone for so long that he had visions of rape or abduction; eventually she came strolling back from a completely different direction looking very sunny with a handful of wild flowers. They ate to the accompaniment of the whoosh-whoosh of cars and the occasional wham of a lorry. Carrie pored over her flowers and then read *Emma.* Mark went through three quite stunningly uninteresting articles in *Le Monde* and had some rather incoherent thoughts about the connection or more probably the lack of connection between expectation and realisation. When he got home he would consider this constructively, possibly in its application to Strong. He said, 'Shall we go on – this isn't all that nice a place.' 'O.K.' said Carrie amiably.

Twenty kilometres further on she gave a kind of squeak and started groping around the floor.

'What's wrong?'

'I'm awfully afraid I've lost my book.'

He pulled up. They searched the car.

Carrie, with a look of dreadful guilt, said, 'I think I put it on the roof while we were packing the things up and forgot to take it off. Can we go back?'

'Honestly,' he said, 'I don't think we'd ever find it, Carrie. It could be anywhere.'

'Oh dear.'

'It wasn't anything very special as an edition. You needn't feel too guilty. I'll get a nice replacement when we're back in England.'

'But I need it now,' said Carrie. 'Can't we buy one here?'

'Well . . . I don't think it would be all that easy. We'll get you something else to read.'

'But I want to know what happens now I've started it.'

He suppressed the thought that if this had been Diana he would be taking a rather different line. 'All right. We'll stop in the next big town and find a bookshop. But I do rather doubt if we're going to be lucky . . . I mean, an English edition of Jane Austen . . .'

'French would do.'

He had entirely forgotten that of course she presumably read French. And spoke it. She had not, hitherto, opened her mouth to anyone but him. He recalled, with irritation, a tiresome exchange with the proprietress of the hotel stemming from his inability to catch something she was going on about to do with a surcharge. 'Why didn't you come to my rescue with that old harridan at the reception this morning?'

'I thought you wanted to do it yourself,' said Carrie, opening *Michelin*. 'Do you think Le Mans would have a bookshop?'

He said he thought it very well might.

The place, of course, was jammed with cars and it took almost half an hour to find somewhere to park. The acreage of metal was unbelievable; Mark, blinking in the flash and dazzle of bumpers and windscreens, reflected that at this rate it wouldn't be long before the entire continent vanished under the spread of it. He drove vainly round and round while Carrie pointed out bookshops. Eventually he slid gratefully into an empty space in a street some way from the centre.

The first bookshop could not help. The second, after some head shaking, produced a translation of *Pride and Prejudice*. 'Actually,' said Mark, 'in point of fact I think you might well prefer that. I almost suggested it back at Dean Close.'

'But I've started the other one,' said Carrie.

They continued. There was not, he decided, a lot to be said for Le Mans. A somewhat featureless town. Still, any new experience has some point. They trudged around crowded shopping streets and found at last another *librairie* whose proprietor could not, alas, provide what was wanted but had a colleague in La Flèche with a small establishment specialising in foreign works. 'We're not actually going in that direction,' said Mark. Carrie's face fell. 'Oh, all right, it's not that far out of the way.' They retraced their steps to the car. It was nearly four o'clock.

By the time they reached La Flèche and went through the parking process again it was after five. Carrie hurried into the shop and came out beaming. 'They had it!'

'Good,' said Mark. 'Splendid. Let's get on – we'll have to start looking for somewhere for the night soon.'

There were some difficulties on that front, also. The first place selected turned out when they got to it to be sited on a main arterial road. The second was full. The third, however, was pleasant enough and had a room. Mark, exhausted, made straight for the shower; at that moment even the sight of Carrie sitting on the bed peeling off her T-shirt could do nothing for him. Subsequently, though, he began to revive after an aperitif and then another aperitif in the café of a market square that really was quite bosky. He said, 'Tell me about when you were in France with your mother.'

Carrie replied that she had forgotten most of it.

'What exactly was she doing?'

'Nothing, mostly. Finding things to do. Meeting people for lunch or drinks and getting tired of the place we were in and going off to another one.'

'Was she married to anyone?'

'No. She doesn't often get married. Only once, actually.'

'You should visit your father,' said Mark.

'Why?' enquired Carrie.

'Well . . . You should get to know him. He is your father, after all. It would be natural.'

'Perhaps we wouldn't like each other.'

'Lots of parents and children don't like each other. That's neither here nor there, in a way.'

There was a pause. Carrie reflected. 'I don't quite see what you mean,' she said politely.

'Well . . . It's a charged sort of relationship, with all sorts of obstacles built into it but most people feel there's a lot to be got out of it.'

'Like being married?' suggested Carrie.

Mark swallowed. 'Well . . . Yes. In a way.'

'I see. I'm not sure about seeing my father and anyway it would mean going abroad again but I expect being married is nice, at least most of the time. The trouble is I could only marry someone who didn't mind about me doing the Garden Centre. Still, I suppose some people wouldn't . . . I just don't seem to have met any yet.'

Mark was silent. The thought of Carrie marrying anyone, even in the most distant future, was violently offensive. Gloom filled him. He waved to the waiter and ordered another drink. Then he reached out and took her hand. They sat in silence, with Carrie's hand lying rather limply in his. Presently she said, 'Do you think we could go and have something to eat soon? I'm starving.'

He woke up at four o'clock in the morning and knew with awful fatality that he would not be able to get to sleep again. Beside him, Carrie gently breathed. She was naked. She had apologised for this the first night, saying she didn't own any nightdresses. He had been, at that moment, so overcome by the sight of her that the only thing he could think of to say was, 'Don't you get cold in the winter?' 'I borrow Bill's pyjamas then,' she replied.

He had the feeling that he might be hallucinating; this whole odd experience seemed to have been going on not for thirty-six hours but for an indefinable length of time. Since it was so very much the kind of thing that he, Mark, did not do he could no longer see how it had happened. He tried to think of Diana; she had the affectionate familiarity of someone known well in the distant past. He told himself that he would be seeing her in five days time; the fact made no impression at all.

The hours inched past.

10

AS THEY MOVED south, in strategic jumps across the map on her lap, Carrie began to suffer from an apparently impossible emotional schizophrenia. The closer they got to Hermione, the more her spirits sagged; but all the time her enjoyment was increasing. She hadn't wanted to come in the least. She had agreed to because she had been pushed into it. And now it was all more interesting than she had expected. She held the map, obediently, and told Mark whether to go right or left and what name they should be looking for next on the road signs, and the cool dispassionate print of the map translated itself into sights and smells. In all the years with her mother, when she must have covered thousands of miles, she couldn't remember ever having felt like this. Had she read maps then? Presumably somebody had; it was inconceivable that her mother had been capable of reading maps for herself. Carrie could remember many absorptions in private landscapes: places of retreat that she had found wherever they happened to alight – a hidden corner of a garden, a room, a favourite walk. But there had never been this rather heady sense of progress – of moving on and leaving behind. Travelling, evidently, was a state of mind quite as much as a physical undertaking.

Mark was less of a problem than she had expected. He seemed rather on edge and he had taken to swearing when other drivers did things he wasn't expecting which was most of the time. But he didn't start embarrassing conversations as often as she had feared; she hoped he might be getting over it. Actually the making love part was fine. And he wasn't often irritable (except about the driving) and didn't mind her wandering off to look at things or find plants. He must be rather nice to be married to, she thought; Diana was lucky. But then Diana must be nice to be married to also – if you weren't alarmed by her which Mark presumably wasn't. Even at this distance the thought of Diana was slightly disturbing, as though she might suddenly materialise in the car and demand to know what exactly was going on, as well she might. Carrie wriggled nervously.

'What's wrong? Do you want to stop?'

'No. I'm all right. We're coming to the Loire soon. The red book has masses of stars and exclamations and things.'

'Yes,' said Mark. 'It would. We might pause and do some sightseeing.'

He stood in a room that had been restored with aggressive good taste and stared out and down through mullioned stone windows. The river wound in fat loops through a painted green landscape, like the background of a fifteenth-century portrait, seen over the shoulder of the subject. The guide was quite the most governessy fellow Mark had ever heard. Tendentious, with it. Clad as for a day at the Bourse, he funnelled his party through the chateau with sharp instructions about where and when to halt for enlightenment. He then harangued them loudly and with infuriating deliberation, as though taking an elocution class, the spiel of information larded with '*voyez-vous*' and '*vous comprenez*' and '*ecoutez bien*'. Right now he was describing the middle ages as '*un climat social très difficile*'; one way of putting it, Mark supposed.

He looked round for Carrie. She waved from the far side of the room, swamped by a gang of Scandinavian adolescents. In the tapestry room she had said happily, 'Isn't it lovely?' On the ramparts, to his horror, he had seen her leaning precariously over to investigate some plant leading a dangerous life in a crevice. He looked at his watch. This, clearly, would be about as far as they would get today. The guide was now going on about this being '*un château sérieux*' – as opposed presumably to some Walt Disney set-up down the road.

And then later in the evening what now seemed to him this systematic traduction of history continued. 'What's *son et lumière*?' asked Carrie, studying notices in the hotel entrance hall. He explained. 'Oh . . . Can we go to it?' And so with gathering resentment he sat in the floodlit forecourt of yet another meticulously face-lifted building while figures in wimples and surcoats and all the flummery of a theatrical costumier paraded up and down and a disembodied sepulchral voice intoned about '*le passé . . . cette pays de mystère et de fantaisie*'. Carrie appeared to be entranced. She sat on the edge of her seat and gazed around her. When he made a move to leave she said, 'But there's more. We haven't seen it all yet.' Resignedly, he sat. The *pays de mystère et de fantaisie* gave way to a *lutte sanglante*; cries and shrieks rang from within the castle walls, steel clashed, troops of phantom horsemen clattered past.

He drove back to the hotel through a musky velvet night out of which headlights hurtled at them like rockets. Carrie, undressing, said, 'It's been a really nice day.'

'Good. I'm so glad.'

'You didn't like the play thing very much, did you?'

'Well . . . Not a lot, no.'

'It was all right for me because I don't know any history. I suppose they'd got everything wrong?' She took off her bra and pants and got into bed.

'Pretty wrong, to my mind.'

'Oh well . . . I did rather like it, I'm afraid. Is it tomorrow we'll get to Ma's?'

'The day after, I should think.' He went into the bathroom, where he was numbed by the sledgehammer realisation that there was one more day and night of this at the most. He would never be with her like this again, ever, in all probability.

'Are you all right?' she said solicitously, as he got into bed.

'I s'pose so.'

'You looked a bit peculiar. I thought p'raps you'd got something wrong with your insides. That's the thing I remember most about abroad – nearly always having something wrong with one's insides.'

'I'm perfectly well. I was simply thinking that when we get to your mother's it's not going to be like this any more.'

'No,' said Carrie. 'I s'pose it won't be.' After a moment she added cautiously, 'Are you . . . sort of getting over it at all?'

'No. Frankly.'

'Oh. Oh dear, I thought you might be.'

There was a silence. 'We might at least,' said Mark in distant and injured tones, 'make the most of what there is.'

Carrie moved across the bed to him.

He lost her, the next day, twice. Once she vanished up a hillside on yet another plant-hunting expedition and later he mislaid her in an abbey and found her eventually in the market-place, wandering among stalls of fruit and vegetables. She looked absorbed and content and gave a start of surprise when he came up to her, as though she might have forgotten all about him.

She wrote a postcard to Bill. Mark, furtively reading it upside-down across the café table, saw that she had said 'Having a lovely time . . .' and then something about not forgetting to check the alpines.

'Aren't you going to send Diana one?'

He said he doubted if it would get there before Diana left London.

When they were on the road she was frequently silent. He realised that she had no compunction about silence; if she had nothing to say, she did not speak. He was never able to decide if this was restful or faintly unsettling. The latter, probably, since he found himself impelled to make conversational overtures to which, equally, she did not always respond. He told her about the Albigensian crusades and then realised with unease that he had pursued this topic over some ten kilometres in the face of Carrie's more or less persistent silence. He said, 'All this has bored you stiff, I don't doubt.'

'No. I wasn't not saying anything because I was bored but because I hadn't got anything sensible to say. Go on.'

'That's all,' said Mark, somehow dampened. The curious thought came to him that whatever it was he derived from her company it wasn't exactly pleasure. So far as company went there were half a dozen or so people who would rate a good deal higher; Diana very much amongst them. Did he *enjoy* being with her? He mulled over this, as sunflowers unreeled gaudily at either side of the road. Enjoy, in fact, was not the relevant word; he had to be with her – a good deal of the time she exasperated him but he had no choice in the matter, she was essential now, like some addictive substance.

He continued to examine his attitude and found that it did not bear inspection. He was a married man yearning for a woman who was not his wife; his main preoccupation was that he could not have her and his secondary one was that given that he couldn't then he could not endure the idea that anyone else should. Betrayal and selfishness, all in one go. He didn't even want her to be happy, since any presumed happiness of hers would exclude him. It is far from true, he thought bitterly, that love is an ennobling emotion.

'I'm hungry,' Carrie announced. She had taken to eating copiously, saying that she hadn't quite realised that she liked food – 'I mean apart from it being something you've got to have.'

'We'll stop and have some lunch then.'

Over the meal he said, 'I suppose if we pushed on hard we could in fact get there this evening.'

She looked up in alarm. 'Oh . . . Do we have to?'

'No. You'd rather not?'

'Much rather.'

The shadow of Hermione, he assumed, rather than the charms of his company. 'Then we'll take it slowly.'

They were now deep in a landscape that made its living by neatly exploiting two different kinds of natural resource. It grew things, lavishly – sunflowers and vines and maize and prosperous looking cattle and other less identifiable but equally picturesque crops – and it cashed in on all this in a more elusive way also. Regional menus, historic sites, scenic routes, châteaux, abbeys and notable towns clamoured from all sides. Woods and river valleys were bright with tents, latter-day fields of Agincourt. Every other car was topped with a plastic-wrapped mound of belongings or a glittering bicycle, as though an army of refugees was on the move. Flocks of cyclists sprawled on the verges or spun head down along the narrow roads. The rivers were busy with canoes. You could buy *pâté de foie gras* in every conceivable kind of container, postcards and T-shirts and washing-up towels printed with prehistoric paintings. It was as though, Mark thought, the manifold pasts of the area had fused into one lush and inexhaustible crop. A trading commodity that required neither factories nor raw materials nor a labour force.

They ate in a small town that offered a monastery, visits to the *caves* and several *menus gastronomiques*. Carrie worked her way through four courses. 'That was lovely.'

'Good. Do you want to see the monastery? Ruins of.'

'O.K.'

'Don't forget this,' said Mark, picking up *Emma*. 'I draw the line at searching out yet another copy.' Carrie's marking slip, he noticed, had crept half-way through the book. He, at one point, had browsed through a few pages, finding the Box Hill picnic curiously transposed by being in French, both more florid and somehow a little arch. But that, of course, was because a foreign language has resonances that would not be there for native readers. English cannot sound to others as it does to the English. This brought to mind some of Strong's more stridently unperceptive literary comments which were on Flaubert – criticism had not in any case been his strength and clearly where the French novel was concerned he suffered from a total absence of sympathy; nevertheless, being Strong, he had had a go. It was the first time in several days Mark had thought of Strong; his bombastic personality was as out of place here as . . . well, in fact, as the pastoral and crumbling France peopled by gnarled peasants, goats and quaintly-spoken *curés* described in Strong's only writings on the place, a handful of essays published in the twenties. No doubt, Mark recollected, at the time when he was swanning around the south with Stella Bruce instead of doing serious travelling in the Caucasus. The France of *supermarchés*, fibre-glass canoes, chromium racing cycles and a Renault to every household was as alien to then as Strong's merrie England of the shires to the Dorset or Wiltshire of today.

All this prompted a line of thought about travel being as much a temporal as a physical process that distracted him from the matter in hand – which was the extrication of the car from the crammed car park in which they had left it. Someone had parked a Citröen right up against his bumper; with gathering irritation he shunted to and fro, getting hotter and hotter. Carrie sat tranquilly at his side. Diana would have been issuing instructions, or hopping out in search of the Citröen owner. His foot slipped off the clutch and the car leaped forward; there was a thump and the splintering sound of breaking plastic. Two passing women stared at him censoriously. He got out; it was his light that was broken, of course, not the Citröen's. He set about further shunting, grimly, and at last freed the car. He was now streaming with sweat. 'Where are we going next?' asked Carrie cheerfully.

'Let's have a look at the map.'

They were no great distance now from Sarlat. 'I should think the best thing is just to push on until we find somewhere that looks nice to spend the night. The last night,' he added, looking at her.

Carrie was intent upon the map. 'There are *points de vue* and *châteaux* and lots of stuff like that ahead.'

'I don't doubt,' said Mark.

Carrying their cases, for the fourth time, up strange stairs and into a strange bedroom, it seemed to both of them in independent ways as though they had been doing this for ever. For Carrie it was a small revelation about the nature of marriage. If you were married to someone you were with them all the time, pretty well; being alone was when there was just the two of you, as opposed to the two of you and other people. Being alone in the proper sense was only when you were in the bathroom, or suchlike stray moments. Of course, living with Bill had its affinities with marriage but was different in a significant way. Going to bed with someone, both literally and in its euphemistic sense, was more important than she had quite realised. Whatever was it like in perpetuity? Pondering this, she sat down on the edge of the bed and rummaged in her case for a fresh T-shirt. Another thing she had forgotten about abroad was how hot it was.

For Mark the whole thing had moved from heady and unsettling unreality to a dreamlike dailiness. Last Monday was now as long ago as last month, last year; Diana was as benign and remote as some friend long unseen. He had to remind himself that in three days time she would arrive in Sarlat. So far as his feelings were concerned, they were beyond analysis: a horrid ferment in which surfaced now delight, now guilt, now boredom, now irritation. With Carrie almost constantly at his side he no longer had the pain and pleasure of thinking about her in the abstract. He could not envisage what things would be like once all this was over. Lust had been satisfied, supposedly; but of course lust is never satisfied, that is its awful power, it is forever regenerated. He watched Carrie putting on an emerald green T-shirt with a small rip under one arm and thought, simultaneously and quite detachedly, of his small, book-crammed study at home in London. It seemed like a lost paradise – the contentment of a perpetual autumn afternoon in there, in front of his typewriter, amid his papers and card-indexes, with Diana shortly due home, bearing gossip and maybe something tasty for supper. Time before Carrie; time when this insanity was unconceived and inconceivable. Time before Strong, come to that. Confound him.

The hotel was an old building with a central courtyard in which were set out tables and chairs with sun umbrellas. There were tubs and pots of trailing plants of which Carrie was grudgingly appreciative, as they sat there for a pre-dinner drink. She had been relentlessly critical of French gardening. Mark drank two Cinzanos in rapid succession and felt better. Here they were, and that was all that mattered at this moment. The future, right now, could take care of itself. Carrie too seemed relaxed and more conversationally forthcoming than usual. She chattered about her first job, at the big plant nursery in Hertfordshire.

'Who was Jim?' interrupted Mark.

'He was the owner's son.'

'I suppose he was your boyfriend.'

'Well. Sort of.'

'Why didn't you marry him?'

'He didn't ask me,' said Carrie. 'Anyway,' she added, 'I was talking about how I got interested in alpines, really, not about Jim.'

Mark sighed. 'Sorry.' He put his hand on hers and they sat in silence. After a few moments Carrie said, 'Would it be O.K. to have another drink? Is there enough money?' She had insisted on handing over to Mark a lump sum on which to draw for her share of the expenses.

'Of course.'

He went in search of the waiter. When he returned Carrie was reading *Emma*. She looked up, smiled, and returned to the book. Mark, mildly affronted, sat watching other patrons of the hotel. From time to time he glanced at Carrie, who continued to read; her eyes moved, pages turned, there was no pretence about it. Eventually he said, 'Shall we have some dinner?'

The menu was extensive. Carrie worked her way through five courses.

'You'd better make the most of it,' said Mark. 'What's your mother's cooking like?'

'Oh gosh, I'd almost forgotten we'll be there tomorrow.' She looked suddenly downcast. 'Well . . . She can't cook much. Usually there were people who did it.'

The dining-room had filled up, The service became slower. Coffee, it seemed, was failing to materialise at all. Carrie, furtively, reopened *Emma*. After a few minutes, Mark said petulantly, 'Still reading?'

'I have to read more slowly in French.'

'You don't *have* to read at all.'

She lowered the book and gazed at him. 'But I'm enjoying it.'

'It is our last night together.'

'Sorry.' She closed the book, marking the place with a toothpick, and regarded him with kindly expectation. Mark could think of nothing whatsoever to say. They sat in silence while the waitress swept plates from around them and dumped the bill beside Mark. 'Café,' he snapped, 's'il vous plaît.'

'Sorry,' said Carrie again. 'I remember now – it's bad manners to read at meals, isn't it?'

'It wasn't the manners part I minded about.'

He and Diana, in fact, frequently read through breakfast, lunch and even occasionally dinner. Which was beside the point. That, somehow, was perfectly all right but this wasn't.

'Well,' he went on, 'I'm glad it was such a success. You'll have to try the rest of your grandfather's library now.'

'Yes.' Carrie was also thinking of domestic practice. She and Bill frequently listened to the radio while eating; this, since it was a shared activity, was not bad manners, she supposed. Actually Bill never minded what she did anyway, which was why being with him was so comfortable.

'What do you particularly like about *Emma*?'

Carrie reflected. 'I want to know who she marries in the end.'

'Can't you guess?'

'No. Don't tell me.'

'I wouldn't dream of it.'

There was a pause. The coffee came. Mark laid his knee against Carrie's under the table. 'Never mind *Emma*. Tell me something honestly.'

'Mmn?'

'Have you enjoyed this?'

'Being with you?' said Carrie cautiously. 'Or being in France?'

'The first.'

'Oh yes.'

All right, he said to himself savagely, ask a silly question and you get a neutral answer. 'Well, I have, Carrie.'

'Actually, it was better than I thought it would be. I mean, I don't really like abroad so I didn't specially want to go there again but it's been more interesting than I expected. It hasn't been like before, with Ma, when I was a child. It's much nicer being with you.' She went pink, but continued. 'So I just wanted to say thank you very much for bringing me and telling me about things like those Crusades and that abbey. I'm sorry I sometimes don't talk very much. And I'm sorry about not feeling about you the way you do about me but in fact it's just as well, isn't it? I mean, it would all be rather awful if I did. So we should be thankful in fact. But I've really liked being with you and you've been very nice.' She beamed. The waitress returned, offering more coffee.

Mark sat on a terrace gritty with crumbs of cement and contemplated Hermione. He was not required to do anything else since Hermione seldom stopped talking for long enough to allow intrusion by others; when this did happen she did not listen to what they were saying. One of the several disquieting things about contemplation of Hermione was the way in which there were about her faint echoes of Carrie. In fact they did not look at all like each other but nevertheless some perverse genetic prank allowed a hint of Carrie to show from time to time: an expression, an inflection of the voice, the turn of a wrist. And, conversely and distressingly, he could see now the occasional whisper of Hermione in Carrie.

Actually, he had not seen much of Carrie at all since their arrival. She had undergone a total transformation from the moment they had stepped out of the car and Hermione, sunbathing in a lime-green bikini on the rubble-strewn terrace, had waved a languid hand. Carrie had simply effaced herself, literally by vanishing into some other part of the house or into the wilderness surrounding it, and otherwise by retreating into passive silence, as though she could escape from what was going on around her by hiding somewhere deep inside herself.

The house was the shell of an old farm now in the process of undergoing massive abuse by builders who were nowhere to be seen but overwhelmingly evident in the form of ladders, cement mixers, rusting empty tins and mounds of ginger sand. Hermione's act of welcome had been to take Mark and Carrie on a tour of the place with explanations of how heavenly it was all going to be eventually. They had gazed into skeletal rooms with square glassless spaces where windows would be and crunched across bare cement floors and inspected the pit where there was going to be an amusing little conservatory and the half-demolished pig-stys that would become this super guest annexe. All this, it became apparent, had been going on for some three or four years now.

'I dare say,' said Mark politely, 'builders are as slow here as in England.'

Sid Coates snorted. 'Aggro about lolly, mate. *Niente* dollars. No more loot.'

'Oh don't be silly, darling,' exclaimed Hermione. 'That's just a tiny snag – till that stupid Mr Thing who handles the Trust sees sense.'

Sid snorted again. He spoke, with strident south London diction, a fractured language composed entirely of colloquialisms spattered with foreign words and rendered in phrases rather than sentences, like a character in a comic fettered by the requirements of balloon speech. He was sunburnt to the colour and texture of cardboard and wore nothing but a pair of jeans shorn off above the knee. He was, Hermione had respectfully explained, working on a major sequence of murals that would adorn the walls of the farmhouse. Preliminary jottings for some of these were already apparent around the whitewashed studio and as a backdrop to the terrace. Mark had taken a dislike to Sid so violent that he had to avoid looking at him. Every time Sid spoke Mark's irritation became physical: his crotch itched and his head began to ache.

And now, at the end of the day, they were all four on the terrace having what Hermione called an aperitif and Sid a jar of vino. And Hermione was talking. She had dealt exhaustively with the plans for the house, given a run-down on Sid's career which apparently had been blocked at every step by the prejudice and lack of perception of London art galleries and had moved, at last, to her father and the reasons for Mark's presence.

'Of course I remember him absolutely even though I was terribly young when he died. He and Mummy were quite old when I was born, you know.'

Mark nodded, reflecting that she was getting herself in a fine fix about what was considered old and what was considered young. Hermione herself must have been in her late thirties when Strong died, and he in his early forties when she was born. Subjectivity is all. She was, one had to admit, a handsome woman, and well-structured for sixty-two. Even the bikini, now replaced by a long flowered skirt and top, had been just about tolerable.

'I adored him. And he absolutely doted on me of course – we were very close.' She sighed. 'I still miss him. I can see him now – in the rose garden at Dean Close, sitting in a deck chair, and I came running over the lawn – I suppose I must have been about ten or eleven – wearing a little blue gingham frock, I can see that still too – and he put down his book and held out his arms and I simply rushed . . .'

There was so much amiss with this spiel that Mark had to look away. In the first place the Strongs had not been living at Dean Close when Hermione was ten or eleven. On a more general level, there was little evidence in fact to suggest that Strong had been particularly paternal – indeed references to Hermione were rather infrequent in diaries, letters or anything else; Hermione's own sentiments, admittedly, were her affair.

'. . . Of course he had his little quirks, no one was allowed in his study and one wasn't to make a noise when he was working but after all he was an *artist*, Mark, a genius in fact, he simply wasn't like other people. I so wish Sid had known him – they'd have had so much in common.' She threw a fond look at Sid, who said, 'Sure thing.'

Mark glanced at Carrie; she sat gazing into the distance.

'And of course sometimes he was a tiny bit brusque with Mummy but in fact they were devoted. It's all total nonsense, you know, about him having ladies on the side, not of course that he wasn't frightfully attractive. He was utterly heart-broken when she died, Susan was just a sort of housekeeper really. Do you want me to remember specific things or just sort of go on in a general way like this? And do you think my voice will come over right or should I be more – more *emphatic*?'

So this was a run-through for the recording. Mark, who had been silently considering how ruthlessly he could prune this, or if it would be feasible even to lose it totally at some later date, said, 'Oh, something along those lines will be very nice. And you sound fine.'

'Good. We'll work on it properly tomorrow, then.' Hermione's attention at this point was diverted suddenly to Carrie; she had a way of being apparently preoccupied and then pouncing in an unexpected direction. 'Darling, I'm determined to do something about your hair. There's a frightfully good salon in the town – I'm going to take you there tomorrow.'

Carrie blinked, but made no comment.

Hermione turned to Mark. 'Of course, I've always thought this garden shop thing was quite mad. Daddy would turn in his grave frankly. I've never understood why Mr Thing at the lawyers gave it the go ahead. And now Carrie just slaves at it night and day, like some sort of peasant.' She homed in on Carrie again. 'You ought to get married, anyway.'

Carrie looked across at her. 'You're not married.'

'That's different,' said Hermione snappishly. She patted her hair and flexed an ankle. 'Pour us another drink, Sid.'

Deciding it might be prudent to intervene, Mark asked a question about Strong's working habits. Hermione, whether or not these were known to her, was prepared to hold forth at length. At some point Carrie simply evaporated. One moment she was there and then when Mark looked across again to her chair was gone. Hermione, running out of steam, sent Sid inside for another bottle. It was now a quarter to nine. Mark wondered when, if ever, there would be something to eat, and who was going to cook it. It seemed unlikely that it was for that purpose that Carrie had departed. Sid returned with more drink. 'Where's Carrie?' demanded Hermione.

'Alfresco. Watering the bloody garden. Peculiar bint, your daughter. *Encore* booze?' He waved the bottle at Mark, who shook his head, struggling against a compelling need to get up and hit the man.

Hermione sighed. 'She has this obstinate streak. Frightfully independent, as a child. Sweet, of course, in her way, but with this craze for flowers and so on. One always thought she'd grow out of it but then she simply took off like that when she was eighteen, nothing one said made any difference. I was worried sick, of course – a girl of that age. And after one had devoted oneself to her for so long. It's not easy, bringing up a child on your own, believe me. And after all the lovely opportunities she'd had with me, travelling and meeting interesting people.

she had to go off to that dreary college place, when she could have gone to some super finishing school in Switzerland.'

'My mum,' announced Sid with uncharacteristic fluency, 'always said the biggest kick up the arse you'll get in life is from your own kids.'

'She must have been so amusing. I wish we'd known each other.' Hermione turned to Mark. 'Sid grew up in the most fascinating part of London. The sort of place one doesn't know at all. He has the most marvellous stories about it – we'll get him to tell you some after dinner.'

Mark, momentarily uplifted by the final word, said, 'Ah. What part of London would that be?'

'Balham,' said Sid, with great promptness. It occurred to Mark with sudden insight that this was probably quite untrue; a nice semi in Camberley, more like. Social posing takes various forms, nowadays.

At nine-thirty Hermione and Sid moved into the kitchen from which, after much noisy bickering, they came up with a large and watery omelette and a salad. This, with cheese and fruit, was eaten off the dusty table on the patio. Carrie reappeared. Hermione said she couldn't understand how people could bear to live in England when they could be somewhere like this. At midnight Mark went to bed with a headache.

11

'THAT WOMAN's half-witted,' said Diana. 'And as for the boyfriend! Proper Lady Chatterley set-up, I must say. What the hell are we doing in this menagerie, I ask myself.' She shot Mark a look. 'Don't you ask yourself?'

'Sssh . . .'

Throughout the farmhouse you could hear pretty well everything anyone else said. The Lammings' bedtime exchanges were conducted now in harsh whispers. It is extraordinarily difficult to give vent to the full range of emotion in a whisper; Diana, in moments of unendurable frustration, would break the sound-barrier.

'All *right*. And it's like spending one's holiday on a building-site. We'd do better to take off for some nice *pension* in the town. How much longer do you need on this tape, anyway?'

'Not sure,' said Mark, hedging. 'Anyway, you're usually so keen to come to France.'

'There's France and France. This particular version of it is unfamiliar to me.'

'I could do with another couple of days here. Then maybe we might push on somewhere else. Provence? I dare say it would be a kindness to take Carrie along,' he said casually. 'She doesn't exactly love it here.'

'All right. I must say I'd like to see Avignon again.'

Carrie, of course, was the problem. In fact he had done pretty well as much recording of Hermione as he wished to do and would be only too happy to see the back of her; what he could not endure was the thought of separation from Carrie. Carrie a reluctant prisoner in the back of the car would be better than no Carrie at all. If she would agree to come.

She had continued to efface herself. That morning he had managed to waylay her for a few minutes in the garden – or rather, the parched and whiskery wilderness called by Hermione the garden. Wearing shorts, bra and a large sun-hat she was doing something intricate to a geranium with secateurs and twine. Diana was sitting on the terrace reading. From the swimming-pool – the only completed feature of the landscape – came the sounds of Hermione and Sid engaged in noisy horse-play. Carrie said, 'Hello. Could you just hold the end of the twine for me?' He had sat down beside her and for a few minutes all had been peace and pleasure. And then Hermione, draped in a towel that matched her bikini, had come up and said she must redo that last recording, she'd had second thoughts about it. So that had been that.

Diana had now been at Sarlat for two days, her initial good humour and sociability abating by the hour. She remained outwardly genial towards Hermione but was barely able to conceal her contempt for Sid. 'Christ!' she had muttered, on first sight of the studio and demonstration of Sid's professional skills. 'We get plenty like him at the gallery. And he no more comes from Balham than I do. It's taken years of cultivation, that accent.' She had sought out Carrie, in so far as Carrie could be found – presumably in desperation. Mark had recorded Hermione: a far more lengthy and tedious process than ever he had anticipated. In the first place most of what was said turned out to be more about Hermione than about Strong; and then no sooner was a sequence taped than Hermione would decide she had said it wrong and demand to do it over again. In all his experience of interviewing and listening, Mark grimly reflected, there had been no one to equal Hermione for irrelevance, egotism, inaccuracy and sublime stupidity. It seemed quite extraordinary that she could be Strong's daughter. He even entertained, lying in bed one morning, a wild fantasy involving successfully concealed cuckolding by Mrs Strong. At any rate, clearly that rich vein of perception, intuition, intellectual application and so forth had stopped short of Hermione. He thought, with new understanding and sympathy, of Mr Weatherby in the London office of Weatherby and Proctor, for whom Hermione was an inescapable and remorseless professional hazard. Hermione spoke frequently of Mr Weatherby, to whom she referred as that little man or Mr Thing. Mr Weatherby, evidently, was doing a grand job in preventing Hermione from acquiring and spending any more money than she already did. Sid, too, it was clear, had interesting powers of perception when it came to financial matters, despite the artistic status which, according to Hermione, raised him above such matters. He treated Mark to a disjointed tirade which appeared to mean that he had thought out a scheme whereby, with Carrie's consent, the entail could be broken and Dean Close sold for the general benefit.

'I doubt,' said Mark coldly, 'if she'd agree. Apart from anything else she happens to earn her living there. And there's the small matter of the Strong Society, and their administration of the house.'

'The old guy,' admitted Sid, 'buggers things up. *Pas de joie*, then, you think? No dice? Shame. Nice little bit of capital there for the girls.'

Mark raised his eyes from the tape recorder, which was giving trouble, and gave him a withering look. 'How nice of you to have their interests so close at heart.'

'Hermione,' Sid confided earnestly, 'is an O.K. *señora*. Believe me. *Molto* good fun.'

'I'm sure,' said Mark. He glared into the tape recorder. Sid, with some breezy remark about having work to do, slopped away into the farmhouse. It was insufferably hot. Hermione was asleep on a lilo by the pool. In the evening there would have to be another tape session which, with any luck, could be curtailed by mechanical failure. And then there would be no further reason to stay here. At some point soon he must get Carrie on her own and see if she could be persuaded to come with them. There was no sign of her in either the house or the garden at the moment, nor indeed of Diana. He wondered where they both were.

Diana sat at the café in the main square in Sarlat drinking Pernod. The town, its antiquity groomed to museum standards, seethed with people. Carrie sat at the other side of the table, an ice-cream in front of her that she did not appear to be eating.

'All right,' said Diana. 'Let's sort this out. Have you been to bed with him?'

Carrie found that it was quite impossible to look away. She gazed at Diana in acute discomfort. She felt herself get redder and redder; she blazed; her insides heaved. 'Yes. About four times, actually.'

'I don't want to know how often,' snapped Diana. 'I just want to know yes or no. At least you're honest.'

At the convent Carrie had briefly attended when she was twelve you got a credit mark for owning up to things you'd done wrong before you were found out; this felt a little like that. She bowed her head.

There was a silence. At last Diana said, more to herself than to Carrie, 'He's temporarily off his rocker, I imagine.'

'Yes,' said Carrie with enthusiasm.

'You simply are not in any way his type.'

'No, I know.'

Diana took a swig at her drink and waved at the waiter. 'I suppose he may have to have therapy when we get back to London. If I can get him to a therapist.' She eyed Carrie. 'Do you do a lot of this?'

'No,' said Carrie.

'Neither does Mark. At least not so far as I'm aware.' Diana continued to study Carrie. 'And, not to put too fine a point on it, you're about the last person I'd have expected.'

Since Carrie entirely agreed with this she could think of nothing to say.

Diana ordered herself another Pernod. 'Would you like one?'

Carrie shook her head.

'Well,' said Diana briskly. 'It's got to stop.'

Carrie agreed with alacrity. 'Anyway I think he might have

been getting a bit tired of me, on the last day or so. He didn't like me reading at dinner.'

'Reading?' Diana stared. 'Reading what? Oh, never mind . . . I must say you are . . . well, not quite like anyone one's come across. I suppose that's precisely why . . . Are you in love with Mark?'

'No,' said Carrie apologetically. 'I'm afraid I'm not.'

Diana, for a moment, looked distinctly offended. 'I see. That simplifies things, I suppose. The point is, what's to be done from now on? There's still the rest of this damn book.'

Carrie decided to eat her ice-cream before it melted. She was, she realised with relief, being regarded as some kind of natural hazard, a nuisance rather than an object of blame. She had expected worse than this. Indeed, from the moment that morning when Diana announced rather than suggested a short tour of the town by the two of them she had feared that this was in the offing. Since she could think of no way of getting out of it she had allowed Diana to tow her around the churches and the museum and through the narrow streets and finally they had come to rest at this café table, precisely as she had known they would.

'I suppose,' said Diana, 'I shall just have to come down to Dean Close with him every time, which will be a damn nuisance.'

Carrie nodded sympathetically, thinking of the guest room mattress.

'So it'll have to be weekends, because of the gallery.'

Carrie's relief grew. She was always busy at weekends anyway, what with extra customers and the girl in the office not there. She and Bill could just keep out of the way. Her attention began to wander, straying to the curious ginger-coloured stone houses with their balconies and discreet notices tethering them to some other century and the rivers of polyglot people that flowed around them. Hardly anyone seemed to be French. There were Scandinavian families with flaxen-haired children, matching clean-limbed blond parents, droves of young Americans, Japanese slung about with photographic equipment. They were sitting in the midst of the old town, which seemed to have been efficiently rinsed of both residents and any manifestation of age that was decrepit rather than engaging: what remained was a convenient and antiseptic receptacle for passers-by.

'. . . sit around twiddling my fingers all day.'

Carrie jumped. 'Sorry?'

Diana, it seemed, was offering the benefit of her administrative expertise at Dean Close. A face-lift for the sales office, which she'd had a glance into once and frankly . . . A once-over of the book-keeping.

'Well . . .' said Carrie awkwardly. She wasn't sure how Bill would take to that. Diana had moved on to an energetic consideration of redesigning the main part of the house.

'But it's supposed to be kept exactly like it was,' protested Carrie.

'There's keeping things like they were and keeping them like they ought to have been,' said Diana. 'Now take your grandfather's study . . .'

At the farthest end of the scrubland that would be Hermione's amusing formal French garden, because this was the closest she could find to privacy, Diana attended to Mark.

'She has the educational attainments of a check-out girl in Marks and Spencer. She has read about five books in her life. She can't spell. She doesn't know if the Prime Minister is Labour or Conservative. She isn't even pretty. And you're in love with her.'

'Up to a point,' said Mark.

Diana snorted. 'Up to a point, my foot. I thought better of you, frankly.'

Mark gazed at a plant: a disagreeable plant with fleshy leaves that looked as though it should be in a hot-house, not sprawling around in the dust. 'I'm assuming,' he said in a distant voice, 'and indeed fervently hoping, that it will pass. In the meantime I can only apologise. Humbly.'

'You *told* her,' he said.

'She asked,' said Carrie, 'if we had or not.'

'And you told her we had.'

'What else could I have said?'

'Various things,' said Mark at last. 'You always tell the truth, don't you? Now I know what it is that's so disturbing about you.'

'I'm sorry.'

Hermione, presiding over pre-dinner drinks on the terrace, said, 'Everyone's very *quiet* this evening, I must say. Here am I, feeling gay and forthcoming and none of you will take me on.'

'All dressed up and nowhere to go,' suggested Sid.

Hermione laughed indulgently. 'I want to be entertained. And you're all off tomorrow. I must say I think it's awfully sweet of you to take Carrie with you. Not that she couldn't have stayed here, of course – darling, I never did find a moment to take you to that hair place, for heaven's sake get something done about it when you go home. And she's been to Provence lots of times – we had that gorgeous little villa in Grasse on and off for years.'

Mark, with an effort, remarked that no doubt Carrie would see changes. He felt at the moment like an invalid, as though he were in a fragile state of health and must take great care of himself. He was beyond, even, being irritated by Sid. Hermione, by now, seemed merely an unavoidable fact, like some landscape blight that eventually becomes so known that the eye digests without seeing. She was remarkable only for being connected to Strong. That she had sprung from the loins of Gilbert Strong was indeed something to be wondered at. She was off on a final round of filial reminiscence.

'. . . And of course one grew up surrounded by all those famous people. *Everyone* used to come to Dean Close, and to the London house before that. I can remember, um, Shaw and H. G. Wells and um, someone with a pointy beard, terribly well known, goodness who was it, I know so well . . .'

'D. H. Lawrence?'

'That's right. Him. I sat on his knee. I sat on his knee and he told me stories, I was only about six or seven. He was sweet.'

'How extraordinary,' said Mark. Since Strong's only meeting with Lawrence had been disastrous and all his references to him scathing, and since Lawrence was in Italy at that time in any case, it was indeed.

'I know. It's wonderful how vividly one remembers things like that. He had a dreadful wife, you know, Erica or something, but he was charming – I've always loved the books, of course. And then there was that women with the long face and what's-his-name, the one who wrote that novel about India, and . . .'

Uncle Tom Cobley and all, thought Mark. Of course. Shaw, possibly. Certainly not Virginia Woolf, whom Strong detested. Ah well, what did it matter? At this particular moment and in his frail emotional state he was in no condition to cope either with Strong or with the complexities of truth and falsehood. Hermione's various testimonies would serve only to confirm what he had already learned: that what people remember is distorted not only by the shortcomings of memory but by the myth-making of the rememberer. The various Strongs recreated by friends, foes, former mistresses and the seed of his loins were performing functions far more intricate and impenetrable than ever one knew. He was required to bolster egos, confirm alibis, glamourise his daughter's picture of herself. He may or may not have faked a travel book, exercised bribery and/or intimidation, been a loving husband and father, a domestic tyrant and marital trickster.

Mark looked across at Diana, who wore an expression of patient interest, and Carrie, who was picking at a patch of peeling sunburn. He didn't understand why it had been quite so simple to establish that Carrie would come with them tomorrow; nobody had raised the objections he had expected. How things would proceed now he had no idea, nor did he very much care. He would have liked to go to sleep for a long time. Diana, he supposed, would be hatching forms of punishment. As for Carrie, she seemed simply to have switched off; he wondered if, at this precise moment, she was seeing or hearing any of them.

Hermione was talking about D. H. Lawrence for some reason and the awful boyfriend was drinking too much and Mark looked like a zombie. Diana, inspecting Carrie, felt a further uprush of the energy and planning ability that had seized her ever since that moment in the café in Sarlat. Crises always brought out the best in her; she actually enjoyed episodes like burst pipes or scalded limbs or domestic drama among friends requiring immediate bustle and organisation. She had seen what to do at once. You stepped right into the centre of things and took over. What you certainly did not do was send the girl packing or heap recriminations or stow Mark away under lock and key (as if that were possible). No, what you did was establish control.

She would drive. Mark would come in the front, because he would have to map-read. Carrie and the luggage would go in the back. She, Diana, would draw up an itinerary which Mark in his present shell-shocked state would be unlikely to query. She would see to it that everyone was kept busy, fed and slightly overtired. They would be under her eye. The whole thing would be domesticated and once she got them back to England she would have had time to work out the next phase. Carrie, who was basically docile, would have accepted her as administrator and decision-maker. Mark . . . well, Mark would probably be all too ready for the comforts of home and routine.

The sound of her mother's voice induced in Carrie a Pavlovian response: she simply blotted it out and concentrated on something else. She had mastered the art of doing this when she was seven and was surprised at how easily it came back. Occasionally odd words or names broke through (D. H. Lawrence – prompting the memory of an uneasy evening at the film of *Women in Love* with the plant nursery proprietor's son) but on the whole she heard nothing. She felt Mark looking at her and sternly did not look back. Her feelings of joyous anticipation at leaving here quite extinguished any apprehension about what might happen next. She had agreed to go with the Lammings because it seemed the obvious and only thing to do.

It started to rain almost as soon as they left Sarlat. Thunder rumbled from a queasy yellow sky and torrents of warm water descended. Diana, her eyes bright and her shoulders tense, hunched forward over the driving-wheel; the car splashed along black shiny roads, skirting strings of cyclists shrouded in yellow plastic. The roadside fields were dotted with blue and scarlet tents, buttoned up and lashed down like ships weathering a storm. And then all of a sudden the rain ceased and the sun came out and the whole place furiously steamed. Diana said, 'Right. We'll stop at the next town and buy stuff for lunch.'

In the supermarket, somewhere between the soft drinks and the delicatessen counter, Carrie decided to leave Mark and Diana and go back to England. She glanced furtively at them – they were busy arguing about a melon – and slipped away to the check-out. There, she got in a slight panic and picked up a packet of sweets so as to have something to proffer. Once outside she hurried to the car. It was locked, of course, which she had forgotten, so she could not take her hand-grip. Her sweater and her copy of *Emma*, which she regretted, were on the back seat and also inaccessible. But her passport was in the bag over her shoulder, along with her money and the travellers' cheques that Mark had made her bring, so that was all right. She could buy some T-shirts and a change of jeans; she had not had much with her in any case by way of clothes and she supposed the Lammings would bring the rest of her things back. She tore a page from her address book and wrote, 'I decided to go back to England.' She stared at this for a moment and then added 'Sorry. Love, Carrie'. She stuck it under the windscreen wiper, looked quickly back in the direction of the supermarket and set off down the road, fast.

∽ 12 ∽

CARRIE, IN PARIS, in a large cool room, sat gazing at a unicorn in the midst of a flowery meadow. The unicorn wore a jewelled collar and was encircled by a little wooden fence, but it was the carpet of flowers surrounding it that entranced Carrie. There were violets both white and blue, clover, daisy, bluebell, white campion, an orchid of some kind, iris and lily of unidentifiable species, persicaria, ramsons and many other things. She wrote down on the back of an envelope everything she could put a name to, but that still left a dozen or more, neatly stitched there apparently in the sixteenth century. Of course, when you stopped to think about it obviously there were the same flowers then as now, but this precise and lovely demonstration made the fact more startling. Lions and unicorns and those fairy tale people were gone, but violets and daisies and clover flowered away unconcernedly through the years. This was somehow reassuring; it also, in some way that was difficult to define, made you believe more firmly in the sixteenth century.

She had been doing a lot of sightseeing. That was not really what she had at first thought of coming to Paris for – it was simply that the first train that turned up had been an express going only there and it had also seemed to be a good place in which to hide from possible pursuing Lammings. But once she arrived she knew it was the place she wanted. She had been here often enough with Hermione, but all the time seemed to have been spent eating or drinking or shopping. Notre Dame amazed her. She took a train to Versailles and was further astonished. She wished she wasn't so ignorant. The guide books told you a good deal but they also left out a lot; what was left out, she suspected, was what most people already knew – even the scruffy chattering fellow-tourists by whom she was surrounded. She decided, resenting her own deficiencies, to do something about this. She would buy some books.

There were a number of bookshops near the tapestry museum. In the first she found an *Histoire de la France* that looked about right for her purposes. But it could not supply her other need, which was a further copy of *Emma*. She had spent the entire train journey from the Dordogne regretting having had to abandon hers. A helpful assistant suggested a neighbouring establishment which again was unable to oblige. She bought a book about the Revolution – it had illustrations and was less off-putting than its companions – and continued down the road.

She had also acquired a guide to *Paris et environs* and a map. Her purchases were quite weighing her down. She put the carrier-bag on a chair while she scoured the shelves of the next shop for *Emma*. She found Hardy and Henry James but no Jane Austen. Reminded of Mark and one of their first conversations she took down *The Golden Bowl* – the editions were in English – and dipped into it. The sentences were distressingly long; she fought her way through a few and then tried some dialogue. Her reservations increased; it was hard to see exactly what the speakers meant. She returned the book to the shelf and took out *The Mayor of Casterbridge*, again remembering Mark. Casterbridge was Dorchester, was that right? But what was the point of all this – presumably there were copies of these back home at Dean Close. She put the book back. At this point a man standing near, whom she had vaguely felt to be watching her, spoke. He said, with an inescapable English accent, 'Hardy est plus . . . plus agréable que James, à mon avis. Vous l'avez déjà lu?'

'I'm English,' said Carrie.

'Ah. The cut of your jeans fooled me.' He was not in the least disconcerted. Carrie eyed him coldly. And you don't fool me, she thought – trying to pick up French girls in bookshops. Huh. He was around thirty, thin and dark and with very bright eyes. Carrie prepared to leave.

'Would you agree?'

'I've never read either of them,' said Carrie. At that moment she caught sight of a row of Jane Austens on the top shelf and among them – hurray! *Emma*. She reached up for it; the shelf was too high.

'Allow me . . . Which is it you want?'

'*Emma*,' said Carrie, annoyed at her disadvantage.

'My favourite.' He handed the book to her.

'Thank you.' She moved towards the cash desk. The man followed her, holding a couple of French novels. Carrie delved in the carrier bag for her purse.

Which was not there. She delved further, went brick red, remembered, now, setting it down at the cash desk of the last shop and, presumably, not picking it up again. She explained, getting redder still. 'Je reviens . . . dans quelques instants. Si vous voulez bien garder le livre je . . .' 'Oh, don't be silly,' said the man. 'I'll loan you the cash and we'll go along and collect your purse together. If it's still there. If not you're in trouble anyway.' 'Please don't bother,' said Carrie. 'I can perfectly well . . .' By which time he had swept *Emma* up with his own purchases, slapped down a wodge of francs and that was that. Carrie followed him out of the shop, feeling even further disadvantaged.

They proceeded down the street. He talked. He was called Nick Temperley and he was a journalist. 'Not one of your glamorous Sunday paper journalists, I'm afraid. What's called an educational journalist. I write specialist stuff about teaching and schools. I used to be one – a teacher.' He was in Paris on holiday and partly to collect material for a piece about the French *baccalauréat*. Carrie conceded her name and that she was on holiday. And then half way between the two bookshops – on a traffic island, to be precise – something rather curious happened. He laid a hand on her arm to prevent her stepping into the path of a manic cyclist; she felt him looking at her, she glanced back at him and was seized with the thought that she was scruffy, that her hair urgently needed a wash, that her T-shirt was grubby and she very much wished she was looking nicer. Whatever was the matter? She hardly ever cared what she looked like, except from a vague sense of compunction.

The purse had been rescued by an assistant in the bookshop, who produced it with exclamations of triumph. Everybody thanked everybody else. Carrie counted out the right number of notes to repay Nick.

'Buy me lunch instead.'

'Oh . . .' said Carrie. 'Well . . .'

'Unless you're meeting someone?'

'All right,' said Carrie.

An hour and three quarters later, over the cheese, Carrie was struck at one and the same moment with the realisations that she was hugely enjoying herself and that this was someone she wasn't actually ever going to see again. The enjoyment sagged; she fell silent; Nick continued cheerfully with an anecdote about the Japanese who lived next door to him and a bottle-opener and the man from the Gas Board. Carrie sat with a listening expression on her face and observed the fan of little lines that spread out from his eyes when he smiled and a front tooth off which a piece had been chipped. She wondered when and how.

'Hmn . . .' he said. 'That's the first time that story's fallen as flat as that. It's usually considered amusing.' He contemplated her. 'By the way you've never said what you do.'

'I run a Garden Centre.'

He roared with laughter. 'You never.'

'What's so funny about it?' enquired Carrie, hurt.

'Well . . . It's just so unexpected. And not the sort of thing anyone I've ever known did.'

'*I've* never met an educational journalist before,' said Carrie with dignity.

'How long are you staying here?'

'I'm not sure.'

'I'm here another week or so.'

'Oh,' said Carrie.

'I thought of going to Fontainebleau tomorrow.'

'Oh.'

'Have you ever been there?'

'No,' said Carrie, suppressing an unwelcome recollection of a jaunt with Hermione and some exceptionally awful friends of Hermione's.

'Why don't you come along, then?'

That warm glow of enjoyment came flooding back. Carrie beamed. 'O.K.,' she said.

'Good,' said Nick, beaming also. So lunch came to an end, they stepped out into the street, parted, and Carrie set off back to her hotel, stopping on the way to buy shampoo and, in a moment of heady abandon, a rather nice dress she had caught sight of in a shop window.

The Lammings, after the initial surprise, did not much discuss Carrie's departure. Diana, reading her note, said, 'Well, that's a bit abrupt, I must say. Frankly she is the most peculiar girl.' Mark said nothing. He felt . . . well, he was not even entirely sure what he felt. Bleak. Deprived. Also, possibly, a faint twinge of relief. At least perhaps he could now step off that switchback of emotion. He could merely exist, a condition for which there is something to be said.

They went south and examined with diligence Aix and Avignon and Arles. Diana drove. She complained about the condition of the car; 'What the hell have you been doing to it?'

'It's difficult,' said Mark testily, 'to drive several hundred miles through France at the height of the holiday season without incurring a single scratch.'

'All right,' said Diana, 'I'll let you off that one.' She was not, indeed, going in for recriminations. She was brisk and efficient about maps and hotels and itineraries. They both read at meal-times. Sometimes Diana would glance at Mark sitting beside her in the car, hunched up so that he looked somehow smaller than usual, with his hands in his lap, staring ahead. And she experienced something odd. She felt . . . yes, she felt *sorry* for him, of all things. Occasionally she put out a hand and held, for a moment, his knee, and Mark's hand would move sideways to touch hers. Neither of them spoke. France continued to roll past at either side.

There was Fontainebleau and then the next day there was the Musée d'Art Moderne where Carrie discovered she liked several kinds of picture she had thought she didn't care for at all. And there was an old Chaplin film at a little cinema off the Boulevard St Michel on an afternoon when it rained and lunches at the bistro they particularly liked and dinner with some French friends of Nick's. He had been for a year at the Sorbonne so he knew quite a lot of French people.

In the cinema they held hands and after the dinner with the friends he kissed her and the day after that he came up to her hotel room after lunch and it became apparent that they were going to make love and Carrie said 'No.' 'Why not?' he asked, reasonably enough, she thought. And she said again, just 'No.' Because it's too important, she was saying inside her head, but none of this got spoken; she simply sat on the edge of the bed gazing at him in despair. And he gazed back for a minute or so and then said, 'You may well be right.' And they went for a walk along the *quai* instead, holding hands a great deal.

Carrie telephoned Bill.

'Well! The prodigal partner! How's *la belle France* then?'

'Lovely.'

'Lovely, eh?' said Bill. 'That's a bit of a turnaround. I thought we didn't care for abroad?'

Carrie said it was just that the weather was nice and she'd seen some interesting places. She asked about the alpines and whether the compost delivery had come all right and if Bill had remembered to check the syringas. Bill told her not to teach her grandmother to suck eggs. He asked where she was.

'Paris.'

'How's thingummy – Mark?'

Carrie said actually she wasn't with Mark any more. 'Bill?'

'I'm listening.'

'Would you mind if I stay on a few more days?'

'You suit yourself, duckie. Why?'

Carrie said there were some museums and art galleries she still hadn't seen. Bill replied that he was impressed with this sudden thirst for culture and looked forward to a blow by blow account.

The next morning Carrie did indeed spend in the Louvre. She had arranged to meet Nick at lunch-time. By eleven, though, the gallery was unbearably crowded and she had a slight headache; she decided to make her way across the river and look around the shops.

Half an hour later, wandering along the Boulevard St Michel, she glanced across the road and saw Nick. At first she thought it was just someone like him and then it unmistakably was him. Also wandering along. With a girl. With a girl across whose shoulders his arm casually lay.

Some part of Carrie's intestines turned right over. It was a horrid sensation; she had never felt such a thing in her life. It was like fear and yet not; it was like sudden violent illness and yet not. She stood stock still staring at Nick and the girl and her insides subsided but left her feeling frail and queasy. Then she panicked lest he should see her and plunged away, head down.

She decided not to meet him for lunch. Maybe he wasn't coming anyway. She decided to do something else; she would visit the tapestries again and then tomorrow she would go home. It was absurd staying here all this time anyway. She set off for the tapestry museum, with this huge lead weight implanted somewhere in the centre of her stomach, and half way there she turned round and headed for the bistro.

Landscapes displayed themselves to Mark as though he watched some travelogue: towns and villages and pastoral settings and the Rhone pouring fat and muddy towards the south. He looked, dutifully, at the things he was told to look at. Roman amphitheatres merged themselves into one composite Roman amphitheatre; Romanesque and Gothic passed before him and busy tree-lined squares and fields of vines or maize or Charollais cattle. Diana negotiated for food and beds; he spoke to no one except her. His thoughts, which were largely on Carrie, were like the chronic physical discomfort of flu or some gastric complaint. Indeed he was, he decided, ill – emotionally ill. But the Carrie of whom he thought, detached from any known setting (where was she? In a train or bus? Sitting at a café table? Walking by some roadside?) was already unreachable, removed by distance as finally as though by time. He had begun to think of her in the past tense. Which in no way diminished his distress.

'Cheer up,' said Diana. Irritatingly.

'I'm all right.'

'When we get home,' she went on, in the throw-away tone that, he well knew, concealed hard purpose, 'it might be an idea to see this rather clever man Suzanne knows. Just to sort of chat.'

'Chat about what?'

'About what you've been feeling and that sort of thing.'

'Are you suggesting,' he growled, 'that I take a course of psychoanalysis?'

Diana laughed lightly. 'Heavens, no! This chap's called a therapist or something. It's all very informal.'

'A kind of emotional massage?'

Diana, scenting danger, side-stepped. 'He sorted Suzanne's sister out marvellously after her husband left her. She's completely adjusted now.'

'I have no wish to be adjusted.'

Diana diplomatically suggested a detour to Troyes to take in the cathedral.

They were on their way north. In a couple of days or so they would cross the Channel. And life would be waiting for them on the other side, rubbing its hands: letters and bank statements and card index boxes. The book. Dean Close. Carrie.

Carrie over the *côtelette de porc garnie* which was steadily choking her, said, 'I saw you. Earlier.'

'Did you? I didn't see you.'

'You were with someone.'

'Why didn't you shout or something?'

'A girl.'

'Yes,' said Nick. 'That's right.'

'Who is she?' said Carrie distantly.

'She's called Marie-Claire and I've known her for nearly ten years and she's engaged to a friend of mine.'

There was a silence. He looked at her with what seemed to be concern. He asked if there was something wrong with the chop.

'Oh,' said Carrie, at last. And then, 'Are you sure?'

'Am I sure about what?'

'About her being engaged to this friend of yours?'

'Absolutely certain,' said Nick. The look of concern had changed to one of . . . well, of amusement. 'If you're not going to eat that I'll have it. I'm still ravenous.'

But Carrie had realised that she was, in fact, hungry and outside the sun had come out and maybe there was no point in rushing off to Dean Close tomorrow after all. Bill was obviously managing perfectly well without her.

Diana, at the same time as she expertly drove and busily observed, provided for the future. Mark required distraction. There must be outings and dinners for friends. She would go to Dean Close with him but not every time. Observation and reflection had now convinced her that it was not Carrie who was the threat but Mark's state of mind. Carrie, in a sense, was neither here nor there. She was, Diana decided, a figment of Mark's imagination, in a way; patently she was not the kind of girl he really cared for (his inclinations were, always had been, towards clever well-informed women, women of his own sphere, women in other words somewhat like Diana), so she was a projection of some kind. A projection of restlessness and obsession with the subject of his book and some vague sort of wishful thinking. Figments and projections could be dealt with.

And so, deftly and efficiently, Diana whipped the car through labyrinthine one-way systems, cheated death on motorways and planned the redecoration of the kitchen, her autumn wardrobe and Mark's rehabilitation.

Carrie had never felt like this before in her life. When she woke up in the mornings, in the cheap hotel room with windows opened to the clamour of the early traffic, she was confronted each time anew with this huge sense of well-being. She was not conscious of having been especially discontented, or indeed at all discontented before: it was simply that she seemed suddenly to have been granted an extra dimension of existence. As though you had been sickly, without knowing it, and all at once discovered perfect health. She was waking up very early, partly because if feeling thus it was a pity to waste a moment of it. On one of these occasions she lay reading *Emma* and reached at last the point at which the outcome of everything became apparent: 'It darted through her, with the speed of an arrow, that Mr Knightley must marry no one but herself.' She read the passage several times: of course, how stupid Emma had been despite thinking herself so clever, and how nicely you had been led astray yourself, not spotting until now how it would all work out. Perhaps most people did.

She continued, with satisfaction, to read. And as she did so, at a different level, somewhere below or behind the words that passed before her eyes, recognitions occurred. Arrows darted. With such accuracy, indeed, that she blushed, all alone there five floors up and in a foreign land; she went on reading, sternly.

'Incidentally,' said Nick. 'Why on earth were you buying Jane Austen in Paris?'

They were in the Jardins du Luxembourg. There were children and dogs and flowers hideously trapped in symmetrical beds; even these last could not much subdue the incandescence of Carrie's mood.

She hesitated. 'It's all rather complicated. I'd lost, you see, two other copies.'

'One,' said Nick, 'would be carelessness. Two sounds obsessive. Explain yourself.'

And so she did. From the beginning, more or less. Mark. Her grandfather. Mark's book. Hermione. Diana. The drive south with Mark. The time at Sarlat. Leaving out . . . well, leaving out one or two things. Leaving out is not lying.

'Then why did you ditch them like that?' enquired Nick, eventually. 'These Lammings.'

'I . . . well, I thought maybe they'd be better without me . . . And I sort of wanted to get away by myself.'

'Ah. And do you often do that?'

'No.'

'Good,' said Nick. There was a pause. 'This Mark fellow. What's he like?'

Carrie hesitated. 'He's very nice.'

He scrutinised her. She gazed back: those very bright eyes; the way his hair grew; that face, known now eight days and forever. 'That won't do,' he said. 'That's the most meaningless way there is to describe a person. Do you like him?'

And oh, she thought, why is he interested? What's it matter to him? But it does, oh it does. She sat in exultation – oh shameful exultation – amid the blazing pens of geraniums and petunias.

'We're coming back tomorrow,' she said to Bill.

'We?'

'I mean I. Not we, of course. I. Me.'

'I see,' said Bill.

'So I'll be at Dean Close by . . . well, in the evening.'

'Great.'

'So . . . Well, I'll see you then.'

'So you keep saying,' said Bill.

A long time ago, in fact, Carrie had been given to reading. It was in the year or two after that kindly and observant actor friend of Hermione's had spotted her educational deficiencies and taken the trouble to teach her how it was done. She had been amazed: first at this revelation of ingenuities quite unsuspected, and secondly at what was exposed. Stories. Worlds apart. Other private landscapes in which to hide. The only trouble was how to get hold of these things. The books she saw in shops were in Spanish or Italian or French. Hermione did not have many books because she did not have many possessions; the point, after all, of leading a fascinating travelling life was that one wasn't tied down by boring things like houses and furniture. Consequently Carrie found herself partial to reading but without, for the most part, the means to satisfy the taste. From time to time, though, some thumbed and battered book would fall into her hands and the contents of several had lain in her head ever since. There was *Tales from Ancient Greece* which particularly appealed to her because of the way in which people kept changing into something else: bulls or swans or trees. She would have very much liked to change into a tree herself and indeed selected various specimens against which she would lean hopefully for hours: a certain tamarisk somewhere near Antibes, a pine in Corfu, an immense protective ilex in Tuscany. Subsequently, she read and reread a tattered collection of fairy tales for the same reason; but now this universal tendency to metamorphosis seemed to her to indicate something else, a worrying instability to things, a subtle threat that what should be relied on might very well be snatched from you. Words might become pearls or toads; gold might become dead leaves; men were frogs or beasts and pumpkins were coaches. Don't count on anything, these stories seemed to say, nothing is what you think.

And it was this that came into her head, like an old dark superstition, as she left Paris with Nick and travelled first by train to the coast and thence in the ferry back to the shores of England. She leaned on the rails of the ship, with him beside her, and looked at the gulls hanging at eye-level and the green milky foam-marbled sea beneath and felt as though he might well vanish now or turn into a deck-chair or crumble into a flapping newspaper. Perhaps she had made him up anyway. When he went off to buy coffee and was gone for what seemed far too long she became panic-stricken and sat there with her heart thumping and her eyes wild. When he came back, grumbling about the queue and bearing two paper cups of luke-warm coffee, she couldn't believe in him. She had to keep glancing at him to reassure herself.

But when they reached Dover he was still there. He looked the same and he sounded the same. He did not evaporate when exposed to English air, nor did he turn into a frog or a cat or a German hitch-hiker in the train. They sat side by side and the predictable fields and hills and towns rolled past and gave way at last to suburban London and the Thames and the busy echoing vaults of Victoria, and he was still there. If she had been dreaming for the last week, then either she had not woken up yet or she was not going to wake up. At least not just yet.

13

MARK AND DIANA, at about the same time, also crossed the channel. Mark, on the ferry, thought not of fairy tales but of himself and of Gilbert Strong. He felt himself to be in the condition of some chronic invalid; he husbanded his energies, moved more slowly, acquired a slight stoop. Ensconced by Diana in a deck-chair at the rear of the ship, he watched the coast of France melt into the sea and remembered a photograph of Strong that he had found in an envelope in the trunk at Dean Close. The photograph showed Strong, sometime in the twenties, similarly installed on what looked like the deck of a cruise ship, but tightly shrouded in a plaid rug and flanked by other shrouded figures, as though all of them were convalescents laid out to take the sun. The face of the woman beside Strong was so extinguished by her hat as to make her unrecognisable; it might be Violet, or Stella Bruce, or someone entirely different. There was nothing invalidish, though, about Strong. He stared robustly at the camera, pipe clamped at one side of his mouth and a panama hat on his head at a slightly rakish angle. A book was spread-eagled on his lap; Mark had used a magnifying glass to try to make out the title, unsuccessfully. There was nothing on the photograph to indicate when or where it had been taken; it would remain yet another silence.

Or perhaps the moment was irrevelant. The moment; the voyage; the companion; the book, even. Extraneous matter, to be rejected as, according to Strong, the novelist rejects everything that has no bearing on the action of the novel. Strong himself would have disputed this: the biographer pursues truth – lies and silences for him are areas of failure. There is no extraneous matter.

At this point Mark abandoned Strong to his rug and his book and his woman and allowed Carrie to surface; it was as though he bit on an aching tooth. Diana, beside him, was reading the *Guardian*; she seemed absorbed but Mark was aware of an occasional inspecting sideways glance. He was under observation; in intensive care, perhaps. He found this mildly comforting. In his reduced condition, there was something to be said for being looked after.

'You'd have made a good nurse, you know.'

Diana lowered the paper and looked at him sharply. 'Whatever makes you say that?'

He shrugged. 'It just occurred to me.'

'Are you feeling seasick?'

'Certainly not.'

'Well, you look peaky,' said Diana. It seemed quite on the cards that she might announce he would have to take a tonic. Instead she added, more gently, 'Cheer up. We'll be home by dinner time.'

He realised that he could no longer remember at all clearly what life had been like before he knew his wife. How had it been to go to bed and wake up alone? To arrange for days in which there was no one to be considered but himself? He could remember meeting her, and the onset of passion and all that. What was gone was any recollection of her absence. Of pre-Diana. All of which had nothing to do with love or guilt but was simply a condition of existence.

France had now vanished. Seagulls and cardboard cartons bobbed in the wake of the ferry. Posses of French schoolchildren roamed the decks, shrieking. I have absolutely nothing to look forward to, he thought, no day is better than another day. Self-pity was laced with vigorous self-disgust. Work, he thought, is what I need, months of unrelenting work.

Strong, Mark thought, would have relished this whole

situation: meddling in and manipulating the lives of others even from beyond the grave.

'Yes,' Diana said to Suzanne. 'We had a marvellous time. Perfect weather. Some lovely little places we'd never seen before. Gorgeous food. Well, no . . . the Hermione woman was a bit tiresome but we didn't stay there all that long in the end. Oh, Mark loved it, yes – it does him good to get away. The girl? No, she decided to come back on her own. Just as well, really, Mark had rather a lot of her one way and another, and she's not entirely, well, our sort of person. Pleasant enough, of course, but . . . oh, a bit fey. So it's back to work all round now. Mark's only too happy. His desk is what he really likes.'

'France?' said Mark, to the woman acquaintance who shared his trade. 'Oh, France was all right I suppose. Contaminated in various ways but putting up some sort of fight. They still have a few natural resources to call their own. Material? No, material was somewhat thin on the ground. Fictitious, mainly – not but what that hasn't a certain interest in itself. You'll know what I mean. Do you still insist on my man's carnal weekend in Aberystwyth? Incidentally I came across a letter from your lady at Dean Close – I'll send you a xerox. It's remarkably dull – about some book Strong lent her and the unseasonal weather. Writing? Good grief, no – I'm a long way from writing the thing yet. The man is still a number of assorted pieces. The life . . . well, the life is several different lives, according to who is doing the talking. But you know all about that . . .'

He did not go down to Dean Close. There was quite enough to do sorting and collating material he already had – the stuff in the trunks could wait for a while. He needed at this stage, he decided, to take stock, to see what he had and what he yet needed. Accordingly, he sat day by day at his desk, assessing and allocating. He found it difficult to concentrate. He anticipated nervously the eventual inevitable meeting with Carrie. Diana continued to treat him with brisk and affectionate consideration. When she was at the gallery she would telephone once a day; there were appetising lunch snacks left for him in the fridge. She bought theatre tickets and invited friends to dinner. He found himself dependent on her.

He began to plan the book. His attitude towards Strong had undergone many changes, he realised. Initially respectful, anxious and faintly propitiating, it had entered a familiar, companionable and critical phase and had progresssed from there through every degree of cynicism, admiration, distaste, irritation and reconciliation. It was, when you stopped to think about it, disconcertingly like the progress of relationships with the living. Plenty of love affairs, come to that, run along these lines.

But now something new had entered the field: a rising tide of suspicion. He became daily more convinced that Strong was holding out on him. The more he examined and reflected upon the evidence – especially the Dean Close papers – the more he was persuaded that the cunning old so-and-so had been manipulating him right from the start, providing precisely what it suited him to provide and making away with anything at odds with his own preferred version. A much subtler process than the Hardy system of dictating your account of things to someone else and much more difficult for the biographer to rumble. Widely practised though, no doubt.

For instance . . . Nowhere was there so much as a passing reference to this fellow Hugo Flack; no way at all of confirming or refuting Stella Bruce's tale of Strong's purchase of his Caucasus travel notes. No letter, no mention anywhere. Strong's diary for the relevant period survived – the Red Notebooks series at Dean Close. The Red Notebooks were silent about the Caucasus, but this might not be significant. Strong had made a practice of leaving large gaps in his diaries, ignoring several months at a time, and often used separate books for material of a particular kind, like travel notes. That the diary made no reference to the Caucasus neither supported nor disposed of Stella's story. Equally, there was nothing to relate in any way whatsoever with Edward Curwen's allegations that Strong had tried to bully him into retiring from the *TLS* row about the *Disraeli* book. Mark had traced the two friends of Strong's at the Cambridge college in question and written to their relatives enquiring about possible Strong correspondence: none survived.

But, over and beyond these specific items, he found himself increasingly suspicious of the very nature of what was left. The shortage of letters from Strong, for instance, as opposed to letters received by him. Of his correspondence with Violet, for instance, only her letters remained – and an oddly random selection of those. None, for instance, telling him what a wretch he was – which, according to some accounts of the marriage, there ought to be. Susan's letters existed, but none of Strong's to her. Why? Because some of them didn't suit the Strong version of things as to be presented ultimately to the public? A man like Strong would have been highly unwilling to hand himself over lock, stock and barrel to anyone, let alone some prying stranger. Mark Lamming.

Mark, increasingly obsessed by the idea, vented all this upon Diana. 'He must have been perfectly systematic. Either all along or at some point quite late. Selecting and destroying. There were some things he simply didn't want me to see or know about.'

'Not you specifically.'

He barely heard this. 'Which means that I have got to work with this always in mind. That the silences may be points where he is trying to outwit me. Equally, at other points he may be trying to lead me astray.'

'Darling,' said Diana, 'the man's dead. Not is – was. And he didn't know you from Adam. If he was doing that sort of thing it was aimed at the world in general, not you specially.'

She was looking at him with concern. 'Yes, yes,' said Mark testily. 'I know all that. Sorry,' he added after a moment. 'I didn't mean to be cross.'

Diana laid a hand on his knee. Mark, in confusion of spirit, thought yet again that she was really being quite extraordinarily nice these days. When she would be fully entitled to be the very opposite. He couldn't explain what he meant about Strong and resolved not to bring the matter up again.

Diana, gently withdrawing her hand after a moment, decided to have a quiet word with Suzanne's sister about this therapist.

A week after this Mark went down to Dean Close. He did so on the spur of the moment, deciding when he woke that morning that it had to be done and could be staved off no longer and that there was stuff he needed to look at. He telephoned and got Bill. So far as Bill was concerned it was fine for him to come down. Suit yourself. Everything ticking over here as usual. See you later then, mate.

Diana raised no objection. Neither did she offer to come too. She said, 'I suppose you'll stay the night.' Mark replied that he supposed he would.

When he arrived there was no sign of Carrie. He went through to the kitchen and put on the table Carrie's grip that she had left in the car at Sarlat and, on top of it, the French copy of *Emma*. Then he climbed to the attic and immersed himself in selecting the bundles of letters and notebooks he wanted to work on next. He had decided to take them away with him. At lunch-time he came down to the kitchen and found Carrie there. Alone. She jumped to her feet, went bright pink and embarked on an incoherent sequence of apology.

He looked at her: at the ginger curls and her wrists which he had always especially cherished and her mouth. He tested himself. And yes, it was profoundly painful. There she was, and there, also, she would no longer be. Untouchable and unreachable. Exactly as one's rational self had known all along she would have to be. He wasn't after all, the kind of man who went in for this sort of thing.

Carrie had stopped gabbling explanations. She said, simply, 'Sorry.'

'It's all right. It was probably the most sensible thing to do.'

'Was Diana very cross?'

'Yes and no. She's not throwing me out, if that's what you mean.'

'Actually,' said Carrie, 'I meant cross about me going off, not about you and me, um . . .'

'Going to bed together?' said Mark remorselessly.

Carrie stood chewing her fingernail. 'Mmn.' She threw Mark a quick, guilty look. 'I just felt you and she would have a nicer time if I wasn't there any more. And . . .'

'And you wanted to get away?'

Carrie did not answer. There was an uncomfortable silence into which the rooks cawed and the kitchen tap dripped.

'Well,' said Mark, 'there it all is. I'd better get on and do some work. That, after all, is what I'm here for.'

'I finished *Emma*. I got another copy.'

'Ah,' said Mark. 'Where?'

Carrie turned and became suddenly very busy at the sink. She said she didn't remember, exactly. In Paris, possibly.

'So now you know how it all turned out.'

'Yes,' said Carrie. 'The arrows.'

'What?'

And at that moment Bill came in so that Carrie's reply, if reply there was, was extinguished by greetings and then by Bill's demands for food and so by the preparations for and the having of the well-remembered appalling Dean Close lunch. During which Mark forced himself to glance at Carrie. It occurred to him that she was looking extraordinarily well. She glowed, indeed. He looked away.

In the attic, dust and dead flies had gathered upon the ranged piles of papers from the trunks. Diana's neatly lettered date-and-content cards had warped a little in the strong sun through the skylight: '1930–1935; corresp. from eds of *TLS*, *Spectator*, *Horizon*, A. P. Watt, Heinemann, photographs, notes on Morocco visit, incomplete diary for 1932.' The piles grew larger as time progressed. Very little before 1900; toppling heaps for 1940 onwards. It was the content of these piles, and their extent, that Mark wanted to check.

He had, on the wall of his study at home, a chart, recently drawn up. All the evidence from all his sources had contributed to this chart, which laid out Gilbert Strong's life year by year and told Mark, at a glance, where he was living at any given points and what, broadly speaking, he was doing. It was lettered in several colours (domestic circumstances, books in progress, contributions to periodicals etc.) and was inspired by similar and even more intricate charts created by the senior history master at Mark's school, who had liked to see the collective past as capable of being thus simply and neatly displayed.

The trouble was, of course, that there were gaps. For 1938,

say, or 1951, it was possible to pin Strong down for almost every week and for almost every day. At other points there were disconcerting tracts of virgin white paper. And the most extensive of these tracts ran from 1905 to 1915. Where was Strong in his vigorous late twenties and early thirties? Unmarried, working on the life of Napoleon, publishing swingeing opinionated pieces, reviewing, bouncing around in those allegedly halcyon expansive pre-war years. For a time he had rooms off Baker Street. He popped up for a few months in Maidenhead or Weymouth or St John's Wood. But there were long uncharted stretches. It was unsatisfactory. And, in Mark's present mood, provocative.

Throughout the afternoon he sorted and checked. Once he heard Carrie's voice outside, calling something to Bill. He wished he were elsewhere. He wished he did not have to come here any more. He wanted never to see Carrie again; then in the next minute he fought the urge to get up and go downstairs and outside and find her. He read, and searched, and made notes, and endured. He put into cardboard cartons those items he wanted to take home with him. The afternoon became the evening and he went down into the house. There was a smell of frying from beyond the green baize door.

They ate, once more. Carrie came in late, when Mark was giving Bill a forcedly spry account of the summer. He did his best to look at her as little as possible (every now and then there arrived within his field of vision a sunburnt arm on which gleamed ginger hairs). He enquired if she had heard from Hermione. She had not. 'Incidentally,' he said. 'How do you feel about me taking some of the material from the attic up to London to work on?' That, it seemed, would be perfectly all right by Carrie. 'Good,' he went on. 'In that case I probably won't be around for a while. I'm getting to the stage of gathering all the threads together.' Carrie was silent. From relief, he presumed.

He could not sleep. The hair mattress, *angst* and the indigestion commonly induced by Dean Close fry-ups combined to produce an intolerable restlessness. The only book he had to hand was

Gilbert Strong's third novel, *Once in Summertime*, an undistinguished but in some ways persuasive account of rural love. The novels, poised somewhere between Ford Madox Ford and Galsworthy in style but with an occasional disconcerting whiff of Mary Webb, were hard to take. There wasn't much of a case to be made out for them, if any. Good thing Strong had packed it in fairly early on. Grudgingly, Mark opened *Once in Summertime*; truth to tell, he'd only read it rather cursorily.

Carrie had been consumed with guilt about Mark. Guilt for having walked out on them like that in France; guilt for what had happened in Paris because now she knew – oh, how she knew – what Mark must have been feeling like. And when he had walked into the kitchen all this guilt had surged forth like some shaming disease. Above all, she didn't want him to know about Nick. She had worried about this all afternoon. And then, at supper, everything had been unexpected. In the first place he hardly looked at her. And then he had asked, quite casually, if she minded him taking stuff up to London, which she didn't – she never had, indeed, but previously Mark had somehow implied that this was out of the question. But now, apparently, it was perfectly practicable.

He'd got over it, she supposed. He wasn't in love with her any more. Which of course was an entirely good thing. Why, then, was she both melancholy and somehow queasy. She went out to shut up the greenhouses and the feeling stayed with her. She contemplated the alpines and a sad confusing anxiety gnawed at her. And then she had to come in because Bill was going out and the telephone could never, nowadays, be left unattended: Nick might ring. He might ring and not get an answer and then not ring again for hours, or for a whole unendurable day.

She was glad, for Mark, that he didn't feel like this any more. She wasn't at all sure that she wanted to feel like this herself, but, of course, there is no choice. And at the same time, in the midst of it, she was assaulted by a knowledge of the treachery of things. That one condition slides into another of its own volition; that you can cope with what you do, but not with what you are. She had never seen this before with such sharpness. Perhaps it was of this instability that those fairy stories warned, for all their talk of living happily ever after.

Diana, alone in London, decided not to telephone Mark. In the same way that she had seen it would be best for him to go to Dean Close alone, so it now seemed to her more sensible to leave him unsupported. She had no qualms about the Carrie business; that would not start up again. Her observation of Mark, which combined the shrewdness, experience and folk-wisdom of an old-fashioned nanny, had convinced her that he had been going through a difficult phase which was, given continued astute treatment, well past the critical stage. For Diana, although to all appearances in the vanguard of fashion in every way and especially ideologically, retained a view of men that was not only pre-feminist but in fact somewhat in advance of feminism. She regarded men as different; not as inferior or superior but quite simply as apart in a sense that transcended discussion, or made it superfluous. You treated them differently from women and expected different (and, by implication, irrational) behaviour from them. Accordingly, you perfected certain lines of approach, changed strategy and studied form – much like any professional handler of a related but crucially distinguishable species. She was often surprised that other women did not seem to know about this, or that men apparently were impervious to it.

She had known, when she first met Mark, that she would have trouble with him. This affected not in the slightest her decision to marry him. So far as she was concerned, not only should any girl worth her salt be prepared to confront difficulty, but that was what she was there for. Nor did this state of conditioned readiness have any bearing on her feelings for Mark; she loved him. But love was not a matter for brooding or analysis; it was simply the climate in which you lived, and you dealt with it appropriately, with the help of barometers and umbrellas and air-conditioning.

Right now, she was no longer concerned about Carrie but about Mark's state of mind within a wider context. It was not unusual for him to be abstracted or mildly evasive or periodically irritable. He was all those things at the moment but with a manic tinge that was new to her. She mistrusted it. This book, she suspected, was at the bottom of everything. Personally, she didn't care for the sound of Gilbert Strong at all; from what she had read, both at Dean Close and in Mark's study, he was the kind of man whose resources matched her own. Had he been alive, this would have been both a compliment and a declaration of war.

Twenty-four hours later the Lammings confronted each other across Mark's desk, from which Mark was feverishly and somewhat inefficiently gathering papers and notebooks.

'*Somerset*...' said Diana. 'All that way. The whole thing could turn out to be a wild goose chase. Can't you just write to people?'

Mark, stuffing things into his briefcase, replied that no, he couldn't. He emptied photographs from an envelope onto the desk and made a selection: Strong as a young man, moustached and Norfolk-jacketed leaning against a gate, a beetle-browed cottage with a water pump beside the door and a monkey-puzzle tree alongside.

'That's the place?'

'That's it.'

Diana picked up the photograph and turned it over. 'Porlock, 1914. And the tree is in this novel? Very Edwardian trees, monkey-puzzles, mind. It's all a bit tenuous.'

'I know it's tenuous,' said Mark. 'Lots of things are tenuous. It's a hazard of the trade. But this has to be followed up.'

Diana sighed. 'Well, drive carefully, for goodness sake. I wish I could come too, but no way, the state Suzanne's in about the new exhibition.'

'I'll only stay a night or so. See if I can find the cottage. Talk to people a bit.'

He couldn't wait to be off. He was possessed. He had lain, last night, in the Dean Close guest room bed, persecuted by *angst* and the hair mattress, and on page eleven of *Once in Summertime* there was the description of the cottage somewhere in the west country with the monkey-puzzle tree at the door. And on page twenty-five, when the sensitive young hero met his lady-love, who is not named throughout the book but exists only as a pronoun, a pre-*Rebecca* conceit which had demanded of Strong much grammatical contortion, there was the mention of the amber necklace, lying against the curve of her strong young neck. And so forth and so on. And at that point he had been able to contain himself no longer but had crept up to the attic to ferret in that inadequate and therefore provocative '1910–1915' pile. And there, as he thought, was the photograph, mildewed in an envelope with others of Strong himself, of an unidentified cricket team, of his parents in old age. And the letter, in an unknown hand, with no address, dated September 1914, saying simply, 'I am sending you my sister's amber, with the thought that you may wish to have something of hers to keep. We are as well as can be expected.' Signed, merely, M.

Tenuous indeed. Straight, in fact, from the pages of a fiction more romantic and popular than Strong's wordy, somewhat heavy-handed account of love and separation in a rural paradise. The girl in the book had gone away, mysteriously and precipitately, leaving her lover to mourn through the final high-flown chapter.

Strong's other two novels were indisputably autobiographical. Despite his pontificating on the subject of fiction, Strong's own attempts at it were fatally crippled by his inability to reach beyond the confines of his own life for subject-matter. Admittedly all novelists are subjective to some degree, but Strong was unswervingly so. Novel number one was about his time at Cambridge, novel number three was about high jinks in literary circles in the south of France. Novel number four, happily, had never seen the light of day.

So, by deduction, novel number two was also about some Strong experience. A person and a place. A person and a place, moreover, for which there existed no other evidence. The envelope of photographs and the letter had been pushed into a folder of newspaper cuttings – reviews and articles – as though they might well have been overlooked. As though, in fact, they might be the only murmur out of what was intended to be a silence.

14

IT WAS SEPTEMBER. The landscape sliced by the M4 had the wearied look of late summer: the fields scoured, the hedges dark and shaggy. Long, rough-looking clouds were strewn around the horizon. Mark, stopping only at the anonymous concourses of motorway services, had the sensation of the country through which he passed as being detached, an elsewhere in some other dimension of time or space from himself or from these other travellers hurtling through. It did not seem possible that one could stop and step out of the car into it. The fields and hills and clustered houses seemed as removed as the scenery in a photograph.

He was decanted from the motorway into the narrow roads of west Somerset and at once was reunited with a tangible and contemporary world: hedgebanks that brushed the side of the car, a whiff of manure, a flock of little birds skirling from a tree.

He reached Porlock and found a pub that could let him have a room for the night. The place, strenuously manicured and catering, it seemed, only for people without occupation beyond riding horses or going for walks, did not appeal to him. He left the car in the pub garage and wandered around, a little disconsolately. The venture now seemed impetuous. The long drive had tired him; he wished Diana were there, with some reviving proposal.

He left the centre of the town and followed a lane that began to wind up a steep hillside. He rounded a bend and there, in full colour and distorted only by a new porch and a television aerial, was the cottage. With tree alongside. And the pump, painted sparkling white.

The Bed-and-Breakfast sign outside said 'Vacancy'.

Mark went back to the pub and said he had changed his mind about staying. Ten minutes later he was presenting himself to the lady who opened the door of 'Pump Cottage'.

By the morning he knew that if Gilbert Strong had slept under this roof there was no whisper of him left. Mrs Cummings, a widow from Manchester, had retired here with her husband five years ago. Before that there had been the so-and-so's for three years and before that someone for another five. The cottage's memory was brief and disordered. The neighbours all appeared to be similar refugees from the Midlands; indeed, Mark had an impression of the urban retired as descending upon the West Country in a gentle nostalgic snowstorm, in search of those summer holidays of yesterday.

She served him a lavish breakfast, hovering inquisitively. 'A writer? You don't look like a writer, if you don't mind my saying. I'd have thought you did something quite ordinary. I like a good biography. Winston Churchill or the royal family. You haven't written about the royal family?'

'Unfortunately not,' said Mark.

'And this person you're interested in was a writer too? What was his name again? No, I can't say it means anything to me.' She patted a sculptured grey curl. 'Pity. If it had been Bernard Shaw or someone I could have had a sign up, couldn't I? Well, if you send me a copy of your book when it's done I don't mind putting it out on the hall table for visitors to have a look at.'

Mark nodded, ambiguously.

'I suppose you could try asking Major Hammond. He's been here donkey's years. He might remember something.'

'Major Hammond?'

'Up the road. Big house with white gates. I only know him to pass the time of day with, he's not all that what you might call forthcoming. Bachelor, of course. But he's local. They let you know it, round here.' A *frisson* reached Mark: a hint of complex matters of status and position. 'You could give him a try, anyway.'

'Thank you,' said Mark. 'I might at that.'

'That's the fellow.' Major Hammond turned the photograph over and then handed it back to Mark. 'Before the war, that's right. Had the cottage down the road.' He eyed Mark. 'What d'yer want to know for? Lawyer johnnie, are you – something like that?'

Mark explained. The Major, though upright and spry, appeared to be in his eighties which made him ten or so when Gilbert Strong was in Porlock. Well, ten-year-olds can be observant.

'You'd better come in,' said the Major. He led the way through a windy hall and into a large sitting-room in which crouched innumerable battered leather or wicker chairs, giving the impression of a club premises. Bits of stags and foxes hung from the walls, alongside photographs of polo teams in Burma or Karachi in 1920-something. The Major was dressed in sports jacket and grey flannel of awe-inspiring antiquity. His white moustache was kippered a delicate tan on the right hand side. The room smelt resoundingly of tobacco and dog. An enormous labrador lay on its side on the hearth-rug, as though recently shot.

'Whisky?'

'No, thank you,' said Mark. It was half-past ten in the morning.

The Major took a cigarette out of a chrome case and stuck it under the moustache. 'My doctor tells me I should pack these in. What I say is, I pay the feller but that doesn't mean I have to take his advice. Write books, do you? I've done a bit in that line myself.' He got up and went over to a glass-fronted bookcase and picked a slim volume from amid a run of bound copies of *Punch* and freckled editions of Dornford Yates, Charles Morgan and A. J. Cronin. 'Verse,' he explained.

Mark inspected the title page. Privately printed by someone in Dulverton. Dedicated to the rabbit whose untimely positioning of its burrow had caused the fall from a horse which occasioned the enforced leisure enabling the Major to produce this work. The poems celebrated Exmoor, home leave, a good day with the hounds and once or twice something rather more unexpected. One described an evening in London, date unspecified, when the Major had gone 'To the Trocadero, And on . . . To see the girls with nothing on'. Mark laid the book down on a large leather pouffe with a murmur of appreciation. He found himself rather taking to the Major.

'Why write a book about this particular fellow?'

It seemed an apt question. Mark began to answer as best he could. 'I happen to think he wrote a number of good books himself. He was a forceful man and more influential than has been realised. He . . .'

The Major cut him off. 'Interesting sort of life, I should think. Could fetch you up all over the place.'

'Yes, he travelled quite a bit . . .' Mark began.

The Major brushed this aside. 'For a young chap like you, I meant. Pay well, does it?'

'No,' said Mark. He noted that 'young', with appreciation. The Major nodded gloomily. He stubbed out his cigarette and lit another. The dog rose to its feet, shook itself with a sound like a rug being beaten, and collapsed onto its other side.

'Know this part of the world at all?' enquired the Major.

This, Mark realised, could go on for some time. Not that it wasn't agreeable enough, but it seemed the moment perhaps to direct the conversation a little more firmly. He paid a brief tribute to the surrounding landscape (blurred now beyond a curtain of thick grey rain) and went on, 'You actually met Gilbert Strong, then, when you were a boy?'

'Went fishing with him,' said the Major promptly. 'Mackerel and that sort of stuff. He didn't ride, that I remember. Talkative fellow. I'd forgotten he was a writer. I'll have to give one of his things a try.'

'You knew him quite well, then?'

'Oh yes.'

There was a pause. The Major sucked on his cigarette and blew, in quick succession, two perfect smoke-rings. Mark, who hadn't seen that done for years, was temporarily distracted. He pulled himself together and continued, 'Did you see him later on – after you were grown-up?'

The Major shook his head. 'Lost touch. Or my mother did, rather. Never heard from him again. After. Well, um, afterwards.'

Mark, alerted, said, 'Afterwards?'

The Major peered at him through a drift of smoke. 'Fact is, the man was, um, how shall I put it, associated with my aunt.'

'Oh. Really?'

'Yes.' The Major hesitated. 'Well, not to put too fine a point on it, we're both men of the world, they were living as man and wife.'

'But they weren't? Man and wife?'

'Dear me no. Irene was married, d'you see.'

Mark, feeling slightly heady, gazed at him. The Major's cheeks were a crimson fretwork of broken veins; his eyes were a light whisky brown and had the kindly look of an equable dog. It was odd to think that here lurked a boy who had gone mackerel fishing with Gilbert Strong.

'I didn't know anything about all this,' said Mark. 'It's very interesting to me. I suspected something of the kind, because of a novel of his. I suppose your aunt couldn't get a divorce?'

'She intended to, I've understood. All a bit of a fuss, in the family. Upset my grandparents. But then there wasn't time, in the end.'

'There wasn't time?'

'She died,' said the Major. 'Poor girl. Too bad, really.'

They sat, for a few moments, in silence. The Major cleared his throat and looked away; he seemed, now, embarrassed at this revelation of past irregularity. Mark was thinking that for the first time Gilbert Strong had surprised him. He wondered why he did not feel more excited. Instead, he felt a faint unease, as though inadvertently stumbling upon the privacy of some acquaintance.

The Major cleared his throat again. 'Yes. Tragic business. My mother was very cut up. Nasty bout of pneumonia and that was it. Didn't have the right sort of pills in those days, did they?

Strong was very cut up too, I understand. Did he get married in the end?'

'Yes. Yes, he did.'

'Ah well.'

'Have you any pictures of her?' said Mark. 'A photograph or anything?'

The Major frowned. 'Come to think of it, there may very well be one with my mother's things. She kept some of Irene's papers, I know. Whole lot of junk in boxes upstairs. Don't know about you, but I'm very bad at throwing things away. I give these women who come to the door an armful of things for the local jumble sales from time to time, old clothes and that, you know, but I never get around to a proper turn-out.' He sighed, evidently daunted now by the immensity of the task. 'I dunno, though, could be wasting your time . . .'

'Perhaps we could have a look,' Mark suggested.

The Major, shaking his head doubtfully, led the way upstairs. The hall was lined with old mackintoshes, voluminous, stiff and pink with Somerset mud. There were dozens of pairs of wellingtons, racks of walking-sticks and riding-crops, bowlers and deerstalkers hanging from pegs. On the stairs and the landing above hung more framed photographs: the Major with his foot on a dead tiger, another polo team, a group of army officers. The labrador followed them, wheezing dreadfully.

This was not, the Major explained, the family home but the house he had built himself in the thirties in anticipation of the early retirement from the army which he had indeed taken immediately after the war. His parents had lived a few miles away, in Wootton Courtney. His mother's more personal possessions had come here after her death, including, he remembered, boxes of letters.

He opened a door into a large dank room with many gloomy pieces of mahogany furniture and an iron bedstead. There was a washstand furnished with the kind of jug and basin that would have gladdened the heart of a Camden Passage antique dealer and, above the mantelpiece, an engraving after Landseer's *Monarch of the Glen*. The Major went over to a high cupboard in the wall and opened it to reveal crammed shelves reaching right up to the ceiling. The labrador, at his heels, began to make snuffling noises as though about to expire. 'Poor fellow thinks there might be a mouse,' explained the Major. 'Very likely, too.'

The Major pulled out various boxes and files and examined them, rather hopelessly. He gave Mark a look of appeal. 'D'you really think it's worth the trouble?'

'Well, I think it might be,' said Mark. 'I'm sorry to be such a nuisance.'

'Not at all, dear boy,' said the Major valiantly. 'Tell you what, bring the chair over and see if you can reach that stuff at the top. I have a feeling what we're looking for might be up there.'

Perched somewhat precariously, Mark reached up and delved into an open shoe-box. He dropped a packet of letters down to the Major who fished a pair of glasses out of a breast-pocket and said, 'Ah. Getting warmer. These are mother's, all right. From my father, in the war. Try again.'

Standing on tiptoe now, Mark took out another thick wodge of packets. He peered at the top envelope and saw with a thud of the heart Gilbert Strong's unmistakable handwriting; at the same moment the dog gave a hoarse bark and lunged at the leg of the chair, which lurched sideways.

He crashed to the floor. He tried to rise and felt violently sick. He head the Major say, 'I say, my dear chap, you did come a purler.' He rose, groggily, felt a grinding pain in his ankle and another somewhere in his chest, found that everything for some reason was turning grey, and fainted.

When he surfaced again the Major was offering him a cup of tea and talking about mice. The dog was nowhere to be seen. The Major had tucked a rather smelly tartan rug under Mark's head. The tea was Jacksons of Piccadilly, he confided, a regular order, not from the local people. He peered at Mark, 'I say, I am sorry about that. What a thing to happen. How d'you feel?'

Mark heaved himself up, gingerly. Both pains were still there. 'I'm rather afraid I've done something to my ankle. And possibly a rib.' He tried to stand, and subsided hastily onto the edge of the bed. The bundle of envelopes was still in his hand.

He undid the string and flipped through them. Each one was addressed to Mrs Irene Lampson, in Gilbert Strong's handwriting. He closed his eyes, opened them and looked again. His ankle hurt abominably. This whole episode, his presence in this place and this house, seemed like a bad dream. He felt like the victim of some malevolent conspiracy and stared with a mixture of distaste and suspicion at the bundle of letters. The Major was talking about doctors.

'I simply do not follow all this about a dog,' said Diana. 'But never mind. However it happened, it's happened, that's all that matters. I suppose this local GP knows what he's doing. You'll certainly have to have another check-up with our man when you eventually do get back. A week before you can use your foot! What on earth will you do with yourself?'

Mark replied that he thought he would have a good deal of reading to keep him busy.

'I could try to get down.'

Mark hesitated, tempted. Diana's sympathy would be brisk and practical. Part of him yearned for it, and then he thought of the conjunction of Diana and the Major, and shuddered, more for the Major's sake than for Diana's. 'Don't bother. It isn't worth it. I'll be all right.'

'Well . . . Suzanne would go spare, just at the moment. So if you're sure . . .'

The Major had himself walked down to Pump Cottage to fetch Mark's overnight bag and settle the account with Mrs Cummings. The car could be left where it was for the time being. The exercise of trying to envisage the exchange between the Major and Mrs Cummings gave Mark his only brief passage of cheer. And now he was installed in an enormous leather armchair in the Major's sitting-room, his bandaged foot stuck out on the pouffe and aching dreadfully. The Major was upstairs making up a bed for Mark. He had insisted on providing hospitality and would not be gainsaid. ''Fraid you may find the place a bit spartan, but I can knock you up some grub in the evenings and I daresay we might find time for a spot of backgammon when you're not going through these letters. No trouble at all, I assure you, my dear chap, least I can do . . .' The dog, banished to the kitchen during the doctor's visit, had reappeared ('Poor fellow says he's most frightfully sorry') and was once again unconscious on the hearth-rug.

Mark apparently had a badly sprained ankle and a cracked rib. Rest was the only treatment required. And so, for the second time, he was absorbed into Gilbert Strong's territory. In this instance, imprisoned there. Discomfort and annoyance destroyed any possibility of a rational response to what had happened; so far as Mark was concerned, Gilbert Strong was responsible, whether directly or indirectly. Just as he was responsible for all the disorders of the previous months.

Grimly, he began to read the letters.

∽ 15 ∽

BILL HAD DIAGNOSED Carrie's condition within a week. 'You,' he said, 'have got yourself involved with a bloke. And high time too. Come on, then, give. Where did you find him?'

Carrie, puce, denied everything.

'All right, have it your own way. But since when did you jump a mile high every time the phone rings? Let alone spill a can of spray and lose your pruning knife. Or stand in the greenhouses staring into space. When do I get a look at him?'

That, then, was something Carrie hadn't known herself. She had parted from Nick at Victoria and he had vanished into Suffolk to visit his mother and for four fearful days she had heard nothing from him. On the third day she knew she had never been so unhappy in her life and on the fourth she began to contemplate suicide and that evening he telephoned. He said, 'What's the matter? You sound funny.' And Carrie had taken a deep breath, discarded the hours of anguish and despair, and replied that she was fine, thanks.

He came to Dean Close for the weekend. He inspected everything with the same energy and application that he had devoted to pictures and statues in Paris: the house, the greenhouses, the stock fields, the display area. He made Carrie explain mist-propagation and layering and the application of fertilisers. He spent a long time in Gilbert Strong's study, pulling books out of the cases and looking at the pictures on the walls while Carrie hung around nervously. He said, 'You're something of an iceberg, do you realise?'

Carrie was alarmed, suspecting criticism.

'You hide seven-eighths of yourself. All this . . . Extraordinary museum of a house and a flourishing business alongside. And there you are apparently half-dotty, wandering around Paris in a grubby T-shirt.'

'I told you.'

'Up to a point,' said Nick. 'Up to a point.' He came across the room and put his arms round her. 'Don't look like that. I'm not finding fault. It's part of your charms. What are we doing this afternoon? I'm prepared to put on gumboots and perform manual labour, if need be.'

He struck up an easy relationship with Bill. They had a long conversation about Bill's resistance to paperwork and Nick devised a more effective system of processing orders. On Saturday evening they all three went out to the pub, where they ran into the journalist from the cottage down the road with his girlfriend. It was very convivial and Carrie found herself talking a great deal more than she usually did and indeed making people laugh. She hadn't thought she was the kind of person who did that.

And, later that night, Nick came to her room and this time there seemed absolutely no reason why they should not make love. It was no less important, she knew, but in some way what would have been spitting in the eye of fortune back there in Paris no longer was, here at Dean Close. When she woke in the morning Nick was beside her and for a moment she was confused and thought, with various kinds of guilt, of Mark. And then Nick awoke and said, 'If this sort of thing is going to go on, you'll have to get a bigger bed. You kick, in your sleep.'

'Do I?' said Carrie, in blissful contemplation of that 'going to go on . . .'

'Yes. There have been problems of *lebensraum* all night.'

'What's that?'

'It's what happens when nations feel themselves constricted. Don't you know any history?'

'No,' said Carrie happily.

He wanted to go for an outing. Maiden Castle, he suggested, or Dorchester – that's in these parts, isn't it? And Carrie said, yes, let's, but somewhere else maybe. So they climbed another hill, elsewhere, and lay on chalky turf in the last sunshine of the year and Carrie knew that all her life she had been living in a state of semi-consciousness. She had been neither unhappy nor discontented, except occasionally; but, quite simply, she had not known that this marriage of feeling and seeing and being was possible. She lay in the sun and the wind and looked sideways at Nick, at his face and his hands and his green sweater with one elbow out, and her whole body hummed in accord with the world, an accord that she had never suspected, as though she were putting out buds or leaves in response to the season. She wanted to know if Nick felt the same but could find no words that were right. She said, 'Are you happy?' and Nick replied, 'Oh yes, I'm happy all right.' He put his hand on hers and above them birds floated against the enormous heights of the Dorset sky.

Mark, ensconced now in what the Major called his study, which was devoid of books but hung about with guns and fishing-rods, read Gilbert Strong's letters. The Major, from time to time, would appear with another cup of Jackson's tea, brewed unnervingly strong. He would then retreat, with a conniving nod of the head, as one who fully recognised the demands of intellectual life. He had produced a Remington typewriter of venerable age and minus a couple of keys; Mark, to demonstrate his appreciation, had felt obliged to write a letter to his publisher with which the Major had happily trotted to the post-box. The house was the dampest Mark had ever experienced; some of the shoes in the rack in the hall had a green fur of mildew and the books in the sitting-room case had that ripe and vaguely nostalgic smell. There was also an atmosphere of melancholy which Mark, for reasons he could not fathom, found not unpleasant. He sat, his aching foot propped on another battered leather pouffe of oriental origins, and read.

My darling . . . Only five hours since I left you and already I am in a wretched state. How I shall contrive to get through the next two weeks lord only knows. All the way to London you were in my head and there I sat with The Times *and the* New Age *and a heap of books, frowning and reading, every inch the literary gent, and not a word did I see . . . The day we walked to Luccombe . . . Last night, oh Irene, last night . . .*

The Major put his head round the door. 'Don't want to interrupt, but there's a spot of dinner ready as soon as you'd care for it.' Mark, obscurely relieved to be able to break off, said he would come at once. They went into the kitchen, for which the Major apologised ('Fact is, I don't get a lot of visitors these days – dining-room's a bit dusty, I'm afraid.') where the Major served a hefty meal of baked potatoes and tinned stew followed by tinned suet pudding with golden syrup and culminating with what he called a nice bit of mousetrap from the village shop. After dinner the backgammon board was produced; the Major turned out to be a nifty player, gallantly (Mark suspected) allowing his visitor to win a respectable number of games.

There were a great many letters. Disordered, in no kind of sequence, some with envelopes, some without, some giving the address of origin, some not, dated and undated. They had to be sorted, listed, read. Chronology had to be established; the cold eye of the future and of an undreamed-of stranger must be cast on these words of love and confidence.

'Everyone sends commiserations,' said Diana. 'Suzanne and the Milburnes and Liz Fryer. But look, is it really all right at this Major Whatsit's house? I mean, the pub can't be that expensive and from what you say it's all somewhat grotty . . . You'd be more comfortable. What? Well, officers' mess circa 1935 sounds like grotty to me. No, I'm not fussing, I'm merely showing a little natural concern.'

Dear Mrs Lampson . . . Thank you for your letter and comments on my article. No writer, I assure you, resents an expression of informed interest and I found your remarks most stimulating. So far as Mr Conrad is concerned I do feel that . . .

You were not as I expected. No, that's not right – part of you was as I expected and part was not. Spectacles, I thought, and a touch of the schoolmistress and maybe you would jaw me a bit like clever women tend to. And instead there was your wonderful laugh and the way you tilt your head when you're listening and I never met a girl before who could walk farther and faster than I can. May I talk like this? May I say such things? Probably not, but I am, I can't help myself, and if you are cross, well, you are cross . . .

'Lampson?' said the Major. 'Truth to tell I can hardly remember the fellow.' He paused, stroked his moustache – a characteristic gesture – and shook his head regretfully. 'Years older than she was, you know. Married her at eighteen, straight from school. Business associate of my grandfather's, you see, legal walla, solicitor I think. And then Irene turned out very different, poor girl. Had a mind of her own, read books, strong opinions – that sort of thing. Wrote stories herself, my mother said. Lampson was an old stick-in-the-mud, I daresay – they hadn't a thing in common.' He shook his head again. 'Caused no end of a rumpus, of course, her going off like that. But you know, when one thinks about it, well . . . Poor girl . . . And she and Strong just fell for each other hook, line and sinker, I suppose . . .'

So I have taken the Porlock cottage for three months and you will be only four miles away. We can walk and talk and I shall persuade you that Stendhal is superior to George Eliot and you shall lecture me (just a little) on Christina Rossetti. Isn't it a good prospect? I am bringing down a cargo of books to start work on Napoleon and plan to shut myself away and buckle down to it, with your company please as the icing on my cake . . .

It is after midnight and there is a blazing moon hung over Bossington Point and this note is the treat I allow myself after working all day. May I come on Friday afternoon? May I inflict more Napoleon on you and if your sister comes over may we all three do the walk on the hill?

Your lovely letter came when I had been writing a piece for the New Age *all day and was quite knocked up, head aching, ready to chuck up books once and for all, and with it the sun came out and I walked on the beach and read it again by the rock against which we sat last week . . .*

I lay awake all last night. I should have gone away, Irene, that first time we met, and never returned.

'Fact is,' said the Major, 'my mother took their side. Stood up for them, d'you see, against her parents. She'd never cared for Lampson, apparently. Thought he was a dry old stick, not worth Irene – there was some name she used to call him, afterwards, she and my father – Cas . . . Caso-something . . .

'Casaubon?'

'That's right.'

What are we to do, my darling? What am I to do? Do you want me to go away?

Your letters . . . I lie in wait like some spider, a pipe-smoking typing spider – one eye on the paper, the other on the window, pretending to work. I hear the postman's bicycle before it rounds the corner. I hear if he is slowing down for my door or if this morning he is spinning past and if he spins my heart drops unfathomable depths into my boots and the morning is ruined, it lies in ashes around me, it can rain black cats for all I care, the world is a foul mean dingy place . . .

Not at the weekend, you say. So be it. Five whole days, then.

Midnight. You are four miles away, and four thousand. After we said goodbye I watched you go down the hill – you stopped at the oak by the gate, as I knew you would, and looked back, and waved – and walking home through the valley I went over every word we said. I love you. You love me. God knows why you should do so, but you do. I am happier than ever in my life, Irene, happy in a way I didn't know possible. And in black despair.

'Wondered if you'd care for a spot of music tonight?' said the Major. 'Make a change from backgammon?' He had produced from the depths of one of the many cupboards in the house a heap of 78s. The curious sounds that Mark had heard from time to time during the day were, he now realised, the Major's attempts to limber up the ancient radiogram in the corner of the sitting-room. He now opened it and demonstrated with pride the revolving turntable. 'Going nicely again. Wretched thing went phut for months but I've had a go at it with the oil-can and a screwdriver and hey presto!' He looked thoughtfully at Mark. 'I imagine you'd prefer classical stuff? This sort of thing your cup of tea at all?' He held out a record from the pile.

'Certainly,' said Mark.

They sat at opposite sides of the fireplace. The Major lay back in his chair, gazing at the ceiling, and as 'Pomp and Circumstance' got under way his right arm lifted from time to time and made stabbing gestures at the floor, not quite in accord with the beat but evidently deeply felt. At one point his lips moved, soundlessly, as though in song. The room was filled with Elgar; the Major got out a large handkerchief and wiped his face once or twice. When the record was over he sat up, blew his nose vigorously and put on the other side. 'Fine stuff, eh?'

Mark nodded.

They moved from Elgar to the *Nutcracker* Suite and thence to Borodin and part of one movement of the Grieg Piano Concerto (the rest had been broken). The Major's stabbing gestures gave way to more expansive movements of the arms. At the end of each record he would shake his head and say, 'Amazing, isn't it?' or 'Wonderful the way those fellows think up stuff like that.' Mark was invited to make his own choice and found some excerpts from *The Magic Flute*; the quality of the sound was somewhat distressing at points but the Major listened rapt. When it was finished he said, 'I like a nice bit of singing. 'Fraid there isn't anything much else in that line – except . . .' He went over to the pile of records and picked out another, which he put on the turntable, with glance of apology in Mark's direction. 'You may not care for this sort of thing.'

A little distorted, as though coming from a long way away, the strains of thirties dance music filled the room. 'Blue Moon, you saw me standing alone . . . Without a dream in my heart . . . Without a love of my own.' The Major crossed the room to the tray on which stood the whisky bottle and poured them each a tot. He returned to his chair. It was beginning to get dark. The room, always somewhat gloomy, became twilit except for the single bar of the electric fire in the empty fireplace before which the dog lay, snoring like a simmering kettle.

Oh isn't it heavenly . . .
To be so romantically and frantically in love with you . . .

The Major, one hand gently tapping the arm of his chair, had a beatific smile on his face. Once or twice he nodded absently, as though in agreement with the lyric. He looked at Mark, 'This all right for you?'

'Very pleasant,' said Mark.

Love is the sweetest thing,
The only and the neatest thing . . .

There hung in the room an atmosphere of unspoken recollection, a hint of passions dried out like rose-petals but to which a faint scent still clung, a whisper of the girl and the song and the moonlight. Mark, infected, was filled with indefinable yearnings which seemed to have little to do with love or anything pertaining thereunto. He felt a sense of loss that was general rather than specific, a grief that was not entirely unpleasurable at departed emotions, at the scheme of things, at the passage of life. Once or twice images of Carrie or of Diana, long ago, flitted before him, causing a twinge but drifting away again as the singer on the gramophone, his voice creaking at points and employing a curious exaggerated pronunciation, moved on to another theme.

> The rose that you caress
> Is willing to die
> It loves you so very much
> And so do I . . .

It seemed indelicate to break the mood with conversation. The Major sighed. He got up to change the record, brought the whisky bottle over and put a dash more in each glass, murmuring, '. . . little of what the doctor ordered does no harm.'

> Smoke gets in your eyes . . .
> Yet today my love has flown away,
> I am without my love . . .

They sat on in the darkening room. The Major leaned back in his chair, tapping on the arm with one finger and softly humming. Mark, in a limbo just short of melancholy, roved around various moments and feelings and people; none of them, now, seemed of intense importance and perhaps more significant in this state of contemplation than at the time. He wondered, but did not like to ask, what the Major was thinking about, or feeling. The rapport between them was too comfortable and discreet a thing to rupture with intrusive enquiry; emotion, the Major implied, was perfectly acceptable but a matter for private indulgence. When the record finished and the needle ground to a halt he sighed again, looked at his watch, stirred the dog with his foot and said, 'Well, time to take the poor fellow for his walk, I suppose.'

'I wish I could offer to do it for you,' said Mark. 'I'm a total parasite, I'm afraid, as a visitor.'

The Major peered into the radiogram, blew at something and closed the lid. 'Think nothing of it.' He paused. 'I'm only sorry you're having to pig it rather. It's not exactly the Ritz here, I know. When a chap's lived by himself for a long time things get a bit out of hand. Needs a woman's touch.' He straightened, shoved the dog absently with a foot and pulled his moustache. 'Could have been a different story, of course . . .'

Mark looked enquiring. The dog put its nose against the Major's knee and snorted loudly. The Major patted it and shook his head briskly. 'Ah well – all for the best, I dare say.'

The moment passed.

∽ 16 ∽

THE LETTERS, chronologically sorted in so far as this was possible, lay in neat piles on the table: those read, those yet unread, those from which transcripts should be taken. And each time Mark sat down in front of them again his unease grew.

He had never felt like this before. He had read without flinching and frequently without response of any kind the most intimate and revealing documents; he had marched resolutely into the privacies of strangers. It was, after all, his job. He could not, therefore, understand why it was that, now, here amid the dusty weaponry of the Major's study, he confronted Gilbert Strong with greater and greater reluctance.

One of the surprises – one of the imponderables – was that this was a different Strong to any he had met before. Here was a Strong with all defences down, without any of the bombast or calculated stances, sincere, vulnerable and . . . doomed. For, as Mark read, he was unable to lose sight of his own foreknowledge. He felt like some cold omniscient Olympian eye, knowing as he read these words of love and hope and expectation that none of it would come to pass. Knowing what would happen.

Irene, after months of anguish, had decided to tell her husband of her love for Strong and ask for a divorce. His response – deduced from the Major's recollections through his mother and from passages in Strong's letters – had been unexpected and chilling. He had admitted that he did not love her, at least not in any sense of love that she recognised, but had cited her duty and her position. Divorce was out of the question, unless eventually he so chose and he implied that he never would.

And so she left, and went to Gilbert Strong in the Porlock cottage.

Do you know that this is the first time I have spent more than two hours away from you in two months? Confound London – confound editors and libraries and Napoleon. What are you doing at this moment? I know – you are walking up onto the moor, with your hair coming unpinned as it does at any excuse. No you are not – you are by the fire, reading and frowning and making notes of things to get our teeth into next week . . . And I am wretched without you . . .

I want children, Irene. I want a daughter who will grow up as a further dimension of her mother. Never mind about sons – oh well, them too, maybe, eventually.

When we are married – and we will be married, I know we will, I see the long years of our marriage ahead like a great spacious welcoming firelit room – when we are married we shall have a house in London because I want to show you off. I want to wave you around in pride. We'll have that – but we'll also have Porlock, or somewhere like Porlock, because we're going to want to be alone, and work, and shut the door on people . . .

Friday, my love . . . Napoleon or no Napoleon, I cannot stand another day away from you.

I suppose there are other women in the world but if so I do not see them. I think you are the first woman, you are how the whole idea began, there has never been a woman before. And don't frown, I shall talk nonsense if I wish – there is nothing you can do about it, two hundred miles away. Let me tell you why you are the first woman. Let me tell you about your eyes and your hair and your breasts . . .

Mark pushed the letters to one side and got to his feet, forgetting momentarily his ankle and uttering a yelp of pain. He reached for the stick lent him by the Major and limped to the door. Enough. A half-hour respite, at least.

Nowhere, subsequently, in all the mass of Strong's preserved papers, was there any mention of Irene. This could not be fortuitous. He had deliberately set about eliminating any reference to her. Had Violet known about her? Had Susan? Undoubtedly Hermione did not. And why? The reason, it seemed to Mark, was manifest in the nature of the letters themselves: his relationship with her had had an intensity unequalled by anything that came after. Her death, it was easy to deduce, had shattered him; and his complex and somehow typical reaction had been to hide her away. From his wives, his friends, his colleagues and, finally, from any potential biographer. These letters were not supposed to be read.

And I wish, thought Mark with violence, I were not doing so. His response amazed him. Anyone else would have regarded all this as a stupendous piece of professional luck.

The Major was out on one of his protracted and complex shopping excursions. Mark went into the sitting-room and sat at the window, looking into the dank and untended garden. He thought about Gilbert Strong. He tried to come to some conclusions about the man. The point was not far off when he would have to stop accumulating and reading and questioning, and start to write.

And as he considered – piling up Strong's qualities of tenacity, contentiousness, application, intellectual breadth, deviousness and so forth – it came to him that what was in question was not only an assessment of Gilbert Strong but the progress of a relationship. An entirely one-sided relationship: intense on his part, non-existent on Strong's. Two weeks ago, Mark thought,

I was having paranoic suspicions about the man: I was fully persuaded that he had gone to considerable lengths to frustrate and mislead me. Me personally, mind. And now that I am in possession of knowledge that seems intrusive – now that I have the upper hand, so to speak – I feel as guilty as though I had stumbled upon the privacies of some friend or acquaintance. I would much prefer to discreetly withdraw.

He sat, his ankle giving the occasional twinge, and stared at the Major's rampant greenery; a light rain misted the view, as it usually did. Thoughts of Strong himself gave way to reflections upon the effect of Strong. But for Strong, but for the events of Strong's life, but above all for Strong's emotional condition in 1912, he would not be where he was – sitting with a sprained ankle in the house of a stranger. Nor would his own emotional state over the last few months be as it had been. Carrie; France. And, as the garden gate clicked and the Major hove in sight, draped about with plastic carrier-bags and with the dog stumping along at his heels, it occurred to Mark that, in some eerie way, by means of these two people, Strong's life had extended into his own. The relationship was not entirely one way after all.

Carrie no longer thought of Mark with guilt; truth to tell she did not think about him a great deal at all since it was no longer possible for her to devote thought – if it could so be called – to anyone but Nick. But occasionally she returned to those days driving through France, and to the times before that, and she found that they had subtly changed, seen now through the enlightenment of experience. She felt, oddly, closer to him, with the arbitrary intimacy of people who share survival from some natural disaster. She would have rather liked to see him.

And then one day Diana telephoned, which at first induced in Carrie familiar symptoms of alarm. But Diana was perfectly friendly, matter-of-fact and without recriminations. She had discovered that Mark forgot to return to Dean Close with Carrie's other possessions a jacket left in the car at Sarlat. He would do so at some later date. But not for a couple of weeks or so as he was stuck down in some neck of the woods place in Somerset with a sprained ankle, poor darling. 'Incurred in the course of duty, apparently. Don't ask me how, but this is the tale. So he's being put up by a peculiar old boy in some way connected with your grandfather.'

'Oh,' said Carrie. The last statement interested her not at all. After a moment she went on, 'Gosh . . . Poor Mark. Is he . . . I mean how does he . . . Well, how is he otherwise?'

'Fine. Working.'

'Oh. Well . . . good.'

'That business in France,' said Diana, 'is overcome, one way and another. A passing aberration. As these things usually are.'

'Are they?' said Carrie, in sudden apprehension, thinking not of Mark at all.

'In my experience.'

Diana's experience, Carrie had no doubt, was not to be questioned. Her uneasiness increased. She fiddled with the lead of the telephone, worrying.

'Hello?'

'Hello.'

'I thought we'd been cut off,' said Diana. 'Well, I must go. I'm at the gallery and we're up to the eyes, as usual. I just thought you might have been wondering about that jacket.'

'Thank you. Could you give Mark my love?'

Diana appeared to reflect. 'Yes. I don't see why not. Any other messages?'

'No. No, not really.' Carrie hesitated. 'I'm glad he's O.K. I mean, except for his ankle. But what you said about, about passing . . . passing aberrations. Not *everything* is.'

There was a silence. 'How do you mean?' enquired Diana cautiously.

'Well, you and Mark weren't. When you met.'

Diana cleared her throat. Behind this, Carrie could hear a woman's voice telling someone, in tones of ringing authority, not to put the damn thing down that way up. 'Well, we got married, for heaven's sake.'

'That's what I meant,' said Carrie.

'Oh.' Diana conveyed a quiver of the antennae. 'Are you . . . Is there something else you were thinking of?'

'Oh no,' said Carrie hastily. 'Anyway, thanks very much for ringing.'

Mark, too, received a call from Diana. The Major summoned him into the hall saying respectfully, as usual, 'Your good lady.'

Diana delivered a quick run-down on domestic and professional life. 'Are you all right?'

'More or less,' said Mark.

'What about these letters? Useful?'

'I'm not sure that useful's quite the word.' He pondered; impossible, thus, or indeed perhaps at all, to explain. 'I had this dream last night in which I was struggling through this enormous field of lettuce. Commercially grown lettuce, you understand. Trying to reach something or someone. Row upon row of crisp green lettuce.'

'*Lettuce*?'

'Word-association. A well-known dream phenomenon, apparently.'

'Oh,' said Diana. 'I've never heard of it. By the way, I rang Carrie about that jacket. She sent her love. Have you seen the doctor again and when are you coming back?'

A further dimension of the lettuce dream, not communicable, had been that what Mark had been trying to reach was in fact a girl, a stark naked girl who both was Carrie and in some way was not. He had been stark naked too: a good conventional unimaginative dream, that. He had been forging his way towards this girl, placidly waiting there amid the lettuce, and when he reached her at last the expected processes had got under way, or been just getting under way when, of course, he woke up.

He went into the sitting-room to join the Major for what had now become the customary glass of sherry before dinner. Mark, embarrassed by his parasitic state, had succeeded in persuading the Major to allow him to make an economic contribution towards the household expenses: it had been a matter of the greatest delicacy, the Major furiously resisting until driven into a position where further protests would seem more ungentlemanly than capitulation. They were both now happier about the sherry indulgence, as well as a few mealtime treats suggested by Mark such as pâté, which the Major had never come across.

'Too bad, leaving your poor wife on her own all this time.'

Mark said he thought Diana was probably managing quite well and explained that, given the expected further progress to his ankle, he should be able to manage the drive back to London after the weekend, by which time he hoped also to have completed his work on the letters.

'I suppose you'll be putting it all into your book?' said the Major. 'Irene and everything . . .' He fingered his moustache, a gesture of unease that Mark now recognized.

Mark replied, after a moment, that he supposed he would.

The Major nodded. 'Quite. Not a thing you can leave out, now you know about it. Got to get the record as straight as you can.' He nodded again, as though to persuade himself.

At which, Mark, to his own surprise, began to describe his doubts and scruples; there were moments, he said, when he wished this chain of deduction and accident had never led him to the letters.

'Come now,' interjected the Major, 'got to put first things first, eh? There's this book.'

'Damn the book,' said Mark.

The Major, looking shocked, suggested another sherry.

'How much do you remember about her death?' asked Mark, after a few moments. 'And did you ever see him afterwards?'

She had been taken ill very suddenly, so far as the Major recollected. One day everything had been normal and the next there had been an atmosphere of alarm and distress and his mother had departed in haste for Porlock to nurse her sister. He had been aware of anxiety and tension, of late-night messages and the continued absence of his mother. And then after that all he could recall was the funeral, and his mother's silence and anguish for weeks and months.

'She used to avoid going near this place, you know, because of the cottage. Wouldn't come to see her friends in Porlock. When I came to live here she always used to come to see me by the back road, so as not to pass the cottage. Dreadful business. Everyone loved her – Irene. Must have been an extraordinarily nice girl. More than that . . . Full of life, you know. Laughed a lot – that I can remember.' He sighed. 'It was spring when she died, I remember that too.'

. . . And into an inexpressibly tedious day – hours with Napoleon and lunch with an awful man who dispenses patronage by way of reviewing – there comes your letter, to tantalise and lift me up. And oh indeed yes I shall be in Porlock for the first week in April, and yes, yes you should investigate Vellacott's pony-trap and the hire thereof. Because after April there is May and May is followed by June and if I sweat hard now I can read what should be read and hole up with you there to write for months on end. I shall shake off London and libraries for spring and summer and maybe autumn too . . .

This is for your birthday – which we shall celebrate in full next week. But in the meantime I kiss you – all over, from the top of your beloved head to the soles of your equally beloved feet. Are you really twenty-six? Gracious – what a very great age. When you are thirty-six we shall mark the occasion with a visit to Siena which of all the Italian cities you have not seen is the most incomparable and the one which would almost persuade me to run away from England. Our daughter, devoted as we shall be to her, will be left at home since I do not fancy travel with children. But when you are forty-six (and my darling I very much look forward to knowing you when you are forty-six – you are one of those women who will be at their finest then), she will be allowed to come with us on a brief trip to Venice, because we shall like to watch her enjoy it . . .

The weekend passed. Mark's ankle was tender but usable. The letters had been read, transcribed and returned to the shoe-box in the cupboard; Mark had suggested depositing them with the rest of the Strong manuscripts but the Major, violently tugging his moustache, had demurred – 'Fair enough when I kick the bucket . . . But I may as well hang onto them till then, eh?'

There was nothing left but to say goodbye. Mark knew that any excessive display of gratitude or emotion would be quite out of place. The two men shook hands on the doorstep. The

Major's grip was slightly prolonged, the nearest he was going to allow himself to a show of feeling.

'All the best, then, my dear chap.'

'There is just one thing,' said Mark. 'I was wondering if you might think of taking part in a radio programme about Strong I'm getting together. It would probably mean coming up to London – so I'll quite understand if you'd prefer not to.'

The Major looked alarmed. 'Talking on the wireless? Not really my line, you know – never done it in my life.'

'There's nothing to it, I promise you. It would just be a question of saying how you remember him. And Irene, I suppose.'

The Major pondered. 'London, eh? Long time since I've been up to town. Well . . . I don't see why not. But you'd have to put me in the picture – I wouldn't want to let you down.'

Mark got into the car. He lowered the window to wave. The Major was standing at his garden gate, very upright, furiously punishing a moustache. The dog – the apocalyptic dog – lay slumped at his side. It was beginning to rain.

Beyond the bedroom window, Ealing rumbled into life. Diana was still asleep. He contemplated the nape of her neck, a landscape as familiar to him as – no, more familiar than – the back of his own hand. Very deliberately, he set about substituting, in the mind's eye, Carrie – to see what happened. This prompted various responses, but none of them were quite as intense as he might have expected. Could it be that one was on the road to recovery? And, if so, what did one feel about that?

Relief, undoubtedly. Intensity of emotion is all very well, he thought, but there is a great deal to be said – oh, there is indeed a great deal to be said – for tranquillity of mind. He conjured up France, to see what that would do. What that did was induce a certain melancholy – painful, guilty and faintly enjoyable all at once. Did he wish he were back in those three days, in the Auberge des Fleurs and the château whatever it was? Not really. He ran his finger down the back of Diana's neck and between her shoulder-blades; she wriggled irritably and drew the bedclothes around her. He dismissed the shade of Carrie, firmly but kindly. It would return, he suspected, at untimely moments and might well cause distress, but he believed he might now be able to cope with it.

He got out of bed, drew the curtains and got back in again. Diana sat up and said, 'Christ – what time is it?'

'Half-past seven.'

She subsided. 'I thought it must be later. You bustling around like that. What's the matter?'

'Nothing. I thought it would be a good idea to get the day on the road, as it were.'

She gave him a cautious look. 'You sound very energetic all of a sudden.'

'Lassitude,' said Mark, 'will get us nowhere.' He stroked her bottom, under the bedclothes.

'Porlock seems to have been therapeutic. Despite falling off stepladders.'

'A chair, in fact.'

'What I still don't understand is why you stayed with this peculiar old boy.'

'Sometime I'll try to explain.' He paused. 'On another question, I'm afraid I've been somewhat – irrational – over the last few months.'

Diana propped herself up on one elbow and looked at him. 'What's all this?'

'Inconsiderate – not to put too fine a point on it.'

'What *is* the matter?' demanded Diana.

'I'm trying,' said Mark stiffly, 'to say I'm sorry.'

'Oh. Well.' She lay back. 'So long as it's not going to happen again.'

'I should think that's quite extraordinarily unlikely.'

'It had better be.'

'I can vouch for it,' said Mark. 'In so far,' he added, 'as anything in this life is to be vouched for.'

Diana grunted. She turned sideways and shot him a look of inspection. 'Well. I'm getting up. The new exhibition opens on Tuesday.'

'No great rush,' said Mark. He slid a hand over her thigh.

'I thought you had this cracked rib?'

'I'm hoping,' he said, 'and indeed assuming that lust will triumph over infirmity.'

He filed away the transcripts of the Porlock letters. His study, now, was full of other people's lives. Did examination and contemplation of the experiences of others have a salutary effect on the management of one's own affairs? Patently not. Did the search for a complete view of another life enable you to stand back and thus consider your own? Not that either, really. Diana's account of the summer, or Carrie's, would presumably be significantly different from his; nevertheless he was pretty firmly persuaded that his was the correct version. It takes staggering powers of detachment to accept that other people's view of you might be more reliable than your own.

His professional acquaintance telephoned, in search of a reference.

'I gather you've been laid up in the West Country. Poor you. Was it worth it?'

'Definitely. I found a cache of letters.'

'You lucky so-and-so. Useful?'

'Useful all right. Disturbing, in a way. Tell me . . . Do you ever . . . Have you ever had a feeling of prurience, in our line of business?'

There was a brief hesitation. 'No.'

There speaks, thought Mark, a hardened old literary battleaxe.

'Do you?' she enquired.

'Well. The odd twinge, I suppose.'

'These people, my dear, are dead.'

'True. True.'

'I've begun to suspect my woman of lesbian tendencies, by the way. I always thought it was there in the poetry and now I've come across one or two other pointers.'

'Fancy that. So do you still insist on the carnal weekend with Strong?'

'It would by no means rule that out.'

'We shall never know,' said Mark.

'There are plenty of things,' replied the lady crisply, 'we shall never know. One ploughs on. In the pursuit of truth, or whatever.' Mark suppressed a comment about that 'whatever', which might have been taken amiss. 'It's enough to drive a person to fiction. Have you ever tried that, incidentally?'

'Oh yes,' said the lady, 'I've written me novel. Long ago. Haven't we all? Piece of cake, by comparison.'

They parted, cordially enough. Mark returned to his index boxes. The Porlock letters were entered under various headings. If I could sit down now, Mark thought, and write a novel based on the life of Gilbert Strong I would be very well equipped. The silences and rejected matter would be the appropriate silences and rejections of the novel, as so aptly defined by Strong himself in that oft-quoted essay of his. And my evidently over-delicate attitude towards prying into the affairs of others would not apply, since fictional characters have no feelings. Nor, of course, do the dead, as my colleague rightly points out. In fact, the only feelings in question are one's own, and all that they demonstrate is perhaps some Pavlovian response about the indecency of reading other people's letters. A taboo of one's youth, along with listening at doors and asking impertinent questions. Biographers are much impeded by a genteel upbringing.

He telephoned Dean Close and left a message with Bill that he would come down the following week. Time, now, to get back to the attic.

It was October. The trees around the house, which he remembered in brilliant leaf when first he saw them, were now tinged with brown and yellow. The Garden Centre sales office was full of wire racks crammed with bulbs and sporting gaudy illustrations of the joys to come. Mark, who had gone there in search of Carrie, stood looking at shocks of daffodils and crocuses. Bill, entering, said, 'Half a dozen "King Alfred"? You don't want any of those, mate – bad taste gardening for the undiscriminating, this is. The good stuff is round the back, for our favoured clients.'

'I was just wondering where you all were,' said Mark.

'I'm here, knackered after an hour with a bloody cultivator

that keeps packing up on me. Carrie's in the big greenhouse, mooning over the alpines. Very distracted these days, our lass.'

'Distracted?'

'Love. That old uncertain feeling. And not before time too.'

'I see,' said Mark. Somewhere within him something twinged; a little icy finger prodded.

'Bloke she met in Paris. As far as I can see something might well come of it. She hasn't mentioned him?'

'No. No, she hasn't.' The icy finger was now quiescent – gone more quickly than one might perhaps have expected. Just a slight ache left.

'Bound to come at some point.' Bill, intent with a pile of invoices, looked up at Mark. 'I always thought you had rather a soft spot for our girl yourself, perhaps.'

'Me?' said Mark. He contemplated a display of seed packets. 'Come now, I'm a married man.'

'So you are,' said Bill. 'So you are. It had slipped my mind. Well, back to the grindstone. Or to the blasted Massey-Ferguson.'

Carrie was indeed in the big greenhouse. She was at the far end, a small figure amid ranks of pots, much as when Mark had first seen her six months ago. Now, as then, she did not hear him come in and went on with what she was doing. Then she looked up, startled.

'I won't interrupt. I just thought I'd say hello before I get started on the papers. I'm taking more stuff up to London, if that's all right by you.'

'Oh – yes, do. Is your ankle better?'

'Pretty well.'

Dungarees. Orange socks. A smudge of dirt on her cheek. 'Oh good,' she said. And then, 'I talked to Diana. She rang up.'

'I know.'

'She doesn't seem to be cross with me,' Carrie explained. 'I thought she might be.'

'No, she isn't.'

There was a silence. Carrie tweaked a shoot off a plant, looked at Mark and then away again.

'I stayed with a very nice old man in Somerset whose aunt

was the great love of your grandfather's life. Before he married Violet.'

Carrie's eyes flickered. She tweaked another shoot. 'Why didn't he marry her?'

'She died.'

Carrie's response to this, oddly, seemed to be one of relief. She said, insincerely, 'How sad.'

'As a matter of fact it was. Very. I think possibly he never quite got over it.'

'Are you going to put it in your book?'

'I suppose so,' said Mark.

The sun had gone in so that the ripe yellow glow under the glass drained rapidly away and it became shadowy and greenish, as though under water. It smelled warm and damp; Carrie, it occurred to Mark, had always smelled faintly of earth – clean, woodland earth – even in France. He thought of France; it distressed, but not quite as much as he would have expected.

'I hear you've got a boyfriend.'

She gave him a look of alarm. 'Well, it's not exactly . . . I mean . . .'

'It's all right,' he said. 'I'm not going to go out and shoot myself. Are you going to marry him?'

She was silent for a moment. 'We haven't talked about that yet.'

'Then raise the matter. If it's what you want. This is the age of The Woman, after all.'

She stared into a flowerpot. 'It isn't something to make jokes about.'

'I'm sorry.'

'I think it *may* work out all right.'

'Good.'

'It would serve me right if it doesn't.'

'Rubbish,' said Mark. 'For one thing retribution is the myth of the religious or the credulous and for another you don't deserve it.'

She grinned.

'I dislike him intensely, mind. Don't let me ever set eyes on him.'

'Actually, you'd like him, I think.'

'I doubt that. But in any case we'll be spared the experiment. I shan't be coming down much more.'

'Oh. But . . . we'll see each other sometimes? I mean, I don't want to . . .'

'I'll make sure you get a large embossed invitation to the book's launch party.'

'I didn't mean that kind of thing. I hate parties.'

'I'm sorry,' said Mark. 'I'm making inapposite jokes again. Two years' association with your grandfather has taken its toll. In various ways. Of course we shall see each other.'

'It's funny – suddenly you're the one who keeps saying "I'm sorry". It used to be me. You were a bit irritated.'

True, Mark thought, I was. He said, 'There's something different about you.'

'Is there?'

'Yes.' You seem older, he was about to say, but that sounded mildly rude, and anyway it wasn't quite what he meant. Less detached? More like other people?

'Anyway . . . thank you,' said Carrie unexpectedly.

'For what?'

'Well . . . For taking me to France . . .'

'I think I'd better go,' said Mark, 'before this breast-beating gets out of hand.' They looked at each other. He thought of kissing her, and decided that might be taking masochism too far. 'Anyway, I'll see you . . . we'll see you sometime.'

17

SOMEWHERE DEEP in the intestines of Broadcasting House Mark sits at a table listening to the disembodied voice of Hermione and notes that the fraying flexes of the BBC are bound with black insulating tape, just like one's own. Also that the BBC's microphones are scratched and chipped; somehow these homely signs of vulnerability are interesting. They make him think of the 'Nine O'Clock News' and 'Children's Hour', which he can just remember, and old photographs of radio heroes and T. S. Eliot, poker-faced, reading verse.

'O.K.,' says the producer, 'that'll do, Susie . . . What I thought, Mark, is – let's keep that bit and chuck all the part where she's going on about herself. Right?'

'By all means. My sentiments entirely.'

'Good. So we'll take it from . . .'

And Hermione's voice fills the room again. '. . . My father and I were terribly close of course, he was just like a sort of grown-up friend, we used to have the most lovely times together. He and Mummy were devoted too, and of course it was super growing up in that atmosphere, all those interesting people coming to the house, it's so affected the sort of person one is oneself. What was he *like*? Oh well goodness, I mean when someone famous is your own father you don't really see them like other people do, do you? He wasn't a bit intimidating to me, not a bit, but of course we had this empathy, I suppose. We both loved art and travel . . . that's where my thing about travel comes from, I imagine, actually I've lived abroad now since – goodness, since I was nineteen . . .'

'We'll have that out,' says the producer. 'Pick her up again when she's talking about Lawrence. O.K., Mark?'

Mark snaps to attention. He has been adrift again, because Hermione's voice carries with it now a backing of things that are not really connected with Hermione at all . . . Carrie sitting on the edge of a bed peeling off her T-shirt. 'La lutte sanglante du moyen âge . . .' Towels printed with the bison of Lascaux. Happiness. Guilt. Melancholy.

'And then,' says the producer, 'I thought we'd go over to you . . .'

Mark listens to his own voice (unfamiliar – as though for an instant you did indeed hear what others hear): 'Gilbert Strong was never part of a coterie. He knew Bloomsbury, but was never of it; equally, he rubbed shoulders with the Fabians, with Shaw, but was never much in sympathy with them. He was very much his own man, gregarious but essentially private, even solitary. Perhaps this accounts for the peculiarly diverse pictures of him that we get from friends and acquaintances. Certainly it makes the biographer's task a hard one – a point noted by Strong himself in his well-known essay: "After all, we lie about one another with as much alacrity as we lie about ourselves – lies not of malice but of incompetence. We look at each other square – head-on – we seldom trouble to walk around behind and take another view." '

'Nice,' says the producer. 'I like it.'

Mark is diverted for an instant to the producer, whom he knows hardly at all, head-on or any other way. The producer wears a maroon shirt and no tie and is younger than Mark but balder. He wears wire-rimmed glasses and, Mark thinks, is probably homosexual – but, since Mark's perception in these things is notoriously unreliable, that is by no means certain. He seems a nice person, he has been pleasant to work with; on the other hand for all one knows he may be responsible for untold misery.

'My wife,' says the producer, 'has been reading the *Disraeli* life. She found it rather hard going.'

So much for sexual perception (or, rather, up to a point so much for sexual perception). Mark agrees that *Disraeli* has its *longueurs* and the producer does some more fiddling around with tape and into the room comes Edward Curwen, his twittery old man's voice conjuring up that Charlotte Street restaurant and a waitress who nannyishly hovers for the order, and Curwen's blue eyes and mouth pink-horned with wine-stains. '. . . He was a bit of a bully, frankly. Liked to have his own way, you know – push people around. Hadn't much time for younger colleagues and he certainly didn't care for anyone else muscling in on what he regarded as his preserve, as I had occasion to discover when I made a few criticisms of the *Disraeli* book. His behaviour then, I'm bound to say, was pretty reprehensible. Of course I was young myself and a bit impulsive I dare say but nevertheless . . .'

And Mark thinks not of Curwen nor of Strong but of himself, a switch prompted by that word 'young'. He sees suddenly an *alter ego*, twenty-eight year old Mark engaging in his first round of public contention, an article questioning the judgement of a well-known critic. Incurring, thus, the unswerving hostility of the well-known critic who has probably done him disservices of which he does not even know. Bold and enterprising was how this was seen at the time; Mark got a certain kudos. But what brings a private blush to the cheek is the remembered change of heart when the article was accepted and the panicky phone call to the editor with propitiatory amendments. But fate decreed that the editor should be unavailable and courage once again got the upper hand and none but Mark now know of that craven moment.

'And now,' says the producer, 'I thought it might be nice to go over to the other lady, what's-her-name, Stella Bruce. A mistress, is that right?'

'That's right,' says Mark, and listens to Stella Bruce's plummy girlish voice telling of free living in the thirties: '. . . Yes, I knew Gil extremely well, we were . . . very close for a number of years, in fact I think I can say I was probably more of a . . . how shall I put it? . . . more of a soul-mate than anyone. He used to tell me everything – I *presided* over the writing of the *Disraeli* book.

He did a lot of it at my house in the south of France. I can see him now, sitting on the terrace in that frightful old panama hat . . . He was a man who needed that kind of *bolstering* from a woman . . .'

'Interesting turn of phrase,' murmurs the producer.

'. . . and of course I could understand so well what made him tick – I'd always been with writers and artists, you see, it was the world I knew and to be honest Gil didn't always get quite enough of that at home. Violet led very much a country gentry sort of life with her dogs – beastly little terrier things – and her good works. He turned to me for release, you see. To be honest, he wasn't much of a family man. He wasn't close to the daughter either.'

'So we'll let her carry on along those lines for, um, as far as the bit about this travel book,' says the producer, 'and then over to you again.'

Stella whirrs and gobbles for a few seconds and concludes, '. . . and anyway no one would have believed Hugo Flack, he was the most dreadful line-shooter, so I suppose Gil reckoned he could get away with it. He was, as I've said, an awfully complex person.'

And Mark's voice now breaks smoothly in: 'Well, Mrs Bruce's account of the writing of *Long Weekend in the Caucasus* is of course very interesting. Unfortunately Strong left no notes or letters pertaining to the book and Hugo Flack died shortly after the incident Mrs Bruce mentions. We must suspend judgement.'

'Quite,' murmurs the producer. 'You can't come right out and call the old girl a liar, I see that.'

'As indeed the wise biographer frequently must. We all know, with reference to our own lives, the curious ways in which truth can be not so much distorted as multi-faceted. Give the kaleidoscope a shake and a different picture forms. Each of us sees through a glass darkly, impeded not just by the frailties of memory but by our own convictions. We see what we persuade ourselves that we have seen. The biographer's task . . .'

To hell with the biographer's task, thinks Mark moodily. He does not like his voice: smooth, pedantic – savouring, it seems to him, its choicer phrases. He wonders who on earth listens to this kind of thing anyway.

A girl comes in with plastic cups of coffee. The producer thrusts his chair back from the table and yawns. He glances at the clock and says not to worry, the studio's booked till twelve, we've plenty of time. Anyway, he says, we're getting it nicely tied up – the balance is good, there's some very effective stuff. He remarks that it's a pity the granddaughter didn't want to say anything. 'What's she like?' he enquires, and Mark, busying himself with the removable lid of the plastic coffee (and spilling some in the process on the BBC's already battle-scarred table) mumbles something about her being very pleasant.

They drink their coffee. 'The only thing that bothers me,' says the producer, 'is that we're not getting what you might call a rounded picture of Strong.' He frowns. 'Truth to tell, he seems to add up to about five different people at the moment. I'm worried about confusing the listener. Of course I take your point about . . . what was it you said? . . . Multi-faceted . . . kaleidoscopes . . . nice, all that. But this is a radio programme, not real life.' He laughs. So does Mark. 'Anyway . . . Let's get back to it. I've got a little surprise for you in a minute. But first of all let's decide what we can keep of your nice old boy from Porlock. He was a real find. Marvellous old fellow.'

And the Major comes on, loud and clear, saying, 'Just tell me if you'd like me to speak up a bit, won't you? Eh? Oh, I see – this contraption here' – there is a sudden dreadful surge of sound, the Major bellowing and then abruptly cut off – 'Dear me, I'm afraid I'm letting you down right and left. Is that better? Oh good. Now, what was it you were saying? Well, let's see now . . . I think my first recollection of Strong is fishing off Bossington Point. Used to hire a little boat, you know, trail lines for mackerel, awfully good fun. I had no idea the feller was a writer – not that I'd have been much interested anyway, but he was a very good chap to have a day out with. You know, it's a funny thing – you can't quite clear your mind of everything that comes after. You're asking me to tell you about how I remember Strong, but the fact is all the things that came after get in the way. Know what I mean?'

Oh I do indeed, thinks Mark, I do indeed. And to reinforce the point the producer is fiddling around again and now comes Mark himself, pontificating (or so it seems): '. . . A problem, for the biographer, is this omniscience. We know the narrative sequence. We record our subject's childhood and youth with wisdoms of what is to come – we have this god-like advantage over the person of whom we write. The bearded sage who is Strong in the 1950s lies, for me, across the pinafored child two world wars away. And, in a curious way, this both distances one from the subject and invites more personal feelings.'

'Hmn . . .' says the producer. 'Shall we put that in there or shift it till later? I'm not sure. Let's go back to the old boy again.'

'. . . She was a handsome girl, my aunt, very handsome, yes. Lots of brown hair – always falling down, you remember the way girls wore their hair in those days, all pinned up, stacks of it, very fetching really, very . . . What was I saying? Irene, yes. I remember her and Strong laughing together . . . Walking up a hill, through the bracken, hand in hand, laughing . . . They always seemed to have a lot of fun together – know what I mean?' And the voice stops.

'Funny the way he went dead on us there,' said the producer. 'I thought you'd never get him going again. Actually you sound a bit, well, a bit glum yourself.'

'Could be,' says Mark.

'We'll just run through the rest of him, anyway, and see if there's anything else . . .'

The Major rambles on and Mark, listening, continues to think, but in a more personal way now, about the wisdoms of hindsight. He recovers that heady moment of looking down from the attic ladder at Dean Close onto the top of Carrie's head and feeling as though he had received violent news of some kind. Now that the content of the news is known the *frisson* is lost for ever. He thinks, with various emotions, of Diana, and the several Dianas of the last few months pass before his eyes: peremptory or loving or guileful or reproachful or plain cross. He is attached to them all, he realises; further, he depends on them. He wishes suddenly that he could talk to her. He waits till the tape ends and says, 'Sorry – could we break for a few minutes. I'd just like to . . .'

'Sure,' says the producer. 'End of the corridor on the right.'

'No – could I make a phone call?'

'Susie – get Mark an outside line, would you?'

Mark, in the room beyond the glass screen, huddles over the receiver, feeling embarrassed. 'It's me. I'm at the BBC.'

'I know you are,' says Diana. 'That's where you said you were going.'

'I just felt like saying hello.'

There is a pause. Mark, who knows exactly what is going through Diana's head, says, 'Nothing has passed my lips except BBC coffee.'

'Oh. Well . . . hello then.'

'Are you busy?'

Diana, guarded, replies, 'So so.'

'Ah. The old bag's around, then?'

'In a manner of speaking,' says Diana.

'Oh well. Could we have something nice for supper?'

'We always do,' says Diana, nettled.

'I know,' says Mark, mollifying. 'I wasn't casting aspersions. Just something specially nice.'

'Are you pleased with the way the programme's going?'

Mark hesitates. 'Up to a point. It disconcerts a little.'

'How?' demands Diana.

'Well . . . All these assertive voices. Including one's own. And where's the man himself, amid it, eh?'

'Dead,' says Diana crisply.

Mark would like, all of a sudden, to talk about the Porlock letters. He would like to be able to explain the complexity of his feelings, if only for his own satisfaction. How he wishes, in a way, he had not read them; how he knows this is emotional self-indulgence; how they have subtly changed his relationship with (dead) Gilbert Strong. But he cannot. So instead he says, 'I'd better go.'

'Yes,' says Diana. She adds, 'I'm still not sure what you're ringing up *for*.'

Mark reads a note on the producer's desk-pad and looks away guiltily.

'A sudden rush of blood to the head. Or something. See you tonight.' After a moment he adds, 'I love you.'

'Oh,' says Diana. 'Well, ditto, as it were.' She rings off.

He returns to the studio. 'And now,' says the producer, 'here's my little surprise. How about this, then!'

There is a crackle and a hiss and into the room comes a new voice, an unfamiliar voice, a male voice with that diction heard now only on the lips of very old Tory politicians, Edwardian speech in other words but subtly modified in this instance in a way that Mark also recognises: the speech of the man of letters.

'Strong?' he says.

The producer beams. 'We dug it up from the archives. They trundled him out for Network Three when it first began. Not too long before he died, I suppose. I thought you'd like it.'

And so here is Strong made manifest. And yes, he sounds very much as imagined: confident, a trifle hectoring. Mark listens, fascinated. He believes in Strong, all of a sudden. It occurs to him that at points over the last couple of years Strong has come to seem unreal: a fictional character, almost – none the less powerful, but someone safely tucked away in a book. This voice corrects all that. It is a forceful voice, but the sound is slightly reedy – aptly so, as though reduced by the passage of time.

'I'm an old man. One says these words, let me tell you, with a certain sense of disbelief. It is not an anticipated condition unless you happen to be a person of unusual passivity. And I do not care for it. Age does not come naturally to me, if I may put it thus. When I dream, the ego of my dreams is young, a child even. But I am not dreaming of the past, I am dreaming of here and now, indulging in whatever mysterious activity of the brain dreams fulfil.'

'He waffles on rather,' says the producer. 'It seems to have been one of a series of talks in which they got the eminent elderly of the day to reflect on changing society – or whatever took their fancy, frankly.'

Gilbert Strong, though, does not waste too much time on changing society, apart from a few token swipes at the literary scene, the rape of the landscape and the declining verve of British politicians, in that order. He is chiefly concerned with the changes in Gilbert Strong, which he discusses with a not unengaging mixture of detached interest and personal affront. 'The future,' he says at one point, 'I have always regarded as impenetrable and therefore uninteresting' – not a particularly profound remark but one which seizes Mark for a while nevertheless, so that he misses the next bit and has to ask the producer to run the tape again. He thinks of Diana, that undaunted planner, forever trying to control the provoking random processes of fate. And of himself, whose consideration of the future has been restricted to occasional perfunctory assessments of life insurance or the mortgage.

'Once,' says Gilbert Strong, 'a long time ago, I rested a certain belief in the future which turned out to be misplaced. Since then, I have learned to put my trust in expediency rather than in hope.'

It occurs to Mark, with a sudden sense of conspiracy, that Strong is probably talking about Irene. In which case he is talking to himself, but is also, unknown to him, now communicating with Mark, which is odd and confusing but somehow moving. Strong goes on to discuss some of his own books in a way that seems to be disarmingly blunt and candid but, Mark recognises, includes a classic Strong method of special pleading which presents possible counter-arguments with subtle crudeness and then demolishes them with an apparently superior case. It is like listening to the expected manner of a parent, or of a very old friend. I know him better than I thought I did, Mark thinks. This brings a surge of confidence: maybe the book will be better than he believes, maybe the whole activity is more sound than at times he has felt.

And so he sits on, in the windowless room with its lights and buttons and reels of frozen speech out of which can be evoked people and places and a version of a man's life. Gilbert Strong continues to present an account that is as honest and as dishonest as anything he ever wrote or said and the producer interrupts once to say again that the balance is good but that the programme is perhaps too fragmentary now, are we skipping about too much, what do you think? And Mark, not really paying attention, shakes his head and says no, he thinks it will work like this. And the producer, at last, glances again at the clock and says, that's it, that's our lot, I'm afraid. Anyway, I'm quite pleased with it, except for one or two loose ends . . . And so they part, the producer to his office somewhere and Mark into the street, leaving locked away there Hermione and the Major and the rest of them. And, now, himself.